Through the Ivory Gate

BOOKS BY RITA DOVE

Poetry

The Yellow House on the Corner (1980)

Museum (1983)

Thomas and Beulah (1986)

Grace Notes (1989)

Fiction

Fifth Sunday (1985)

Through the Ivory Gate (1992)

Through the Ivory Gate

A Novel

Rita Dove

for Amanda,
who will recognize the
Ohio landscape in this book —

PANTHEON BOOKS
New York

Rita Dove

Ch'ville, 14 Oct 92

Portions of this work were originally published, often in somewhat different
form, in *Black American Literature Forum, Frank, The Gettysburg Review, The
Kenyon Review, Michigan Quarterly Review, Nimrod, Seattle Review, Southern
Review,* and *StoryQuarterly*. Earlier versions of two passages were previously
published in *Fifth Sunday*, stories by Rita Dove (Callaloo Fiction
Series, 1985).

Library of Congress Cataloging-in-Publication Data
Dove, Rita.
Through the ivory gate : a novel / Rita Dove.
p.   cm.
I. Title.
PS3554.O884T48   1992
813'.54—dc20   92-4456
ISBN 0-679-41604-8

Book design by Laura Hough
Manufactured in the United States of America
FIRST EDITION

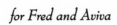
for Fred and Aviva

Acknowledgments

My heartfelt gratitude goes to my husband, Fred Viebahn, who literally "made me do it," to Adrienne Ingrum, who saw the potential and sent me back to the page, and to Robin Desser, my editor at Pantheon, for her enthusiastic support. I also thank Bernardine Connelly, Katie Greenebaum, and Graham Hettlinger for hounding research librarians Marvin Fisher and Roosevelt "Rip" Wilson for information on the racial topography in Phoenix, Ricki Thompson for her passionate discourse on puppets, Dana Weimer for tracking down the Top Ten Hits, Edmund Najera for sharing his memories of Madison, and Robin Waynesboro for resolving niggling details about the history of rubber production.

I am grateful to the National Endowment for the Arts, the Mellon Foundation, the National Humanities Center in North Carolina, and the Center for Advanced Studies at the University of Virginia for their generosity during my work on this novel.

Through the Ivory Gate

Prelude

"You don't want that one."

"Yes I do, please . . ."

"Look at it, Virginia!"

"Why can't I—"

"Just look. What color is it?"

"Black."

"And the mouth?"

"Red."

"And?"

"Big."

"What else?"

"He's smiling—"

"Grinning. What else?"

"Pretty eyes . . ."

"Pop eyes, chile, those are pop eyes. Don't you know who that is?"

"Just a doll a funny doll, Grandma, can't I have it?"

"Girl, don't you recognize an insult when you see one? That's supposed to be you! Shame on you," Grandma Evans said, handing Virginia over to her mother. "Belle, ain't this chile got no sense at all?"

On the bus Virginia eased the new purse out of its wrappings and studied it carefully. It was black and shiny; she could almost see herself in its flat surface. She unsnapped the clasp and peeked inside. A little mirror came with the purse; it dangled from a golden chain.

Skin brown. Hair black. Eyes small and far apart. Un-smiling. *I don't look like that—why she say it's supposed to be me?* Her grandmother didn't say any of those other dolls looked like anybody.

> *There was a pickaninny cryin'*
> *Down in Tennessee one night,*
> *His little heart was nearly breakin'*
> *Just because he wasn't white!*

Her mother sang that song as a joke. Her mother had told her a story about another song; the white insurance man had come to the door and Aunt Carrie was changing the beds upstairs hollering in a loud voice:

> *Someone's gotta pick the cotton,*
> *Someone's gotta pick the corn,*
> *Someone's gotta keep on singin' a song—*

And Mom let the white insurance man in and ran up to the bedroom but not in time to catch Carrie at the top of the stairs

> *That's why darkies were born!*

Virginia liked that story. She would have liked to be Aunt Carrie folding a fresh sheet bigger than herself, hollering at the top of her lungs:

> *That's why darkies were born!*

If you meet a paper tiger, he won't steal your clothes. A tiger in the forest might. That was another song:

Tiger, tiger burning bright
In the forests of the night.

A tiger is also part of a baseball team. A boy cousin from Detroit talked about going to "see the Tigers" and she wanted to go, too, but she was in the wrong state. Her father took her and her brother to see the Indians. It wasn't the same, going to see the Indians. A man stood up in the stands and poured all his whiskey away. He must have been sad, because he hid the bottle under his coat and watched the stream of yellow until it gave out. Ernie Jr. snickered, and she pointed the man out to their father, who took them away for some popcorn.

The puppet's name is Sambo. He is wearing red jacket blue trousers purple shoes with crimson soles and linings and a green umbrella. Oh what a friendly boy he looks to be! Too bad he is so silly! The Negro children laughed.

"Yes, Akron was young and struttin' those days. STANDING ROOM ONLY! the headlines said. Men with their families came up from Georgia to work in the rubber and oatmeal factories. And in the summer when that oats smell got headstrong and those rubber factories loudmouthed the heat, no one was nowhere but in the street. All day, all night the street was the respectable place to be.

"It was 1919, chile. I had on a striped sundress. In those days summers were hot like they supposed to be—that was before them astronauts got to fooling around with God's atmosphere. It was so hot that summer the men got to fainting at the machines. There were traveling minstrel shows, come down from Cleveland with vaudeville for the grown-ups and puppet shows for the children. We stood bareheaded in the sun to see them shows. My dress was red an' white, made out of an old coat lining. It had a yellow sash. When the show started up, Little Black Sambo strutted out in his bright clothes and green parasol. 'Look,' the minstrel said, 'look at little Sambo in his brand-new clothes! How he loves bright colors, little monkey that he is!' "

"I'll never wear bright colors again; I promise, Grandma."

"Hush, chile, don't be silly. But I'll tell you one thing: I don't care how many dolls they make in this world and how bad you might want them—I ain't going to buy you one till they can do them right."

Then there was Penelope, Penelope with the long red hair and plump good looks of Brenda Starr, Penelope of the creamy skin and dimpling cheeks. Aunt Carrie had bought her, Aunt Carrie said she was cute as a penny, she thought up the name. There were also small pink curlers and a comb. Wash and set and place her in the sun to dry. As many as five hairstyles a day—Penelope the Model, Penelope the God-Fearing Nurse, Penelope the Prize-Winning Journalist, Penelope the Girl Next Door, Penelope Had a Man and He Loved Her So. Never a hair out of place unless she shook it loose to let it stream in the wind. Virginia gave her a ride on her bicycle to make sure it streamed.

That summer was Virginia's ninth birthday. Birthdays had their ritual: she was allowed to drink coffee for breakfast, and she chose the dinner menu—chicken and applesauce and pork 'n' beans. She bicycled to Morry's Grocery for a dime's worth of candy buttons and ate them all. Then she took Penelope to the park. When she got back, it was nearly dinnertime; the kitchen clanged and hissed. She had gone upstairs and just laid Penelope on the bed when her mother appeared in the doorway, holding a shiny yellow package.

"Something you've always wanted," she said. "From Grandma."

Virginia ripped the waxy gift paper away. In a blue display box lay a doll in a seersucker playsuit. It had brown skin. It looked like an overturned crab. And the eyes didn't close and—she felt tears coming—it had no hair. Those blistered, painted curlicues on that bulbous scalp could not be called hair.

"Just think, honey—now you finally have a doll who looks like you!"

"I don't want it." Backing away as the doll was thrust into her arms.

"What do you mean, you don't want it? Honey, where are you going? What are you doing—don't you dare—!"

Virginia threw the doll down the stairs.

Her father came running, newspaper fluttering at his ankles. "What's all the commotion about?" he demanded.

"Oh, nothing," her mother said, "nothing at all. Except that your daughter is ashamed of being a Negro. Look what she did to my mother's birthday present. She obviously prefers that fat redhead to her own color." She shook Penelope in Virginia's face.

"Do you know what you're telling us?" Belle spoke under her breath, but her voice was hard and shiny as scales. "You're saying you don't appreciate this doll. Your grandmother goes half across town to buy you the first Negro baby doll and you throw a fit, you throw her down the stairs like dirty laundry. You don't want it? You don't like it? You don't like being a Negro? For years we've fought so there would be Negro dolls for our children, and you'd rather play with—"

"Stop it, Belle."

Her father knelt down, took her gently by the shoulders. "Why did you throw Grandma's doll down the stairs?" he asked sadly. His hair smelled like ginger ale and fresh-cut grass; she knew it was just his hair pomade, but she couldn't help thinking it came directly from him like a magician's smoke, a halo of scent.

"Tell me," he said, "what it is you don't like about the doll."

He took the doll away from her mother and held it out quietly. Virginia stared at it—the bulging eyes, the painted head. She didn't look like that. And if she did, how could her own parents stand there and tell her so? How could they love her and show her at the same time that she was ugly?

"All right"—he sighed—"maybe you need a little time to think it over. I have a suggestion: Keep this doll for a day. Play with it for one day and then, if you still don't like it, we'll take it back. No questions asked. Okay? You tell us you don't like it, we'll take it back."

He put the doll on the bed.

"Come on, Belle."

Virginia was alone. They thought they could leave her up here and she would be too scared to say anything. They thought by tomorrow she'd calm down and say, "Yes, I'll keep it; I'll even give it a name"—and then they would take Penelope away and Virginia wouldn't even notice she was gone.

The new doll lay on the bed in its flimsy, striped sun-suit. She picked it up. It felt cheap—so lightweight, and the hard skin could be dented with the merest pressure from her thumb. She walked over to the window, unlatched the screen, and threw the pickaninny out, hard.

Oh, how smoothly it fell, a mindless spot in the air, toppling lazily, smiling its nonsense smile. A shallow *thwap* when it landed, skipping across the brick street like a ball and coming to rest against the far curb, its body a startled, up-reaching claw.

"You crazy or what?" Ernie Jr. shrieked, making a sharp turn on his roller skates at the end of the drive. The front door slammed, Virginia's mother ran out and across the street; she scooped up the doll and stood there a moment looking up at the window in disbelief. Virginia did not step away.

Sometime after the family had moved to Arizona, Penelope's left arm was punctured by something, a hairpin or a needle, and she soaked up water whenever she got a shampoo; every morning Virginia's pillow was wet. The white girls at the junior high began to iron their hair as if this were a new invention, some kind of revelation. Virginia straightened her hair as always; she cut bangs, used larger rollers, rinsed it sable brown.

She had a recurrent dream: in it she was wearing white shorts and a yellow T-shirt, and she was running through all the streets in the old neighborhood. Though the sun bore down fiercely and the cobbled bricks were precarious, she ran without the least effort. Her hair streamed behind her, long and shining, red as the tulip shedding and the cardinal flashing. *Isn't she lovely*, they whispered as she ran past, *a wild deer, an antelope*. And in the dream her skin was still dark.

. . .

Years later when Afros came into style, Virginia breathed a sigh of relief and got rid of the curlers. It was time to go to college: rummaging through the cartons in the storeroom, she came upon a shoebox. Penelope's hair lay matted and dusty around her rose-pink face; the arm with the puncture had turned dark green, as if rotten with gangrene. She was spongy; even the desert heat hadn't been able to suck all the water out. Virginia took her to show her younger sister.

"What did you ever see in such a fat thing, anyway?" Claudia mumbled, turning back to "Mister Rogers' Neighborhood."

That's when Virginia noticed the stuffing had mildewed. Penelope stank. She took the doll to the bathroom and laid her on the scale: She came to four pounds. There was nothing to do but throw her away.

One

Memory has a reputation for being compassionately inaccurate. Cruising through the neighborhood of her assigned school district, a footlocker full of puppets in the trunk of the Plymouth and a cello on the backseat, Virginia refused to believe that the streets of her childhood, those connected backyards and maple trees and lawn sprinklers of the Midwest, were as scraggly as her eyes took them to be. She recognized the wooden houses, once majestic, that now stood shaggy and cramped between narrow driveways lined with cars quietly rusting away. The knee-high picket fences any tomcat could push over, the plaster models of stable boys posing in the front yards, the silver water tank two streets over that dominated the neighborhood—all footage from a past that had been dim for years.

The woman with the potbelly and bony knees who always wore maroon Bermuda shorts—what was her name? Here was her counterpart standing by a hedge with clippers in hand, yakking to her neighbor, a young mother absentmindedly pushing her baby back and forth in its carriage. *She's probably the neighborhood gossip, and this would be her favorite time of year,* Virginia thought—*Indian summer, when the kids are back in school and the weather is still warm enough for sitting outside.* And outside she would be, by the hedges or on the front porch, with nothing better to do than yell a greeting to every person who had the misfortune to pass by.

This city was no different than a dozen others Virginia had driven through on her trip down from Wisconsin—squat brown and yellow houses boxed in by chicken wire, the brilliant artwork of K Marts and A&P's, thickened air and violet sunsets, plumes of white smoke from grimy factories whose green windowpanes glittered when the sun struck, the skeletal filigree of refineries—except that this one was her birthplace, the place she had grown up in before her father had taken his family so far away. *It should seem stranger,* she thought, pulling into a filling station, glancing around at the weather-beaten shopping center on the other side of the intersection, telephone cables crisscrossing overhead.

Nigel used to say that everything important that ever happened to you happened before you were ten—his explanation for the extraordinary power of puppets to beguile children and adults alike, and why large-as-life puppets were actually larger than life, monstrous, no longer cute but an affront to nature, like dreams and fears blown out of proportion, oversized children almost carnivorous in their demands.

She went inside to pay. The attendant was about her age—maybe a little older, twenty-six or -eight—stocky and dark-skinned. Sculpted chest muscles undulated beneath his kelly-green T-shirt as he handed back the change. His eyes flicked over her.

What kind of future was there in attending a gas station? *I sound like Belle,* Virginia thought, swiping at the air as if she could wipe away her mother's words and tone of voice with her hand.

"What kind of future is that, puppeteering? Tell me, Virginia; is this what we educated you for? Grow up, Doll Baby!"

Belle loved exaggerated nicknames: Sweet Beet, Little Miss (that was reserved for Claudia, always getting in trouble), Girlish Heart. Ernie Jr., who was two years older than Virginia, had escaped most of the sobriquets, though occasionally Belle, in a rare fit of ebullience, would sing out "Oh man o' my heart"; Virginia could picture Ernie's wincing even now. For their part, Virginia and Ernie Jr. exacted their revenge by calling her Belle whenever they were out of earshot, and Virginia always thought of her mother as Belle, although she never would have dared to address her that way in person.

Virginia had been named after Belle's mother, Virginia Evans. Grandma Evans still lived in Akron, in an old folks' home; Belle visited her once a year, hopping on the Greyhound cross-country for three days and turning around four days later for the return trip. She never took the kids along—three kids on a bus for three days and nights was no one's idea of fun, of course, but she had never even suggested it. Once, shortly after they'd moved and Claudia was born, Grandma Evans had come out to Arizona, making the first and only airplane flight of her life.

Now Virginia was supposed to visit her. "Your grandmother is expecting you," Belle had said for the umpteenth time, while Virginia was busy hugging Claudia goodbye in front of the flight gate at Sky Harbor Airport. "She's counting on it, so phone her the minute you get to Akron."

Virginia could barely remember her grandmother. Except for the studio portraits Belle would bring back every couple of years or so of a spectacled, nut-brown face staring carefully from a backdrop of swirled blues, her only memory was a blurred image of a tiny woman leaning over the bars of Claudia's crib, crooning a tuneless tune. Claudia had been born with the umbilical cord coiled twice around her neck, her squashed face forced into a delicate shade of purple. Repeated slaps, mouth-to-mouth—nothing worked until, at the last possible moment before giving up hope, she began to cry.

No wonder, considering what she was coming into. Virginia shivered, recalling the oppressive silence and smoldering angers of her parents' house, Belle blaming everything on the heat—headaches, lackadaisical dinners, melancholy Christmas trees and vacation times that dragged on forever. And her father bearing it stoically, understanding yet at the same time refusing to grasp the hidden message: *You brought us here, now look what's happened.* Sometimes it seemed that Claudia's hesitation to open her lungs and let life enter had been deliberate, and her explosive behavior later—locking herself in the bathroom, hurling shoes against walls—was an expression of her subconscious regret that she had decided, against her better judgment, to join the world.

At last Virginia arrived at Washington Elementary, turning suddenly upon it from a side street. It occupied an entire block, somber and unwieldy as most school buildings of its age. The playground resembled in its abandonment a toppled blackboard, the slide a single blotched tongue. The wind coaxed the swings in their moorings, the grating careful, regular. She'd probably have most of her classes in the afternoon—wasn't Art always the last thing before the end of the day? If she could help it, she wouldn't see many mornings like this, the nine o'clock sun pressed flat into the pasty sky. As she parked she looked past the swings, propelled by their invisible guards, to the hulking building, poised in dark serenity; fitful patches of daylight made their way through the maples on the front lawn,

their shadows adorning the solitary countenance of the second
Washington, Booker T., probably erected in a rush during
black history week a few years ago.

The sleep she'd been able to push back during the long
night drive now inched its way into her body. Hopefully, she
could move into her place right away. What kind of a place had
they—to use the Arts Council administrator's word—"pro-
cured"? Oh, God, please don't make it a family. Or a rooming
house. Were there rooming houses nowadays? A matron in a
starched white blouse saying "Welcome, these are the rules,
read them carefully," flowers blooming in neat patches in the
front yard . . .

Blue and white petals floated in the air, thousands of
them spiraling slowly to the concert stage where Virginia stood
holding the cello by its neck, looking for a chair to sit in. The
petals were humming, and they changed colors as they descended, from blue to brown and from white to yellow, coalesc-
ing into dark copper clouds that broke apart and re-formed as
they dropped closer. After all those years in the Southwest
longing for the changes of seasons, she could feel it singing
inside her: fall was cello season, and she wanted to accom-
pany it.

But there was nowhere to sit, and who can play the
cello standing up, this instrument made to be clasped between
the knees like a lover? Suddenly, out of nowhere Clayton approached in coat and tails, bearing a chair.

Damn, she thought, turning off the ignition and leaning her head against the steering wheel, *here I go dreaming of
him again.*

She reached for the chair, but he swiveled behind her
and pushed it gently under her until she was seated properly.

15

When he began arranging her long concert skirt, spreading the heavy black material so that it spilled around the glowing curves of the cello like dark water, she noticed that his hands had turned ashen, with a bluish tinge.

"What happened to your hands?" she asked.

He lifted the last fold gingerly. "They're ruined," he said. "And if they touch you, you'll be ruined, too."

"Do you think she's okay? Maybe we should call the principal . . ."

Virginia opened her eyes to the dark blue padding of the dashboard, the silver slot of the glove compartment, and faces staring at her from the other side of the glass. She snapped awake, sat up and heard an "Ah!" of relief from the faces.

She rolled down the window. "I guess I fell asleep for a moment."

A tall brown-skinned man in green custodian's clothes turned to the gray-haired woman next to him. "I told you so! What did I say? She was just sleepin'."

"I hope I didn't worry anyone. I'm a day early—I mean, I'm supposed to arrive tonight. My name is Virginia King."

The confusion clouding the stern angular features of the gray-haired woman cleared. "So *you're* the artist!" she said, extending her hand through the open window. "Better early than not at all. We hadn't heard from you since your acceptance letter." Virginia felt the reprimand.

"Well, come inside, come inside! Come on! Mrs. Peck will want to meet you right away."

"I—I don't feel very presentable right now. I better come back later, maybe in the afternoon . . ."

"Nonsense! Where are you going to go?" And with that snippet of logic Virginia was whisked out of the car, across the lot and toward the side entrance. Inside the door she stopped. "May I use the rest room first? I'm a bit groggy."

"I'll show you where it is, honey." A black woman in a white uniform—probably the cook—took her arm. Halfway down the hall, the cook glanced over her shoulder and chuckled. "That old biddy Ludwig. Always trying to take charge of everything. Watch out for her, or she'll have you jumping like a doll on a string!"

LAVATORY in faded brass letters. Virginia leaned against the scarred walnut-stained door and plunged into a cavernous tiled room that looked less like a public bathroom than an underground transportation facility. Right across from the entrance two porcelain sinks had been mounted into a partition that fronted a double formation of toilet stalls.

The sinks came to just above her knees; there was a scratched aluminum paper-towel dispenser above each and a mirror shot through with seeping silver nitrate in the space between. The mustard-colored light seemed to be saturated with the dim odors of soggy paper and soap powder; a cheap, overly sweet air freshener failed to camouflage the vinegary singe of urine and over that, the sharp moral scent of bleach.

Each toilet stood in its own dark wood closet; Virginia nearly fell onto the wobbly seat. She ran two fingers under the rim of her turtleneck. Why were lavatories always overheated? And why the word lavatory anyway? She'd never seen it used elsewhere. "We are going to the la*bor*atory," she used to chant with her classmates, lining up four at a time to pee, wash hands, and traipse back down the hall in orderly fashion, all in five minutes.

Bending over the tiny sink to rinse her hands, Virginia glanced into the bleary mirror, sighed and, fishing a print scarf from her purse, tied it over her mashed Afro.

Mrs. Ludwig was waiting outside. "I would have taken you to the teachers' lounge," she sniffed.

Mrs. Peck was a vigorous pepper-haired woman who had somehow managed to retain a casual manner without losing an ounce of efficiency. "Miss King, you're early!" she said, and held out a hand. "The entire school is delighted you could join us. I understand this is your hometown."

Virginia nodded. "Yes. We moved to Arizona when I was in fourth grade."

"We never forget those early moves, do we? When I was coming out of anesthesia after my second child was born, my husband claims I begged not to leave my friends in Pittsburgh. We had moved from Pittsburgh to Akron when I was twelve." She chuckled. "Well, enough of my past. Now, *yours* has been busy: Dean's List, Thespian Society, Puppets & People Repertory Theater—that must have been exciting!"

"Yes," Virginia replied, stifling a yawn. They both laughed.

"You must be pooped," said Mrs. Peck.

"I'm not as pooped as I am contrite. I should have called when I knew I might arrive early."

"I know how it is when you're on the road. You want to get there as soon as possible. So you drove straight through?"

"Well, yes." Virginia hesitated, then decided not to go into further detail—how she had spent a few weeks in Arizona with her parents after Puppets & People had broken up, then flown back to Madison two nights ago, her friends gone, just her ramshackle car covered with wheat chaff in the padlocked barn.

"We found you a good place to stay. It's an efficiency that rents out by the week, but I'm told there's no dingy beige shag carpeting, so that's a plus. And there's a kitchenette, plus a few additional features to make it look a little like a home. The only trouble is, it won't be ready for occupancy until this afternoon. I'll have my secretary show you over then. Why don't you lie down here? The nurse's station has a cot. It's not the Ritz, but still . . ."

The darkened brilliance of the sickroom was strangely soothing. The shades were drawn. Virginia pulled off her shoes and lay down on the cot, her head sinking into the starched percale of the pillowcase. She waited for her eyes to adjust to the dark. On the counter the pale cotton swabs were arranged in a misty circle around the barely visible rim of a jar. The orange ciphers of a digital clock flared steadily: 9:59, 10:00. Fat packets of gauze gleamed in their plastic wrappings, and she could make out the highly polished surfaces of medical instruments.

Fourteen years ago she had lain in a sickroom like this, in this very town, enveloped in the artificial dark. "Stomach cramps, vomiting for no apparent reason," the nurse had said.

"She usually enjoys her lessons so much," added the music teacher, who had carried her down.

No one guessed the real reason—not even her parents, who had caused it. The week before, at the dinner table, her father had gotten out the atlas and the *Golden Book Encyclopedia,* as if knowledge could soothe the hurt of the shocking news.

"See? This is where our new home will be, right on the Salt River."

But Virginia did not care for salty rivers. She did not care for warm weather. She did not want to eat grapefruit right from the tree, or cuddle up to a saguaro cactus, or experience an Indian powwow. *We must have done something wrong,* she thought, *and now we're being banished.*

She slept until the door opened and the light crashed down on her—a young woman in a pale pink pantsuit had switched on the fluorescent lamp. "I'm Jean Gilroy," the woman introduced herself. "I'm the school secretary."

As they walked to the parking lot, Jean Gilroy kept up a one-way nonstop stream of talk. Virginia in her muddled state only caught snatches: excited children, the upcoming PTA meeting, Mrs. Woods's fourth grade crying for "the Puppet Lady." She yawned; she couldn't help it.

"Oh, I'm talking too much," Jean said, laughing nervously. "I always do."

Two

For a few weeks it would be tolerable: a cube of a room, white walls, white floorboards, daybed with a blue coverlet. A dinette set with two straight-back chairs, the kitchen no more than a counter. Virginia had been expecting a dank linoleum-lined room in a motel complex, or worse, a room in the home of concerned parents, not this postmodern artist's garret built over a languishing shoe repair shop. Venetian blinds shaded the huge windows along the wall that fronted the street. It was actually a miniature studio; whoever had decorated it—a photographer, perhaps?—had used white paint to extend the cramped space, as if the walls were nothing more than reflected light that could squeeze through the slits in the blinds and pick up a few flashes from the stingy scribble of the canal in the background, lifting over the tire factories in the east to be absorbed finally into the chalky sky.

She decided to shower first. She must have seemed like a maniac, rolling into the school parking lot a day early, bleary-eyed and wrinkled like a bum. What did they think of her—Mrs. Peck, Ludwig, the cook, Jean Gilroy?

She started toward the bathroom but stopped at the cello in the middle of the floor, daylight warming along the gray curve of its vinyl case. She had not played seriously since college. Accompanying the troupe's performances and clowning around as Parker picked out old Beatles songs on the piano didn't count—that wasn't *real* music, music that made you forget where you were, made you forget where your arms and legs ended and luscious sound began.

She had started playing the cello when she was nine, shortly after the move to Arizona. At the beginning of the school year in Akron, every child in fourth grade had been issued a pre-instrument called a tonette so the teacher could determine who had an "aptitude" for music. Virginia had liked the neatness of the tonette, its modest musical range and how it fit into her school desk on the right side. Whenever she covered a fingerhole, she felt the contour of its slightly raised lip and imagined she was playing the tentacle of an octopus.

She had chafed through months of scales and simple songs, waiting for the moment when she would walk across the auditorium stage and choose: kneel among the rows of somber black cases, undo the metal clasps and fling open the lid to reveal her instrument, a flute or a clarinet, glowing softly, half buried in deep blue velvet.

But before she could make her choice, they moved to Arizona. There, the music instruments were stored in a classroom trailer, and when she opened the flute case she nearly winced from the glare bouncing off all that polished silver, those gloating caps and hinges. The clarinet was worse—it looked like an overdesigned walking stick, sounded like a clown laughing, and had reeds that needed to be softened in spit.

The music teacher shut the cases with a succession of curt clicks. "That leaves the strings," she sighed, leading the way back through the noonday blaze and into the main building, where the violins, violas, cellos and double basses were housed. There, by virtue of its sonorous name, Virginia asked for the violoncello—and was too intimidated by the teacher's growing impatience to protest when what emerged from the back closets was something resembling not a guitar, but a child-sized android. In her anguish Virginia bowed her head and blindly accepted the instrument. It was not long, however, before she realized that she had made a good choice, for the sound of its name was synonymous with the throbbing complaint that poured out of its cumbersome body.

It took her nearly a year just to learn how to hold it properly. She had been accustomed to practicing after school, but one weekend evening while her parents were out, she dragged the instrument into their bedroom and used pillows to prop the music on the armchair. She was just about to sit on the edge of the bed when something, maybe the shadow thrown from the flowered lampshade or the slats of light sifting from the street, made her want to *do things right*. She got a straight-back chair from the dining room and sat down correctly, bringing the instrument slowly toward her body. The lamp picked up the striations down the back of the wood, each strip slightly different, a little browner, a little more golden, but meeting its mate at the spine, a barely perceptible seam. For the first time she saw that the back of the cello was rounded like a belly, the belly of a tiger she had to bring close to her, taming it before she was torn limb from limb. She had to love and not be scared, and show the cat that it did not need to growl to protect itself. The animal stood on its hind legs and pressed its torso to hers, one paw curled like a ribbon behind her left ear. It was heavy; she sat very straight in the chair in order to support it.

Funny how fantasy works. And memory. I haven't thought about that evening in years. Virginia bent down and lay the cello case on its back, trying, as she knelt to unsnap the metal clasps, to ignore the musk that wafted up; but then she became aware of the dried sweat filming her skin, and the way her stockings had sagged into gritty puddles in her shoes. She stood up and made for the shower.

Virginia gasped in relief at the first gush of hot water on her back. Ah, the pleasure of getting clean! She closed her eyes so as to dissolve in the slipstream, breathing in the steamy clamor of chlorine and almond-scented lather.

Clayton never touched the cello without washing his hands first; more often than not, he'd change his shirt before going to the university orchestra rehearsal. "One must honor the art," he said. "Marcel Proust donned formal attire before sitting down to write *Remembrance of Things Past*."

It had been impossible to miss him that first day of rehearsal. Even from the fourth stand, Virginia could make out the back of his head wafting on the chestnut-colored stem of his neck. *A brother in the cello section—second chair at that!* She leaned over the music stand to get a better view.

Her stand partner sniffed and turned his instrument away, hunching his shoulder as if she was about to bump his raggedy wooden matchbox. For auditions, she had chosen a slow passage from the D Minor Corelli Sonata, hoping the melodic line would camouflage her rusty technique. The sight-reading portion hadn't been too bad, probably because she'd been so relaxed about the whole thing. Her only ambition had been to sit in the back of the orchestra and deposit her modest tones into that gorgeous cornucopia of sound spilling out all around her. No one was more surprised than she when she was positioned before several music majors. She could feel them seething behind her—especially her partner who, as inside stand member, would have to turn all pages.

Who was this dude sitting up on first stand as casual as you pleased? Most black musicians she had met before were either horn men—saxophonists of every stripe, and that lean, arrogant trumpeter from L.A.—or the ubiquitous percussionists who were always clicking out rhythms with their tongues and drumming on tabletops. She hated to fall into stereotyping, but it was true.

At the end of rehearsal the principal cellist, a stocky redheaded guy named Paul, stood up to introduce the new section members. When it was Virginia's turn, Clayton lifted an eyebrow and bowed slightly. Then there was pandemonium as eighty-odd musicians, using their instrument cases as battering rams, stormed the exit.

Heart thudding, she threaded her way through the thicket of music stands to the doorway where he stood chatting with the principal cellist. Paul clapped her on the shoulder in a hale-and-hearty manner. "Welcome to the salt mines, Virginia." He grinned and took off, whistling: *Heigh-ho, heigh-ho, it's off to work we go.* She turned to look up at Clayton, who seemed in no hurry to follow.

He was tall, about six feet four; his nose was flat *and* sharp, like Benin bronzes, with a prominent ridge and flaring nostrils. An Omar Sharif mustache straggled over his lips, and there was a hint of a cleft in the rather small chin. Had he been waiting for her? The thought made her dizzy.

"Yes, indeed. Welcome. My name is Clayton Everett."

She nodded. "Thanks. I mean, it's great to be able to play in an orchestra again."

"Oh?" There he went lifting that eyebrow. "Haven't you played in a while?"

"I've been taking private lessons with Kadinski, but this is the first semester I've been able to work orchestra into my schedule."

He held the door open and started down the hall toward

the cello room, moving along with an off-kilter camel's lope. Every music major had a locker, but cellists and bassists also had a key to humidified rooms where the larger instruments were stored.

"Mr. Kadinski's my teacher also. What are you working on now?"

"The Concerto in D by Anton Kraft. I'd never heard of him before, but the piece is really wonderful."

"Kraft!" he exclaimed. "I had to locate that concerto for my library-science class. We were given obscure compositions to track down, and Anton Kraft was my final exam question last semester." He paused, shifting his cello case to the other hand. "I've never had a chance to find a recording of it. Would you play it for me?"

They had stopped in front of a practice room. Panicked, Virginia stammered, "I'm not a music major."

"That's no reason."

"And I've just started the Kraft." It was a lie, and they both knew it. "Give me a few weeks to get it under my belt, and I'll play it for you."

"Is that a promise?"

"Promise."

He set the cello case down and extended his hand, smiling. The dry warmth of his grip, the tender amusement in his eyes, quietly destroyed her—and the way he spoke, with a deliberate, almost decorous, formulation of the phrases. He reached for the doorknob to the practice room.

"You're going to practice? Now?" she said, bewildered.

"Sure. After orchestra is the perfect time; the muscles are all warmed up."

She had never heard of anyone practicing *after* three

hours of orchestra! Even with the frequent breaks during the rehearsal (the French horns were awful and the conductor had to stop and concentrate on their part), her arm was ready to drop off by the time they were given the sign to pack up.

"What are you working on?" she asked meekly.

"The Lalo. And I would be pleased to play it for you in a few weeks, when I've gotten it under *my* belt. Good evening, Virginia." He bowed his ridiculous but somehow appropriate bow again, and went inside.

She'd met lots of crazy musicians, but no one like Clayton. He was as obsessed as the others, but he had a quirky sense of humor, a slow ironic counterpoint to his own beliefs. And he didn't look quite like anyone else. First of all, he didn't look very black. He didn't look white either, or Puerto Rican. He wore his hair parted dangerously near the middle and combed in little ripples like Cab Calloway, though sometimes he let it fly up a bit at the ends in deference to the campus pressure for Afros. His caramel-colored skin darkened to toffee under fluorescent light but sometimes took on a golden sheen, especially in the vertical shafts of sunlight that poured into his favorite practice room where she'd often peeked in on him—an uncanny complexion, as if the shades swirled just under the surface.

Virginia's friends gave her advice on how to get him. "You two can play hot duets together," they giggled.

As it turned out, she didn't have to plan a thing. She was reading John Hawkes's *Blood Oranges* for Twentieth-Century Lit one afternoon in the courtyard of the Fine Arts Building when the sunny day turned suddenly cold. If she went all the way back to the dorm for a sweater, she'd be late for orchestra rehearsal. So she stuck it out for a quarter of an hour, until a few minutes before rehearsal at four. By that time her fingers were so stiff, she had to run them under hot water to loosen them up. Then she hurried to the cello room, where all the instruments were lined up like novitiates; she felt a strange reverence every time she stepped across the threshold into its cool serenity. There they stood, obedient yet voluptuous in their molded cases. In the dim light their plump forms looked sadly human, as if they were waiting for something better to come along but knew it wouldn't.

Virginia grabbed her cello and was halfway down the hall when she realized she'd forgotten to leave her books behind. She decided against turning back and continued to the basement, where the five-till-four pandemonium was breaking loose. Clayton was stuffing his books into his locker, the music major's privilege.

"Hey, Clayton, how's it going?"

As if it were routine, he took her books and wedged them in next to his. They started toward the orchestra hall. Virginia cast a surreptitious glance upward; five minutes to four or not, Clayton was not rushing. His long, gangling frame seemed to be held together by molasses; he moved deliberately, negotiating the crush while humming a tricky passage from Schumann, sailing along above the mob.

After rehearsal she reminded him that her books were in his locker.

"I think I'll go practice," he said. "Would you like to listen?"

"I'll miss dinner," she replied, and was about to curse herself for her honesty when he said, "I have cheese and soup back at the fraternity house, if you don't mind the walk."

The walk was twenty minutes of agonizing bliss, with the wind off the lake whipping her blue, and Clayton too involved with analyzing the orchestra's horn section to notice. When they reached the fraternity house, a brick building with a crumbling porch and white pillars and weeds cracking the front path, she was nearly frozen through. He heated up a can of Campbell's Split Pea with Ham and plunked the cheese down in the center of the dinette table.

"It's not much," he apologized, but she was thinking *A loaf of bread, a jug of wine,* and felt sated before lifting the first spoonful. The house was rented to Alpha Phi Alpha, one of the three black fraternities on campus. It had the musty tennis-shoes-and-ripe-laundry smell of bachelor rooms, combined with the intensely sweet scent of oil essences she'd first encountered in a head shop David Goldstein, her brother's friend, had taken her to—patchouli, vanilla bean, cinnamon. Books and jackets were strewn everywhere, dishes piled in the sink.

"When did you begin playing?" she asked.

"I began late, I'm afraid," Clayton replied. "Ninth grade. But I felt at home immediately. With the music, I mean. The instrument took a little longer. Everyone said I was too tall to be a cellist." He grimaced.

Virginia watched him as he talked. He was the same golden brown as his instrument, and his mustache followed the lines of the cello's scroll.

"So what did you do?" she asked.

"Whenever my height came up, I would say, 'Remember the bumblebee.' "

"What do bumblebees have to do with cellos?"

"The bumblebee, aerodynamically speaking, is too large

for flight. But the bee has never heard of aerodynamics, so it flies in spite of the laws of gravity. I merely wrapped my legs and arms around the cello and kept playing."

Music was the only landscape in which he seemed at ease. In that raunchy kitchen, elbows propped on either side of the cooling soup, he was fidgety, even a little awkward. But when he sat up behind his instrument, he had the irresistible beauty of someone who had found his place.

Virginia stepped out of the shower and rubbed down until her skin burned, then soothed it with cocoa-butter lotion. Refreshed, nearly pristine, she sat down in the dinette chair that wobbled the least and pulled the cello to her. Now, for the first time since Clayton, she was trying to make music again. Haydn? Elgar? *Tiger, tiger, burning bright* . . . Her fingers found the opening measures on their own volition, those triadic arpeggios of the First Bach Suite that sounded like warm-up scales until the gradual modulations of the high notes in each phrase insinuated themselves into her blood: above the treadmill of chordal progressions a luminous melody unscrolling and floating away, high in the upper ether, where there was no memory or hurt.

Three

"Some of the pupils will be coming from Instrumental Music, so don't be surprised when they troop in," Mrs. Woods said. "It's a lively class, but they'll do anything for you once they get to know you."

Virginia looked over the classroom: approximately twenty-five nine-year-olds in various stages of titter. A chunky black boy poked his neighbor with a ruler, then looked innocently the other way. Two white girls, both dark-haired, giggled. A Goldilocks with green eyes sat very still, hands folded, staring up at her raptly; she would be the type who would volunteer for everything before anyone else. Virginia watched the thin pale boy behind Goldilocks inching toward one of her plump arms with a feather. He moved very slowly, his bad teeth bared.

Mrs. Woods was stout and fiftyish, with graying hair that ended abruptly halfway over her ears. Bifocals hung from a golden chain on her chest. Cheerfully obtuse, she had acquired the habit of speaking very slowly and clearly, even to adults, pronouncing every word as if she were reading it from a dictionary. And every sentence ended with an imaginary exclamation point or question mark.

Mrs. Woods rapped the edge of her desk with a ruler. "Class," she announced gaily, "today we have a very special guest. She will visit us every afternoon for a month, and I think she has some surprises in store for you. Her name is Miss King, and she will be telling you about theater." Someone in the back row snickered.

"How many of you saw *Rapunzel* last month?" Almost all of them raised their hands.

"Well, Miss King works with puppets like Rapunzel. She has been kind enough to volunteer her services as part of the Artist-in-the-Schools Program, and she specifically asked for grade-schoolers, so we're very happy that she likes us so much." She turned to Virginia, who was having difficulty keeping her face impassive. "Miss King, they're all yours."

She gave Virginia the ruler and took a seat in the back of the room. There was a wash of giggles, then silence. Virginia put down the ruler and smiled. A few children smiled back warily. It would take some doing to overcome the results of this woman's daily routine, she thought, turning to the blackboard and writing in letters that filled the entire slate: VIRGINIA.

"My friends call me Virginia, and I'd like you to call me that, too."

Not a breath. Mrs. Woods frowned.

"Okay." Virginia continued, "I need two strong young men to help me bring in my treasure chest. Who'll volunteer?"

There was a general buzz of excitement, and a spattering of hands shot up. She picked the chief snickerer and a shy, light brown boy with high cheekbones, ushering them into the hallway. Soon they returned lugging a bright red footlocker. She had them put it on the table next to the desk.

"What you see here," she began, sitting down to unsnap the metal clasps, "really is a treasure chest. Not one of those chests stuffed with rubies and emeralds that you read about in *Ali Baba*, nor one of those crates loaded with silks and incense like Marco Polo brought back from the Orient. This treasure chest is even more fascinating, because it's filled with life." She threw open the lid. Now she was hidden from view. The children were very quiet.

A small cotton hand appeared along the edge of the lid. It fumbled for a hold, gripped. The other hand appeared, the right forearm, then the left, draped in yellow sleeves, elbowed their way into view. A head popped up: large Afro and wide-spaced slanted eyes. The class laughed.

"Hi, boys and girls. Virginia said I could lead the class today. That is, if I can ever get up here." With a grunt and a heave, the puppet pulled itself into full view: yellow blouse, long denim skirt.

"Hey, that's you!" yelled the fat boy.

"Of course it's me," replied the puppet. "Gina. Who else could it be?" She cocked her head and scratched it.

"No, no," stammered one of the girls, "you . . . I mean . . ."

"Oh—you mean Virginia. People are always saying we look alike, but I don't see how. She's much taller."

The class roared.

"I like being myself," Gina continued. "I can get away with more. That's right! Tall people always think I'm cute. They smile down at me when I say things even *I* know are stupid and then they say, 'Isn't she cute!' "

"Yeah!"

"But the biggest advantage to being small"—she leaned toward the class and whispered—"is that you don't have to do as much work. The ceiling's too high for you to paint. The lawn mower's too big. Believe me, if we all got together and put our minds to it, we could arrange a life of leisure by managing to stay small!"

Virginia could tell by the burst of laughter following each rapt silence that the children were intrigued. She felt a shiver of exhilaration, a heady sense of freedom.

"I have a bunch of friends who came along with me today. Would you like to meet them?"

"Yes" came almost as one shout from the entire class.

"Okay, but they'll need your help. Virginia'll pass them out. Remember, I let her do all the heavy work."

Virginia stood up and began taking puppets out of the locker. She had made them over the course of the past year, whenever she'd had a little time to herself; Parker had helped her with some of them back in Wisconsin. There was an old man with a big nose and a weather-beaten black hat, a Chinese emperor in red silk, a classic golden-haired princess and a not-so-classic Ethiopian one, Captain Hook and Robin Hood, Mr. Punch with his impudent nose already sniffing out profitable adventures, a goateed king, and an assortment of ordinary people. There were animated beagles and Persian cats; one giraffe, his brushed velvet skin dappled with spots shaped like tiny television screens; a witch, an angel. And at the bottom of the chest, creatures whose magical powers were inversely proportional to the probability that they could really exist: an apple tree with a hundred red eyes, a talking bush, a blue-eyed dragon, a ballerina bewitched in the hide of a hippopotamus, a cross-eyed peacock.

"Isn't this marvelous?" Gina took over again, clapping her hands as she skipped along the red ledge. "All my friends are here! It's fun to have so many different kinds of friends. Each one of them has already led a fascinating life. Mr. Robin Hood, for example, spends all his time in the forest with his band of merry archers, robbing the rich people who come through and giving the loot to the poor. And where do you think this little boy in overalls got his nice straw hat?"

"Robin Hood gave it to him!"

"Right-o! I know what we'll do—why don't all of you come up here and pick out a new friend? Ask him or her to tell you their story."

There was a few moments' hesitation; then the children stormed the desk, trying to peek behind the trunk in order to see Virginia. Gina shoved them back.

"What are you, a bunch of robbers? Quiet! Line up, there, you scalawags! Order in the court! What we need is some organization! Now—Virginia will show my friends to you only if you're quiet, and you may raise your hands whenever you find a friend who meets your fancy."

In a short while she had the children back in their seats again, each with a puppet on one hand. Then, out of the corner of her eye, Virginia noticed some movement. Clustered inside the doorway were the students from Instrumental Music, three girls. Caught with Gina parading in front of her, she felt like the Wizard of Oz after his curtain has been pulled away. She decided to play it off.

"Come in, come in! Don't stand there like a pack of frightened rabbits!" Gina yelled, causing another burst of giggles from the class. "Come in! Pick a puppet! The show's just about to begin!"

They trooped up to the desk and shyly looked through the remaining dolls. The last child, a small-boned brown-skinned girl in a blue checkered dress, reminded her of someone; maybe she'd seen her yesterday in the hall. Virginia watched her pick the Wicked Queen and fit it on her hand.

The girl looked up. Her slanted eyes, wide-spaced and framed by thin black lashes—she had seen these eyes before. Unblinking, they held her gaze. Virginia knew that gaze well— a child staring into the mirror wondering if she were a freak, gawking at her own eyes staring back.

"And what's your name?" Virginia heard Gina ask.

"Renee."

"Renee! That's a pretty name. Do you like the Wicked Queen?"

The girl nodded.

"Well, I'm sure she likes you, too."

When Puppets & People, Inc., had no longer been able to escape bankruptcy, Virginia had felt both dismayed and relieved. These people, with whom she had brainstormed and toured for the past year, suddenly seemed to smudge before her eyes.

On one of their last evenings, they had sat around the front parlor, morosely sipping champagne from juice glasses as mosquitoes banged against the screens. The big question hung in the room, as persistent and insinuating as a bad smell: what now? One thing was certain: they would all go their separate ways. They had been a struggling but optimistic troupe, generating their own energy for the offbeat commedia dell'arte performances that were part fantasy, part farce, part soap-box theatrics. A few months back, though, when they'd returned from a tour of the Eastern seaboard, they had felt exhausted in a new way.

We should have stayed here in the countryside, thought

Virginia: fifteen miles outside Madison, where the open-air performances were for anyone who wanted to drive out from the city to see, or the brief forays made into town for those who just happened by. The chalk-white masks, the giant stone heads, the gaudy banners and makeshift signs fit into the stubborn loveliness of the dairy landscape. What they'd been trying to do didn't belong on a stage. Confined by a proscenium arch, the puppets seemed ludicrous, and their improvisational style looked clumsy. No wonder audiences had laughed in the wrong places and found references to White House tapes and CIA-assisted killings in Latin America discomforting, even repugnant.

Parker tinkered at the upright piano, cigarette dangling from his lips and the ever-present scotch glass sweating onto a stack of sheet music. He dove into "Stormy Weather," but no one joined in. When he had finished, Jim came over, shoulders hunched into an imaginary trench coat, and asked him to play it again.

Colette pushed the blond curls off her forehead and sighed. "Lucky Virginia."

"What are you talking about?" Virginia asked.

"Because you've got a job," Jim snorted. "Colette would snap it up in a minute."

Parker chuckled. Colette looked down, shamefaced; they were always accusing her of aspirations to middle-class security. Whenever she opened the refrigerator and complained that they were down to yogurt and bean sprouts, count on either Parker or Jim to pop their eyes wide in mock astonishment and exclaim, "Why, Laura Petrie! Aren't you happy here?" in a perfect imitation of "The Dick Van Dyke Show."

Virginia pursed her lips and put down her glass. "Look, I didn't ask for respectability. I can't help it if it dogs me wherever I go!"

Spontaneous laughter; Colette flashed a wet-eyed smile of gratitude. Parker carefully put out his cigarette, all the while giving her the benefit of his hot, dark gaze. Funny man, Virginia thought, winking at him to keep it light. When had Parker ever acted on his desire?

Nigel's voice boomed from the corner armchair: "But the father said to his servants, 'Bring quickly the best robe, and put it on him, and put a ring on his hand, and shoes on his feet; and bring the fatted calf and kill it, and let us eat and make merry; for this my son was dead, and is alive again; he was lost, and is found.' " Nigel lifted a pale hand in benediction and let it drift gracefully down to the faded crimson velvet. The armchair was tacitly designated as his and his alone: he claimed to have brought it with him from his Bristol flat, though once Parker inspected the underside while Nigel was out hunting down materials and found a label from an antique shop in South Hadley, Massachusetts.

"Hey, Nigel, you can't complain either," said Jim. "The Big Apple awaits you."

"Yes, yes—off-off-off Broadway and no guaranteed pay." Nigel shifted heavily into a more comfortable position. "I am being taken back into the fold—albeit gingerly—just as if nothing had happened. As if there had never been a Puppets & People, an attempt to break out of the bloody *Structure.*"

The first time Virginia had met Nigel, she had marveled that someone so fat could be that energetic and graceful with so little movement. Perhaps it was precisely the effortless quality about him that had sustained the troupe for so long, as if they had been defying the gravity of social apathy.

Nigel had come to the United States at the end of the fifties, on scholarship to study film at New York University; after receiving his degree he returned to London and enjoyed a reputation as radical young filmmaker and occasional director of experimental drama. Then came the Beatles, Vietnam and the student protests. Fed up with the complacent avant-garde in British theater, he threw it all over to participate in the new American Revolution, founding a street theater in Berkeley which evolved into Puppets & People, and moved from the coastal fringes to the swamp and pasture lands of Wisconsin.

Virginia had graduated the winter before, one semester early; after frustrating weeks spent looking for work in theater, she'd taken a job as a secretary for a construction company. She'd had no clue what to do next; all she wanted to do was to fit her existence into some kind of framework. Efficiency was her salvation: she worked through coffee breaks and spent her lunch hour walking the tight gridwork of streets in downtown Madison.

On May Day the bosses bowed to the traditional sentiments of an old labor town and gave the office staff a half day off. Virginia took her usual noonday route and when the hour was over kept going, heading away from the commercial district toward the built-up shores of Lake Wingra to the southwest, at the foot of the campus. She dreaded the free afternoon, although it was an uncommonly fine day: the pale sun warmed her shoulders as she dodged the Frisbee players and baby strollers on the paths leading to the Arboretum.

She heard them before she saw them: the bald thump of tom-toms, and then a clarinet's tootle and wail wafting toward her from a row of boxwoods. *What in the world?* Virginia headed toward what turned out to be a neighborhood park, a little square of green. As she approached, she thought she heard—*could that be Mozart?*—a toy piano plinking merrily off-key.

She entered the boxwoods and stopped, staring: a long table draped in white sheets and above it, on poles, a red banner emblazoned with blue stars and the words LAST SUPPER AT THE BIG HOUSE. Bright helium-filled balloons hovered behind the festive table: at first Virginia thought it was a child's birthday party, for there seemed to be a large birthday cake as a centerpiece; but then a voice croaked through a megaphone: "Due to circumstances beyond my control I find it imperative to render my resignation," and an orange balloon floated up and away, trailing a red-and-blue-striped ribbon—no, a *necktie,* Virginia realized with a start, and then she saw that all the balloons were knotted with neckties that in turn were moored to the table by bronze-colored nameplates—HALDEMAN, EHRLICHMAN, KLEINDIENST, DEAN—and what she had imagined were candles on a cake were actually American flags protruding from a magician's top hat.

Again the amplified voice: "Due to circumstances beyond my . . ." and a blue balloon exploded with a loud *pop!* before the premeditated message could be completed. Scattered applause erupted from the crowd, mostly students and a smattering of curious passersby.

To the right of this tableau sat the ragtag orchestra: on bongos an enormous pink-cheeked man in a rainbow-striped blazer, a female clarinetist in the purple and scarlet scarves of the whore of Babylon, and hunched over the toy piano a black-robed figure with a phosphorescent skullmask—the Grim Reaper shaking back his voluminous sleeves to execute an arpeggio, unaware that behind him a herd of preschoolers had

made off with his broomstick and tinfoil scythe and were playing kill-or-be-killed on the trampled meadow.

After all the balloons had proclaimed their innocence
and floated off, a child-sized puppet appeared and scampered
across the table, inspecting the litter. It was all face, a papier-
mâché potato man, although those jowls, that five o'clock
shadow, those deep-set narrow eyes, were unmistakable—bal-
ancing on tiny brocade slippers with curled-up toes, the scowling head finally scooped up a fistful of flags from the top hat
and stuck them into a ring of Styrofoam to fashion a crown of
thorns; thus adorned, it did a grotesque little jig while from the
sidelines a group of pint-sized marionette skeletons gently
crooned, "Rock-a-bye, Dickie."

Virginia gasped. Nixon's staff had just resigned the day
before; how could they manage to be so up-to-date? It was
more exorcist rite than acting, more pageant than puppetry.
Whenever a person appeared onstage as a character rather than
a technician, he or she donned monstrous masks and shapeless
sacks, becoming oversized human puppets who combined the
dignity of Noh theater with the lustiness of Barnum & Bailey.

The afternoon slipped by. Leaning against an elm, Virginia watched the ever-changing crowd of laughing and clapping students. Every once in a while a pedestrian muttered
disapprovingly, or a nanny hissed her children to safety; one
elderly man even stopped to shake his cane at them. Before she
knew it, they were announcing the last call for donations; a
distinctly cool breeze had picked up from the lake. When the
Grim Reaper came around with the top hat, Virginia dropped
in a hefty smattering of coins. He paused, gazing into the hat
as if it were a well; then the skull lifted and he winked, saying,
"Come out and see us sometime," snapping the mask back

into place and moving on to the next person before she had time to register more than a pair of dark eyes.

"Where?" she blurted out, suddenly not caring what a spectacle she must have made in her jaunty secretarial skirt, standing up against a tree in her sling-back pumps with her prim little purse.

"Route 113," he tossed over his shoulder, "past Waunakee. Just ask for Puppets and People."

Virginia felt as if Fate had dropped a mountain in her path and then, like Ali Baba, had shown her the door that led to the treasure chamber. For the last year she had dutifully pursued her acting career, enduring scores of auditions and casting directors' cheerful impressive-but-not-quite-right-for-us pronouncements, until she'd finally understood that there was hardly any place for a black woman in professional theater, not even in this haven of white liberalism. The few times she'd shown up at a cast call for a mime, the directors just sat there with their mouths open: *A black mime? You've got to be kidding.* And the Black Theatre Troupe, formerly the Ku'umba Workshop, emphasized Marxist doctrine over professionalism. Maybe she should have tried her luck in Chicago or even New York, but she'd been afraid to move to the lion's den all on her own.

The next few days were intolerable. At work, Virginia struggled to maintain a professional attitude, but at the oddest moments—while typing a letter to the cement manufacturer or delivering a batch of purchase orders to the wire basket marked SUPPLIES—snippets of the scene in the park kept popping to mind. She caught herself making mental notes like *Race shouldn't pose a problem; they all wear masks.* Suddenly, the easygoing pace of the office was suffocating. She longed for intensity, fervor.

That weekend she garnered the courage to drive out the county road where Puppets & People had their headquarters. It wasn't hard to find at all; she'd been just about to turn back to the dairy community of Waunakee and ask for directions when she saw an old school bus repainted in psychedelic swirls standing in a gravel driveway: PUPPETS & PEOPLE, INC. screamed out in shocking pink script.

The farmhouse sat on a knoll, behind a small grove of maples. Deep brown earth sprinkled with the erratic beginnings of wildflowers rolled out in dark furrows to the next dwelling, nearly half a mile away, where the fields suddenly erupted in a brilliant pattern of variegated green, crops of young corn and budding hay. Puppets & People, Inc. was obviously not in the farming business.

Virginia pulled into the driveway behind the bus and stepped out. She smelled the wet of earthworms and a light peppery scent on the air. From somewhere came a high-pitched hum, strangely imperious, yet so general a sound there was no telling what caused it—it could have been inside the house or three miles away.

The door stood open. She rang the bell and peered through the screen, then rang again. Finally, from the back of the house she heard the *thlop-thlop* of sandals slapping against a hardwood floor. A door opened at the end of a long dark corridor; in the rectangle of light, the slim silhouette of a man appeared. As he approached, she could see that he wore blue jeans and no shirt, and that he was covered from head to foot in a fine white dust.

"Yes?"

"My name is Virginia King." She didn't know *how* to say it, so she just said it. "I'd like to work with you guys."

43

At his bemused smile she added, "I'm serious. I've studied mime and acted in a few things around Madison. I saw your performance in the municipal park a couple days ago."

His smile deepened, and he motioned her inside, leading her out of the dim vestibule and into a bright and spacious room.

"The name's Jim. Have a seat." Then he disappeared through the French doors in the back.

The room had probably once been the living and dining area of a traditional country house, but the dividing wall had been knocked out, and it was furnished like a studio, with no curtains at the tall windows, a wooden floor without rugs, just a few pieces of furniture. Opposite the couch was a huge stone fireplace and next to it an equally overpowering rolltop desk. Three straight-back chairs were pushed into the corners, and an upright piano, black, stood near the front windows. The room was full of May afternoon light, white with a flush of topaz.

"Well, well, another victim, what?" A merry British voice boomed from the doorway. Virginia started: a man-sized mountain was coming toward her.

"I'm Nigel." He shook her hand vigorously and sat down at the desk. So firm was his fat that it seemed to amass in strict geometrical proportion the nearer it came to the ground. His face was a smaller pyramid, and yet not pudgy. He seemed, in fact, in the best of health and, with his trim brown mustache and bright pink shirt, a bit of a dandy as well.

"Tell me," he said, "why you want to join our family."

Virginia talked about the lack of serious theaters, and how her college drama teacher had merely smirked when she had declared her determination to study mime.

There was a silence. Finally, he sighed. It was a curious sound, like the long note of a singer famous for his breath control.

"So what can you do?" he asked.

"I have a degree in drama, and I studied mime with Nathan Mannheim in Madison. I've played Adele in *Ceremonies in Dark Old Men* and Pandora in *Goin' a Buffalo*, plus bit parts in nonblack dramas . . ."

"Fine, fine. But what *else* can you do?"

She hesitated.

"Listen—I'm not trying to make you nervous. I just want to know what you can do. There are sets to be built and puppets to be made and costumes to be sewn and music to be sung. That means that no one here sits on their ass and studies lines all day long. D'you see that garage back there? Right now Parker is nailing together some stilts and Jim is sawing a three-foot Janus head in half so we can mount a revolving color light wheel inside. Can you do anything like that?"

"I don't know. I mean, I never have, but I think I could. That is, I'm more than willing."

"That's half the fight." He leaned forward. "Now—what other things can you do? Any vocation? Hobbies? What other kinds of jobs have you had?"

"I'm working as a secretary right now."

"That stuff is boring, isn't it? But it can come in handy. I love my 'family,' but they have no business sense whatsoever. Can't answer a simple letter. Anything else?"

"Well . . . I play the cello."

"Excellent! Sometimes we like to use music as background punctuation, you know. Whenever possible, we do it live. Colette plays an atrocious clarinet, but Parker's a mean jazz pianist. Then that's settled. We all pitch in here and get things done. You'll get a chance to do everything from selling tickets to playing the lead."

"Does that mean I'm in?" Virginia asked, amazed.

He laughed and stood up, not an ounce of flesh jiggling anywhere. "Of course you're in! Do you think I would have spent one minute with you if I hadn't known from the first you were one of us?"

What a year it had been! Things happening faster than she could stop to think—actions in the park and stagings that had resulted from late-night brainstorming like *Repression Tango*, a piece featuring Jim and Parker masked and dancing on stilts through a throng of tiny clay marionettes, crushing them underfoot. It had been exhilarating, improvising spectacles to shake up the world, fed by their personal outrage at the times and the land they lived in, a country that conducted a distant war against perfect strangers whose brains were being blasted out on national television.

How strange that she had ended up behind those masks! And yet, not really so strange after all; from the very first moment she'd stood in front of that improvised puppet stage like Ali Baba when he'd just been told the magic word to open the wall of stone, she'd felt the danger. Instead of stepping out into the world, she had entered the cave.

College, too, had been a refuge—not the womb every amateur pop psychologist liked to refer to, but a cave where you made a fire at the entrance, with twigs and sweet resinous pine cones, and then crouched behind it to gaze through the smoky scrim at the infinite stars. In the cave you were free to dream or draw on the walls, or even talk the night through with a few members of the clan; but outside—well, it was better not to think about it, now that everything was falling apart.

Nigel lifted his glass. "From student to secretary to mime and puppeteer par excellence, to Visiting Artist in the Public Schools. And the first gig's in your hometown! You can't lose."

He toasted her. "But if you do—you know where to find me. I mean it, Virginia! If ever you want to follow your dream . . ." He finished his champagne in one silent gulp.

After school, back in the apartment, Virginia called her mother. "Everything's fine here," she offered. "It looks like rain though."

"Really? Lucky you. Of course, it's been dry as bones out here." Belle paused. "I miss rain."

"Come on, Mom. You get rain in Arizona."

"Not that kind of chilly rain. So wrap yourself up good, Sugar Lump, and drink some hot chocolate for me, okay?"

Virginia winced. "Right. Hey, how's Dad?"

"You know your father; nothing fazes him." It was an indictment.

"And Claudia? Has she calmed down a little?"

But if Virginia had been hoping for another soul-sharing like they had had during her visit a few days before, she was to be disappointed.

"What *about* Claudia?" came Belle's retort, a bit peeved. "She's just going through growing pains. You should remember what *that's* like."

And so the conversation dawdled along, with polite

inquiries into the neighbors' health and how Belle and Claudia had gone out to the new mall to get Claudia pumps for the Homecoming Dance. Belle repeated her reminder that Virginia visit Grandma Evans.

"Mother, I just got here! I promise I'll go see her just as soon as I catch my breath, all right?"

"Well, you might just make the time soon. Playing puppets with schoolchildren can't last into the wee hours."

"Mother . . ."

"All right, so you need some time to get adjusted," she said, putting a bite into the last word. "At least you've got a job. Let's hope this one doesn't peter out like that band of *artistes.*"

Virginia put the phone down rather sharply into the cradle, sighing. So often, conversations with her mother had ended in irritation and veiled reprimands; how could she have believed things had changed just because of their reconciliation this summer?

After the members of Puppets & People had gone their separate ways, Virginia had flown to Phoenix. Late summer was the worst time of the year, the dregs of the monsoon season, which meant no rain but the continual threat of a cloudburst and all the accompanying symptoms—muggy days, dry lightning at sunset and even on simmering blue afternoons a constant faint rumbling of thunder from the Superstition Mountains in the east.

Belle had developed a routine: Open the windows at night, but close them and pull the curtains shut by 6 A.M., before the sun had a chance to heat up the house. At noon she'd open the curtains and a few windows just a crack—on the principle that the light, being directly overhead, wouldn't strike the panes—and turn on the evaporative cooler, which really didn't work well on days of high humidity. Promptly at two the sills were bolted and curtains drawn again. In this penumbral gloom they survived the dog days, rolling up the rugs and patting their limbs and brows with a mixture of ice water and witch hazel, and eating tons of fruit—to this day whenever Virginia so much as looked at a cantaloupe, she had to choke down her rising gorge.

The day after her arrival in Phoenix, she'd awoken at noon to find Claudia up and gone, her bed a rumpled mound of sheets. Virginia showered quickly and wandered into the kitchen where her mother was preparing a cold curried chicken salad for supper.

"Where's the C?" she asked, reaching in the cupboard for a water glass.

"Who knows where your sister is. Out with that pack of hoodlum girls, most likely, grilling their skulls."

Surprised, Virginia came over to the table and sat down. Never before had her mother spoken out against her precious last-born, even when Claudia lounged on the couch all day reading teenie magazines.

"She's used to the sun, I guess. After all, she's a native Phoenician." It was a family joke, but Belle didn't smile.

"I don't know how to handle her anymore," Belle said. "She hides makeup in her locker at school and the principal sends her home with a letter of reprimand—as if I'd let her go out of the house like that! And last week she slipped out at night."

Virginia gasped. "How did you find out?" she asked.

"Well, we leave the windows open, you know; but she had taken off the screen and leaned it against the bureau and it fell over. Ernest went to investigate and there was the evidence. It was around midnight; we had no idea where she'd gone. I wanted to go look for her but your father said no, just shut up the windows and she'll have to wake us. And sure enough, about three-thirty the doorbell rang and she came straggling in as huffy as you please."

"Where had she been?"

"Do you know what she said? 'Around.' That's all—'around.'"

Virginia wanted to tell her it was no wonder Claudia had turned out the way she had, coddled before birth and spoiled every minute afterward by a mother disappointed with everything else in life and a father too tired to discipline her. But of course she didn't say anything.

Then Ernie Jr. flew down from Seattle for the weekend. When Virginia expressed surprise that he would come all that way for just two days, he grinned. "Working for Boeing has its advantages. Besides, I had to see my favorite sister."

"Claudia'd love that," Virginia replied, glancing toward the hall, even though Claudia wasn't home—she'd gone to the shopping mall with a gaggle of gum-popping girls.

They were standing in the bedroom they had shared for half a year after Claudia was born; later, Virginia had been moved into the adjacent room with her sister's crib. It was a house full of tiny rooms, a typical southwestern ranch-style, cinderblock construction with the living-dining area and kitchen off to one side and a master bedroom with what was called a three-quarter bath (sink, toilet, shower) branching off to the other side of the front vestibule; there was a narrow corridor leading toward the back and two more bedrooms and a cramped, but full, bath.

After Ernie had gone off to college—first to UCLA and then to Cal Tech—his room had gradually been turned into a sort of den for their father. And now Claudia had completely taken over their joint bedroom; the walls were plastered with posters of Sly and the Family Stone and Rick James of "Super Freak" fame. After one look inside, Virginia didn't feel compelled to set foot in there for anything but sleep.

"Hey, Claudia's not a sister," Ernie Jr. exclaimed. "She's our resident alien." They both chuckled; it had been their private joke back when five-year-old Claudia, despite Belle's scolding, had spent more time outside than in, so that her skin had acquired a brick-red sheen—not burned, more like embers smoldering just under the surface. Claudia, Orphan from Mars.

Ernie was fingering the nougat-colored fringed skirt of a kachina doll on the shelf. "Dad's got this place set up pretty nice," he said.

"Doesn't it bother you, seeing your old room changed?"

"Naw. It looks a hell of a lot better than when I was sleeping here. Course, I never actually *lived* in it." He fell silent and looked around like a stranger appraising a property. *We never really lived in this house anyway,* his silence seemed to say. Then a mischievous glint entered his eye. "But now—*you've* got a right to be pissed. Claudia's done tore your room *up!*"

Virginia smiled. "Remember our trip to the Hopi mesas?"

"Do I? I thought I'd shrivel up from boredom. I was pretty nonchalant in those days. Supercool, you know—James Brown got a brand-new bag. Adolescence is rough." They fell silent again, thinking of Claudia.

Now Virginia touched the leather fringe. "Far Hills Kachina," she said, softly.

"You remember the names to those things?" Ernie asked, incredulous. "But then, you were always in a different bag than me. You were more like Dad—you two liked to get off on weird symbols. Come to think of it, that's what's made you what you are today."

"You mean what I used to be, until Puppets and People folded," Virginia countered. She didn't tell him that he'd gotten it wrong—Far Hills Kachina wasn't the name of the figure on the shelf. It was what they used to call their father.

Four

Virginia glanced down at her brown skirt and green-print jersey blouse. In the apartment it had seemed just the right touch of prim-and-pretty; now in the dreary light of a hazy autumn Sunday, it was plain schoolmarmish.

She found it difficult to imagine her grandmother in an old folks' home. Would Grandma Evans be senile, as Belle had warned? She had sounded fine during their Christmas phone call last winter.

Saferstein Tower was a prefab high-rise named after a local philanthropist who had deeded the land. The alumni of several fraternities had paid for its construction, and its operation was subsidized by the federal government. Designed under the premise that living for the elderly could be pleasant as well as efficient, the building was set on a wooded hill near the center of town and had its own swimming pool and shuffleboard courts.

There was no one at the reception desk and no directory on the wall. Virginia hesitated, looking around. Grinning from a photograph on the wall was James R. Saferstein himself in a yellow polo shirt, posing before *his* tower. By his side stood a stooped-over elderly white woman in a navy blue dress. "Mr. Saferstein and the First Tenant," the caption said. His right hand was extended across his body in the familiar shake-hands-for-the-camera pose; the old woman, however, stood oblivious to his waiting hand and squinted into the lens.

How was she going to find her grandmother's room? Maybe they had visiting hours, like a hospital. She should have checked. Why *hadn't* she phoned? Childish. . . .

"Who do you want to see, dear?" A round-faced woman with pinkish-white hair was looking up at her kindly from a distance of two inches. Virginia moved back a step. Several other ladies stood a little distance off.

"I'm looking for Mrs. Virginia Evans. She's lived here about ten years now, maybe—"

"Mrs. Evans? Oh, Ginny. Everyone knows Ginny!" The others nodded vigorously and came closer. "Are you any relation to her?"

No one had ever dared call Grandma Evans Ginny. "I'm her granddaughter. I just came back to town and thought I'd surprise her—"

"Oh, she'll be a happy soul when she lays eyes on you." They had formed a semicircle around Virginia and were smiling at her with benign curiosity.

"Sometimes it's good to be surprised," the first woman went on. "Better than waiting around for them to come by and then they don't. She's in room 327 . . . or is it 329?" She frowned but cheered up again immediately. "Tell you what: I'll take you there. I know the room by sight. It's just these numbers get me mixed up."

They moved toward the elevators as the other women, disappointed to be left out of the action, milled about in the lobby, whispering among themselves.

"How wonderful that you came all the way to visit your grandmother," the old lady said, beaming.

And here was the door, like every other door on the hall—a knocker, a peephole, nothing more. Virginia wanted to thank her escort, but the woman seemed to have forgotten where she was; she smiled at the door as if it were festooned with streamers.

"Shall I wait?" she asked.

"I think I'd better take it from here. But thank you," Virginia added. "If it hadn't been for your help, Mrs. . . . I'm sorry, I didn't get your name."

"Amy Kepler." The woman tried to hide her disappointment.

"Mrs. Kepler, thank you. I never would have found my grandmother without you."

That seemed to help. Mrs. Kepler nodded, pink hair fluttering slightly, and made her way to the elevator. Virginia watched it slide shut, then she lifted the knocker and rapped twice. The door opened a crack.

"Who's there?" A thin voice, high and imperious.

"Virginia King." That was silly. "Grandma, it's me, Virginia. I just got into town and—"

The crack widened—bright brown eyes behind jeweled winged glasses. "Belle's girl?" Then the door swung open, and she found herself clamped in a set of thin, vigorous arms. "Yes, that's you. I'd know those eyes anywhere. Come in child, come in!"

The same two knots of hair at the temples, only grayer. There weren't many wrinkles on her face, though. "You won't catch me looking like a walnut when I'm eighty," she used to say. "Too much Blackfoot Indian in me for that!" She'd also been right to claim she was too mean to die at an early age. Even now she looked angry at something, scowling as she refastened the chain lock. She brushed past her granddaughter to the center of the room, where she turned and stared.

"I always told them you'd be back to see me. 'If no one else, then Virginia,' I told them. And when Belle called last week from Phoenix . . . well, don't just stand there like a stranger—sit down! Want a peppermint?"

Virginia settled into the fragrant cushions of an armchair. Grandma Evans's sweet tooth! She used to have bags of hard candy hidden all over the house. Virginia remembered the armchair and afternoons spent curled in its flowery depths, reading in the cool parlor. Everything in the room had been transferred from the parlor of the old house: the same dull green sofa, the side tables. And the fringes—fringes on the curtains, on the lampshade, the golden tassels at each plump corner of a pillow with a picture of a girl in a barrel and the inscription NIAGARA FALLS, 1949.

Grandma Evans had taken up the center of the gray-green love seat. This had always been her throne—the *talking seat,* they used to call it, because she had loved to tell stories and give lectures from its cushions.

"I don't reckon you hardly recognize me," she said now, thin voice quavering. "Children never pay attention to a body until you're at death's gate, and then it's too late. But that's old-woman talk. How's your mother? She never tells me on the phone."

"I guess she's fine."

"You *guess* she's fine?" Grandma Evans cocked an eyebrow. "And my girl Claudia—still as wild as ever?"

"Claudia's Claudia." Virginia knew she was being evasive, but she suddenly felt uneasy being scrutinized by this pert, bristling woman. What was she getting at? Why was she sitting there with her arms folded across her chest as if to say, *Uh-huh, I thought as much,* letting the silence bear down as a

56

measure of her disapproval? What was Virginia supposed to say? *My parents live in separate universes and Claudia ricochets between them like a planet knocked off orbit?* That even on holidays Ernie Jr. stayed away, although with his connections he could get a flight nearly anywhere in the world for next to nothing?

"Well," Grandma Evans said finally, "now that you're here, you should visit the rest of the family who ain't seen you since you were knee-high to an Indian. How about your Aunt Carrie—any plans to visit her?"

"Aunt Carrie? Dad's sister? I haven't thought about her in years. What's she doing?"

"Haven't thought about her! She used to baby-sit you and your brother near about every Saturday night, and you haven't thought about her in years? Just like all these young folks—get too busy to think."

"Is she well? How's she getting along?"

"Same as the rest of us. You go visit her soon as you get through with me. She'll be home, she always is." The old woman shook her head. "Sitting all alone in that house on Furnace Street. Folks forget about you before you're even dead. It's a shame."

"I'll visit her, Grandma," Virginia protested, "but not today, please. I've got to prepare for school tomorrow."

Grandma Evans paused, head turned a little to one side. Then she looked up to squint at her granddaughter with a disapproving air.

"Too much makeup," she pronounced. "And those clothes! You're too young to look like a church mouse."

Virginia smiled. Yes, this was vintage Grandma Evans.

"Now that you're here, you might as well get a little advice from someone who knows what's what. You think you know everything just 'cause you've been to the university and all those fancy places people think mean something. They don't mean a thing to me."

"Grandma—"

"Shhhh! Listen, 'cause these might be my last words, child!" She smiled but immediately grew serious again. "I haven't had a chance to help raise you, really, and I know good and well I can't make up for it now. But I'm gonna tell you some things now that I've got a chance, and it's up to you to take it or leave it. Coffee?"

Virginia nodded. "I can make it, Grandma," she offered.

"No, no, child," she said, rising from the love seat with a grunt. "I need to move around some. Makes me feel natural." She shuffled toward the kitchenette.

"Now," she threw back over her shoulder. "There's a way for a lady to act and there's a way not to. Take laughing; there's a way to laugh. Miss Allen in the choir used to say, 'A woman laughs like a saloon, a lady like a music box.' When you laugh, hold your hand over your mouth. Don't clap it over like you're about to burp—hold it straight and a little to the side, like you're going to whisper something to someone next to you. And no whistling. No lady's got no business walking down the street in broad daylight pursing her lips as if there weren't nothing to be ashamed of. Everything in its place, and that ain't the place for that. What my mother told me was good advice and I'll tell it to you:

A whistling woman and a cackling hen
Will never come to a good end.

"Mark that. You're a big girl now, that's why I'm telling you all this. Nice legs and pretty eyes too—wide-set like Belle's. They fill up your face without being cow-ey. You're a good-looking young lady."

She filled the kettle at the stainless-steel sink and turned on the front burner. "Just be careful with them eyes when you get mad. It's got something to do with dark skin and the contrast. When your mama was a little girl, I took her to the park once and told her not to do something, I forget what, and she knew better than to sass me but she rolled them whites at me and I beat her little rump. She claimed she was just looking at me from the side-like, but it sure looked like rolling. So be careful with them. They'll get you into trouble when you least expect. Nowadays, though, no one seems to think about such things. Saucy women, running around with their skirts halfway to their necks and their eyes all blacked with makeup! I never liked it. I didn't like it when they started it, back in the twenties. I saw some movie star on the TV yesterday with one of those mini-skirts on . . . terrible! Knees looked like a couple of turnips."

Virginia had to smile. It was true—knees *were* ugly on white people.

"You're more like me. I feel it. A name ain't just decoration, you know. It's got destiny in it. That's why I told Belle to give you a good one. And she knew what to do. Yes! She did the best thing she could have done. You ain't my namesake for nothing. You like your name, don't you? It's a pretty name. Long and dignified, with a lilt. Not one of those short, bobbed-off names that sound like people's ashamed of saying them. People got to think twice before they say ours. Take their time: Vir-gin-i-a. Couldn't stand it when someone tried to shorten it—like some floozy, Gina or Ginny."

59

"Your neighbors here don't seem to realize that," Virginia couldn't help saying.

"What do you mean?" Grandma Evans cocked her head to one side again, a spoonful of Folger's suspended over the thick lip of a cup whose red trim seemed dimly familiar. Virginia told her about Amy Kepler.

"Hummph," she said. "This place is full of disrespectful people. You can't teach these white folks nothing. I remember how your grandpa said it when he first got a conversation going with me. Set his guitar down real slow. 'Miss Virginia,' he said, 'you're a fine piece of woman.' Seems he'd been asking around. Knew everything about me. Knew I was bold and proud and didn't cotton to no silly niggers. Vir-gin-ee-a, he said, nice and slow. Almost Russian, the way he said it. Right then and there I knew this man was for me. That's how you pick 'em, honey. Listen how they say your name. If they can't say that right, there's no way they're going to know how to treat you proper, neither."

Virginia watched her pour the water in without spilling a drop. Even the cups had survived all those years.

"They've got to take time with it. Your granddad took his time. He knew this lady wasn't going to be pushed over like any old applecart. He courted me just inside a year, came by nearly every day. First I wouldn't see him for more than half an hour. I'd send him away, and he knew better than to try to force me. Fellow did that once, kept coming by when I said I had other things to do. I told him he do it one more time, I'd be waiting at the door with a pot of scalding water to teach him some manners. Fool didn't believe me—I had the pot waiting on the stove and when he came up those stairs, I was standing in the door. He took one look at my face and turned and ran.

He was lucky those steps were so steep. I only got a little piece of his pant leg. No, your granddad knew his stuff. He'd come on time and stay till I told him he needed to go.

"Did I ever tell you how I met him? I was out at Summit Beach one day. That was a place then! Clean yellow sand all around the lake, and an amusement park that ran from morning to midnight. I went there with a couple of other girls. They were younger than me and a little silly—you know how girls are. But they were sweet. I was nineteen then. 'High time,' everyone used to say to me, but I'd just lift my head and go on about my business. I weren't going to marry just any old Negro. He had to be perfect."

Virginia slipped off her shoes and settled back into the cushions, tucking up her legs. She remembered this tone: Grandma was on her talking seat, and there was no stopping her until the story was told.

"There was a man was chasing me around about that time, too. Tall dark nigger. Sterling Williams was his name; pretty as a panther. Married, he was—least that's what people said. Left a wife in Washington, D.C. A little crazy, the wife, and poor Sterling was trying to get a divorce.

"Well, Sterling Williams was at Summit Beach that day, too. He followed me around, trying to buy me root beer. We loved root beer that summer. Root beer and vanilla ice cream—the Boston Cooler. But I wouldn't pay him no mind. People said I was crazy—Sterling was the best catch in Akron, they said. 'Not for me,' I said. 'I don't want no secondhand man.' But Sterling wouldn't give up. He kept buying root beers and having to drink them himself.

"Then I saw your granddaddy. He'd just come up from Tennessee. Folks said his best friend had been lynched down there and he turned his back on the town and said he was never coming back. Well, when I saw this cute little man in a straw hat and a twelve-string guitar under his arm, I got a little flustered. My friends whispered around to find out who he was, but I acted like I didn't even see him.

"He was the hit of Summit Beach. Played that guitar like a devil. We'd take off our shoes and sit on the beach toward evening. Those girls sure loved James. 'Oh, Jimmy,' they'd squeal, 'play us a *looove* song!' He'd laugh and pick out a tune:

> 'I'll give you a dollar if you'll come out tonight,
> If you'll come out tonight,
> Come out tonight!
> I'll give you a dollar if you'll come out tonight
> And dance by the light of the moon!'

All the girls would grin and sigh, 'Jimmy, you oughta be 'shamed of yourself!' He'd sing the second verse then:

> 'I danced with a girl with a hole in her stockin',
> And her heel kep' a-rockin',
> And her heel kep' a-rockin'.
> I danced with a girl with a hole in her stockin',
> We danced by the light of the moon!'

They'd all priss and preen their feathers and wonder which would be best—to be in fancy clothes and go on being courted by dull factory fellows, or to have a hole in their stocking and dance with James. I never danced at all. I sat a bit off to one side and watched them make fools of themselves.

"Then one night near season's end we were all sitting down by the water, and everyone had on sweaters and was in a foul mood because the cold weather was coming and there wouldn't be no more parties. Someone said something about hating to have the good times end, and James struck up a nice and easy tune, looking across the fire straight at me:

'As I was lumb'ring down de street,
Down de street, down de street,
A han'some gal I chanced to meet,
Oh, she was fair to view!

I'd like to make dat gal my wife,
Gal my wife, gal my wife.
I'd be happy all my life
If I had her by me.'

"I knew he was the man. I'd known it a long while, but I was just biding my time. He called on me the next day; I said I was busy canning peaches. He came back the day after. We sat on the porch and watched the people go by. He didn't say much, except to say my name like that. 'Vir-gin-ee-a,' he said, 'you're a mighty fine woman.' I sent him home a little after that. He came back a week later. I was angry at him and told him I didn't have time for playing around. But he'd brought his guitar along, and he said he'd been practicing all week just to play a couple of songs for me. I made him sit on a stool while I sat on the porch swing. I can still remember those songs— silly little things, and I knew he hadn't been up all week trying to learn them. That's when I realized he was proud, too. I liked that.

"He sang the first one. It was a floor thumper:

63

'There is a gal in our town,
She wears a yellow striped gown,
And when she walks the streets aroun'
The hollow of her foot makes a hole in the groun'.

'Ol' folks, young folks, cl'ar the kitchen.
Ol' folks, young folks, cl'ar the kitchen.
Ol' Virginny never tire.'

I got a little mad then, but I knew he was baiting me. Seeing how much I would take. Now mind you, I'm no highfalutin fool would cut off her nose to spite her face. I knew he wasn't singing about me, and I'd already heard how he said my name. It was time to let the dog in out of the rain, even if he shook his wet all over the floor. So I leaned back and put my hands on my hips, real slow. 'I just *know* you ain't singing about me,' I said.

" 'Virginia,' he said with a grin would've put Rudolph Valentino to shame, 'I'd *never* sing about you that way.' Then he pulled a yellow scarf out his trouser pocket. Like melted butter it was, with fringes. 'I saw it yesterday and thought how nice it would look against your skin,' he said. That was the first present I ever accepted from a man. Then he sang his other song:

'I'm coming, I'm coming!
Virginia, I'm coming to stay.
Don't hold it agin' me
For running away.

'And if I can win ya,
I'll never more roam.

*I'm coming, Virginia,
My Dixieland home.'*

"I was gone for him. But not like those girls on the beach: I had enough sense left to crack a joke or two. 'You saying I look like the state of Virginia?' I asked, and he laughed. But I was gone.

"I didn't let him know it, though, not for a long while. Even when he asked me to marry him, months later, he was trembling and thought I just might refuse out of some womanly whim. No, he courted me proper, every day for a little while. We'd sit on the porch until it got too cold and then we'd sit in the parlor with two or three bright lamps on. My mother and father were glad I'd found a beau, but they weren't taking any chances. Everything had to be proper.

"He got down, all trembly, on one knee and asked me to be his wife. I said yes. There's a point when all this dignity and stuff get in the way of destiny. He kept on trembling; he didn't believe me.

" 'What?' he said.

" 'I said yes,' I said. I was starting to get angry. Then he saw I meant it, and he went into the other room to ask my father for my hand in marriage, and that was that.

"Now you'll learn, Virginia, that you can't hide nothing from nobody in this world. You do something vile and no-account, no matter how well you think you've covered it up, there's going to be someone somewhere going to find you out. James came all the way up from Tennessee and that should have been far enough, but he couldn't hide that snake anymore. It just crawled out from under the rock when it was good and ready.

"The snake was Jeremiah Morgan. Some fellows from Akron had gone off for work on the riverboats, and it seems some of these fellows heard about your grandpa. That twelve-string guitar and straw hat of his made him pretty popular. Anyway, story got to town that James had a baby somewhere. And joined up to that baby—but long dead and buried—was a wife.

"You'll find out soon enough in life, child, that nobody'll tell you nothing till everyone else's got wind of it. We'd been married six months and I wager half the town knew it before the honeymoon was over; but I found out from sweet-talking, side-stepping Jeremiah Morgan, who never liked me nohow after I laid his soul to rest one night when he took me home from a dance. I always carried a brick in my purse—no man could get the best of me! Well, Jeremiah must have been the happiest man in Akron the day he found out. He found it out later than most of them—seems things like that have a way of circulating first among those people know how to keep it from spreading to the wrong folks—then, when the gossip's gone the rounds, it's handed over to the one who knows just what to do with it.

" 'Ask that husband of your'n what else he left in Tennessee besides his best friend,' was all Jeremiah'd say at first. But no no-good nigger like Jeremiah Morgan could make me beg for information. I wouldn't bite.

" 'I ain't got no need for asking my husband nothing,' I said, and walked away. I was going to choir practice. He stood where he was, yelled after me like any old common person.

" 'Mrs. Evans always talking about being Number One! Looks like she's Number Two after all.'

"My ears burned from the shame of it. I went on to

choir practice and sang my prettiest; and straight when I was back home I asked him.

" 'What's all this Number Two business?'

"He broke down and told me the whole story. How he'd been married before when he was seventeen, and his wife died in childbirth and the child not quite right 'cause of being blue when it was born. And how when his friend was strung up he saw no reason for staying. And how when he met me, he found out pretty quick what I'd done to Sterling Williams and that I'd never have no secondhand man, and he had to have me, so he never told me.

"I took off my coat and hung it in the front closet. Then I unpinned my hat and set it in its box on the shelf. Then I reached in the back of the closet and brought out his hunting rifle and the box of bullets. I didn't see no way out but to shoot him.

" 'Put that down!' he shouted. 'I love you, Vir-gin-ee-a.'

" 'You were right not to tell me,' I said to him, 'because I sure as sin wouldn't of married you. I don't want you *now*.'

" 'Virginia!' he said. He was real scared. 'How can you shoot me down just like that?'

"He had something there. I couldn't shoot him when he stood there looking at me with those sweet brown eyes, telling me how much he loved me. 'You have to sleep sometime,' I said, and sat down to wait.

"He didn't sleep for three nights. He knew I meant business. I sat up in this very chair with the rifle across my lap, but he wouldn't sleep. He sat at the table there and told me over and over that he loved me and he hadn't known what else to do at the time.'

" 'When I get through killing you,' I told him, 'I'm going to write to Tennessee and have them send that baby up here. It won't do, farming a child out to any relative with an extra plate.' I held on to that rifle. Not that he would've taken it from me—not that that would've saved him. No, the only thing would've saved him was running away. And he wouldn't run, either.

"Sitting there, I had lots of time to think. He was afraid of what I might do, but he wouldn't leave me, either. Some of what he was saying began to sink in. He had lied, but that was the only way to get me, I could see that. And except for that, he was perfect. It was hardly like having a wife before at all. And the baby—anyone could see the marriage wasn't meant to be, anyway.

"On the third day about midnight I laid down the rifle. 'You will join the choir and settle down instead of plucking on that guitar anytime anyone drops a hat,' I said. 'And we will write to your aunt in Tennessee and have that child sent up here.' Then I put the rifle back in the closet.

"That child never made it up here—it had died a month before Jeremiah ever opened his mouth. That hit James hard. He thought it was his fault and all, but I made him see the child was sick and was probably better off with its Maker than it would be living out half a life.

"He was a good man, your granddaddy. He made a good tenor in the choir. The next spring I had your mother and we decided to name her Belle. That's French for beautiful. And she was, too."

Grandma Evans nodded once, satisfied, and finished her gone-cold coffee in one decorous gulp.

Five

Virginia turned her car out of the Saferstein Tower parking lot and headed down Copley Hill. She decided to drive around town. Would she be able to find her old neighborhood? She'd been too ashamed to ask Grandma Evans for directions. She could hear her exclaiming: "You mean to tell me you forgot where you come from?"

Halfway down the hill she turned right onto Edgewood Avenue, skirting the southern perimeter of an appropriately woodsy municipal park. A carved signpost loomed into view— PERKINS WOODS—and in a flash she saw in her mind the corner where she used to stop on her way home from school before crossing the busy intersection—*Look both ways and don't run*—black letters on the white metal street sign that now was white on green: MONROE ST. Here Karen would say good-bye and turn into her white neighborhood. They walked together through most of second grade, up to this traffic light, until the day . . .

How does one forget a word? Virginia could hear it as clearly as God pronouncing the Ten Commandments to Moses, each letter burning into the stone tablets. And the moment surrounding the word was as precisely marked off in her head as a few feet of film—as if someone had snipped it out, and she could still feel the hole it left. But it wasn't neat, it wasn't excised at all. She would always fit into the blue coat and leggings, snow crunching under Karen's yellow boot and the sky far away, so still it seemed more a surface than a medium, an impenetrable scrim. How does one get rid of that sound, that sky?

She'd shown Karen her report card just because she was happy and wanted to share her very first straight A's—in first grade everything had been charted Good, Satisfactory, or Unsatisfactory. They were monitors for the week, which meant they got to stay after school to clean erasers and sponge the blackboard; then they walked home. Virginia couldn't wait to show her daddy so she could bask in the delicious balm of his praise. She asked to see Karen's card because she never dreamed it could be bad, nothing could be bad on a day like this, the old snow crusty like meringue and new snow just beginning to sift down, Christmas less than a week off.

But when Karen pushed her in the chest so that she sprawled against a speckled mound of bulldozed snow and ice, when Karen flung Virginia's starry report card to the ground and stomped it once, twice, with her boot as yellow as her viciously swinging hair, Virginia felt like a glass jar had lowered around her, closing her off from the world that she could still see, out of reach, on the other side of her fingertips. It was like the crickets she and Ernie Jr. caught every summer and kept in mayonnaise jars; they thought because they'd lined the jar with grass and timothy and punctured air holes in the lid that the crickets didn't mind. Now she knew how those crickets felt; pinned to the hard side of the snow mound, she could feel snow melting under her head as the word floated between her and the paling sky, clearly visible long after Karen had spat out her revenge and run off: *Nigger!*

Virginia turned left and cautiously eased down Monroe, a plummeting street. This was a short, quiet block, bounded at either end by busy intersections; before she had entered school, she had not been allowed beyond this hundred-yard brick path except when holding the hand of Ernie Jr. crossing over into Perkins Woods to play on the swing sets or visit the scruffy ducks and threadbare beavers in the little zoo.

Right side, halfway down. She remembered the house number seconds before she saw the house, a steep A-frame wedged between other A-frames, the handkerchief lawn and the square porch. It had been painted dark red like the brick road; there, up under the eaves, was the single window she had opened to throw that hard plastic baby doll out into the street. Denise Sanders and her brother June Bug had lived next door; June Bug had been to reform school, and the only other thing Virginia could remember about him was how he launched home-made rockets by heating the tips of wooden matches that had been tightly wrapped in aluminum foil. On the other side lived senile Anna Everhart and her crazy middle-aged son Floyd. . . .

She turned around in the last driveway and drove back up the street, then back down again, marveling at its compactness, until a large black woman with three children hanging to her skirts came out on her sagging front porch, two houses down from Virginia's old home, and stared at the cruising stranger as if to memorize her face for the police report. Only after Virginia had turned out of Monroe and headed back toward Copley Hill did it hit her: that's where old Mrs. Voltz used to live!

Mrs. Voltz had been one of the last white people holding out in the neighborhood, and she had taken a liking to Virginia. Mrs. Voltz was the one who told her that Akron actually meant "high place." Since she was a foreigner and spoke with a nearly incomprehensible accent, Virginia hadn't been sure whether to believe her or not.

From the porch of Grandma Evans's house, which was on a hill, she had never been able to see farther than over the vacant lot to Plant One, with its scowling brick facade and green windows swung out like parrot wings. Even if she pulled back the thin curtains in her parents' bedroom, all she could see was the city extending in a bog of shingles, antennas, smokestacks and maple trees.

Sometimes when she climbed the stairs to bed, Virginia would close her eyes and imagine she was in the Goodyear blimp. Three steps below the landing she could feel the silver of the moon on her eyelids; if she went slow enough and if Mom didn't snap on the light at the bottom yelling "What's gotten into you, child?" she would keep on rising, through the window and toward the moon, cool and buoyant. Leveling out far above the city, she'd open her eyes and find out just how high Akron was.

She asked her father once if he'd ever been in a blimp, but he just rattled his paper and laughed. "Do I look like the boss's son? What gave you that silly notion?"

Mrs. Voltz knew a lot of stuff other people didn't. When Virginia got the runs from eating forbidden berries, it was Mrs. Voltz's little black tablets that plugged her up. It's all natural, Mrs. Voltz assured Belle; only later did they learn that the pills, a remedy from the Old Country, were made of compressed charcoal dust.

Mrs. Voltz played funny records that sounded like bees and was always elbow-deep in flour, chattering in her own language as she fashioned little triangles of honey and nuts so delicate, it seemed like they disappeared when you looked at them hard. Put them in your mouth, that was another matter altogether. They started the tongue to dreaming; Virginia floated out of the overheated kitchen into the stars she'd been taught were out there, even in the day, waiting.

"It's from the Greek. *Akros.*"

"Greek?" Virginia didn't believe that Greek really existed.

"Uh-huh. In my village where I come from, in Hungary, there used to be a Greek family. A blacksmith widowman with three daughters like a staircase—nine, ten, eleven years old. I spoke Greek to him 'cause he didn't know much Hungarian. They all gone now." Mrs. Voltz smiled sadly and pressed another sugar cookie on Virginia.

Virginia didn't need persuasion, but Mrs. Voltz had her practicing to act like a lady and so she nibbled discreetly on the pale wafer, trying not to roll her eyes in ecstasy as the fragrance melted on her tongue.

"Tell me where it's high," Virginia demanded. "I don't see no high."

"Course you don't. Cities don't like for their hills to show. More tea?"

Virginia shook her head and sat back down. Mrs. Voltz's tea was almost as pale as her skin. Sometimes Virginia couldn't help prickling at the sight of her. She wasn't like other white people, who were actually colored, some pink, some beige, some green like pot liquor saved from turnip tops. But Mrs. Voltz was pure white; her upper arms were spongy as Wonder bread, the old-lady hair brushed into a starlit fuzz. Above the chalky slopes of those cheeks with their spidery map of burst blood vessels—millions of red threads—were the transparent eyes with their black holes. Those irises were the spookiest things, Virginia thought. As if you could peel them off the eyeballs like the silver stars in spelling class and paste them to the back of your hand.

Even Mrs. Voltz's clapboard house was painted white, a white so absolute it begged defilement. Every April a scrawny white boy appeared and scooted up a ladder to slap on the white paint. And every May, Mrs. Voltz stood on her front stoop wringing her hands and wailing over the graffiti left by the neighborhood delinquents—hearts with initials, red and black zigzags, yellow daisies high as the lintels. The spring before she turned nine Virginia had been laid up with a 24-hour virus, so she missed the latest act of vandalism. She was fiddling with a soda cracker on the bed tray when she heard her father's home-from-work-screen-door-slam. Instead of his usual "Hey what's on for supper?" there were only muffled titters. Virginia had already thrown back the quilt and braced her palms on the mattress when he finally exploded into helpless laughter, hooting, "Damn house got the *measles!*" But by the time Virginia was well enough to go back to school, the men in the neighborhood had gotten together and painted over the hundreds of red polka dots.

Now Mrs. Voltz was pouring her more tea anyhow and chattering about being a child once herself and going to a lake in the summer. Virginia picked up her cup and sipped, her eyes traveling over the frilly gauze curtains and dark photographs in oval frames while the wavery voice sprinkled words into the afternoon.

"It was a big lake. Lake Balaton. Fish long as to your elbow, and booths all round to fry them at. Every summer we stay there, it get better. Birds sang. Even the old men danced. We were living not far, not in Budapest—no, Budapest was our Paris, the emerald in the crown of the Austro-Hungarian Empire"—here she flashed Virginia a triumphant look, pleased to have remembered the guidebook jargon. "No, we lived in the provinces in a town called Székesfehérvár . . . can you say that? Székesfehérvár! Try."

"Sheck-ess—fair . . ."

"Székesfehérvár. You gotta rush through it. Székesfehérvár. Beautiful. Gardens with walls and big linden trees down the middle of every road. You stand at the edge of town, you could see forever, except where woods got in the way. Hungary's flat," she added. "Not like Akron. Hungary's flat as that cookie there."

"So why'd you come here?" Virginia was getting impatient. Who cared about her old gardens and summer lakes?

Instead of an answer, Mrs. Voltz jumped up and went over to the corner, where she rummaged among a pile of records until she found the one she wanted, slipping it from its tattered jacket and placing the phonograph needle into the groove.

"Listen."

After a moment's scratch and hiss there was the unmistakable rustle of dry leaves and a stick cracking, the lonely hoot of an owl. A man's voice boomed something unintelligible, and then came the most beautifully sad bird song Virginia had ever heard.

"Nightingale."

"Nightingale?"

"Yes, that is what you call it? Nightingale?"

"But nightingales are only in fairy tales!" Virginia exclaimed.

"Listen! Learn! The city makes you ignorant." Mrs. Voltz stood still, head cocked to one side. The bird gurgled on and on. "They sing better in the countryside. Used to be they come here, in the city, before it get crowded. Ten, fifteen years ago. Before you."

The man's voice boomed again, and again there came a bird, a different one. It went like that for a while, the voice defining species and subspecies as each song was captured by the ornithologist's microphone and the old woman translating: *Robin. Sedge warbler. Blackcap. Reed bunting. Blue throat.* And, in the throes of all that chirping and twittering, Virginia suddenly remembered her parents talking the night Mrs. Voltz's husband had died.

"What a shame."

Her father shaking his head. "That's what sugar'll do to you. Eat you alive."

"And after all they been through. Leaving everything behind, just like that. Running like dogs."

"They did all right."

"What's she going to do now, poor soul?"

"She's tough. Old man told me once how they made it out. They could only take what they could carry on their backs. They walked to the border. All night long, through the woods. She'll make it. That kind always does."

Virginia looked up, then tucked her head quickly; Mrs. Voltz was crying. So Virginia concentrated on the birds until finally the last one came: first the overamplified voice saying something like "Oreo oreo" and then a familiar sweet warble.

"I know that one," Virginia whispered. "That's the Baltimore oriole."

Mrs. Voltz looked up. "We called it *Sargarigo*. Golden Oriole." She dabbed at her eyes with the tip of her apron. "And what you say its name is?"

"Baltimore oriole. That's because they came from Baltimore, I guess. There's a baseball team called that, too. Their uniforms are blue and orange."

What had she said to make the old lady smile through her tears like that? Mrs. Voltz held out the tray of cookies, taking one herself. "Blue and orange," she murmured, now smiling fit to beat the band. "Fancy that."

After leaving Monroe Street, Virginia crossed through the center of town over to the east side, turning away from the main thoroughfares into ever shabbier neighborhoods. The lawns were unkempt and the cars rusted, the clapboard porches dingy with factory soot.

It began to rain, a thin drizzle from low gray clouds. Fourteen years! Somewhere, down these modest streets, under the now leafless maple boughs, the aunts and uncles and maternal cousins twice removed who had punctuated her childhood with their jibes and wry stories had had to give up on their dreams of a good life. Some had been very close to Virginia's family, like Aunt Carrie, who used to baby-sit when Dad and Belle went to the cabarets at the Lodge—or where else did they go, so dressed up and laughing? What lodge could it have been? Back then, the Lodge was the Lodge, whatever a lodge was. Children didn't question further.

On a hunch, she followed the numbered streets until she dead-ended at a row of two-story apartments on First Avenue. Farther down loomed the brick hulk of the First Avenue Factory, Goodyear Tire & Rubber. From here she could imagine the gaping production halls, tiny men in them working the flanges and tire molds, rubber bubbling in red-hot vats and hissing as it struck the cold iron. Around the corner she

77

glimpsed a railroad bridge spanning a small gulch, and beyond, the much-larger facade of Plant One with its gloomy clock tower proclaiming the witching hour, 5 P.M., punch-out time weekdays for the administration, those lucky souls whose white shirts never had a chance to absorb the greasy soot spewing from the smokestacks she could see now, marking off the skyline into blank measures.

Her father used to take the family here on their Sunday evening drives, pointing out the various divisions and their tasks. He had a white-collar job, nothing special, but enough to keep him out of the pits. What had he been working at? Probably something with plastics, like later in Arizona. Too young to care about such details, Virginia never paid attention when he talked about it to Belle, preferring to gaze through the glass from the backseat at the glittering slashes of light escaping from the coated windowpanes cracked open for air, and the gray-streaked smoke that billowed from grates and chimneys and hung at shoulder level like lost thunderclouds. What function had he performed among the reeking tiers of this man-made purgatory, how had his efforts born fruit or withered along the smoking terraces of Babel, how was it that he couldn't resist the compulsion to return to the scene of his daily humiliations on his day off, circling his place of labor like a dog following the scent of its mother back to the house from which he'd been sold?

Grandma Evans's high voice penetrated Virginia's thoughts. *Your Aunt Carrie all alone in that house down on Furnace Street.* Furnace Street must be around here somewhere. Many street names were descriptive, matter-of-fact labels reflecting the landmarks these residents saw every day on their way to and from work—River Street ran along an underground stream; German Alley skirted the cemetery from the

factory to Goodyear Boulevard. There was Pondview and Set-
tlement, Fulton Street and Iroquois Avenue. The cross streets
started at Plant One with First Avenue and ascended, away
from the smell, toward respectability.

After wheeling around for another twenty minutes,
Virginia pulled into a rutted lane and drove slowly past the little
nut-brown clapboard house in the middle of the block, nearly
hidden behind a row of hedges. She turned at the far corner
and parked across the street under a sycamore tree. The porch
was in acute need of repair, with cracked boards and an occasional slat missing from the trellis; the stone steps had sunk
over the years. *A gingerbread house,* Virginia thought, charmed
by the stone urns that had once been planted with petunias.
Then she realized it couldn't be more than one room deep,
since the ferny foliage of the gorge began right behind it;
how cramped and dark it must be inside! There was no movement behind the curtains. *Get out and walk over,* she ordered
herself, but she turned on the radio instead, fiddling at the
dial until some symphonic piece she didn't recognize filled the
car interior.

Each time Aunt Carrie had shown up on their front
porch to baby-sit her and Ernie Jr. while their parents went
out, she'd left this tiny house, locked the flimsy front door and
followed the railroad tracks to the bus stop. She had climbed
out of this valley of smoke to arrive on their porch and smother
her niece and nephew with hugs and her odors of cabbage and
peaches, an old-fashioned purse jabbing their ribs.

It was getting dark, but no lights came on behind the
curtains. Virginia breathed a sigh of relief—so her aunt wasn't
home after all. Or she might be napping; no use ringing the
bell. Virginia shivered; the cold had crept into the car and even
seeped through her pea jacket. She'd better start back.

Six

In the dull late Monday morning light, Virginia dragged herself out of bed. Why was she so tired? She'd had several unsettling dreams, but she couldn't remember a single one. She forced herself to dig into her bowl of Grape-Nuts and yogurt, and by the time she entered Mrs. Woods's classroom, less than an hour later, she felt strangely exultant. As she hefted the red trunk onto the table, the class cheered.

"I want each of you to find the puppet you had on Friday," she began. "Don't try to sneak off with a different one. Puppets don't like to be abandoned; they have feelings, too."

"Hey." It was the boy with the mossy teeth. "Where's Gina?"

"She had a hard weekend, so I let her sleep late. She'll be up in time to hear your stories."

"Stories?"

"Your puppets' stories, I mean. I want you to spend ten minutes or so with your puppets. Find out where they were born, what their parents are like, what the most exciting thing that ever happened to them was."

As the children scrambled for their puppets, Mrs. Woods came over with an encouraging smile and patted Virginia on the arm. "I guess you're in control," she whispered. "I'll be in the lounge if you need me."

The light brown boy who had helped carry in the foot-locker on the first day quickly reached out for a generic girl puppet. The first time he'd been too slow, or too shy, to snatch up one of the bandits or the few more terrifying animals. Virginia caught his attention and smiled: he was fine-boned, somewhat lanky, and his eyes were the color of warm toffee, fringed with dark curly lashes—a startling combination. *I hope those looks don't spoil him,* she thought.

Renee picked up the Wicked Queen, gingerly. What a nice-looking girl she was, actually! Her scalp was neatly subdivided, the crop of pigtails sprouting with rubber bands at their roots and barrettes at the tips. When Virginia was that age, she had thought she was ugly, a poor imitation cheated by some "natural law" that had given white girls all the options for beauty.

Once they'd moved to Arizona and Belle had discovered that the extreme lack of humidity in the air meant Black hair wouldn't "go back," Virginia's "wool" was pressed once a week and styled. She could still hear the angry sizzle of the curling iron as her mother took it from the stove and plunged it deep into the green jar of Dixie Peach. All that grease!

"Now you look elegant," Belle would proclaim, untying the dish towel around her daughter's shoulders; but Virginia stared in the mirror and thought she looked like an oily poodle. Luckily, this hair ritual took place only on Saturdays, in anticipation of church, so she had almost forty-eight hours before the next school day to try to soften the effect with the surreptitious application of a wet brush.

Virginia walked around to the front of the desk. "Okay, who wants to start?"

Not a sound. Even Goldilocks looked down at her hands. All the bustle was quenched when Virginia stepped full-size among them, the figure of Fearsome Authority. But Gina —they would listen to Gina.

"Oh, I'm sorry; I forgot to wake Gina up. She wouldn't miss this for anything. Gina? Gina! Wake up, lazy-bones!"

Gina poked her head up, rubbing her eyes sleepily and peering through her fists. "Where am I?" she mumbled.

"We're in Mrs. Woods's class, and everyone here has made a new friend who wants to tell us about him- or herself. I thought you'd like to listen. Or should I let you go back to sleep?" Virginia made a move to put the puppet away.

"No!" the class cried out.

Gina put her hands on her hips. "Stories, eh? Sounds interesting. Who's going first?" Not a face looked down. "How about you?"

Sitting next to Renee was a girl with glasses and nappy hair. Her skin was "high yellow," but with all the brightness gone. She looked around, then smiled shyly.

"What's your name?" Gina asked.

"Mona," she replied.

"Hi, Mona, I'm glad to meet you. Who's your friend there? She seems a little sleepy, too." The class laughed. "Don't you think so?"

Mona looked at the puppet on her hand to see for herself. She glanced up, relieved, and nodded.

"Has she got a name?"

"Caroline."

"And why is Caroline so sleepy? What did you two do last night that you got to bed so late?"

"We watched television."

"What did you see?"

" 'The Jeffersons.' "

" 'The Jeffersons'! No wonder she looks so sleepy! Look, I'll tell you what. We'll let Caroline get a little nap—right after she meets a few other people in this room. Has she made any new friends yet?"

"No."

"Well, now's a good time to start. Caroline, I want you to meet your next-door neighbor. Caroline and Mona, introduce yourselves to what looks like a real live queen."

"This is Queen Victoria. She's a wicked queen," said Renee.

"Will she cast a spell on us?" asked Gina.

"Oh, no. She's only wicked to wicked people."

"That's a relief," Gina said. "Say hello to the Wicked Queen, everyone!"

A chorus of hellos boomed out. And though a few kids couldn't resist the opportunity to act up, whooping and clowning—one boy even fell from his seat, clutching his chest in mock horror—their antics were drowned out in the swell of general good cheer.

"All right," Gina called out. "Who's next?"

No one moved. "Come on," she cajoled. "I know there are lots of people out there just dying to make new friends. Anyone? What, no one at all?"

"How about you, Gina?" someone shouted.

The children applauded. Virginia looked in the direction of the shout. It was Mosstooth, naturally.

"What's your name?" Gina asked.

"John."

"And your friend there?"

"Uh . . . Peter. He's visiting from Cleveland." The room tittered.

"I'll consent to an interview on one condition; I'll only answer questions asked by another puppet. Interview, puppet-to-puppet. Agreed?" A murmur of excitement.

"All right," John replied.

"Okay, give me your question, Peter!"

"What's your last name?"

"I can do better than that. Not only will I tell you my *last* name—I'll tell you my *full* name. But first I have to take a deep breath. Okay, here goes: Gina Lynn Augusta von Claybourne-Prince. Gina Prince for short."

"Do you have any brothers or sisters?" This from the boy who had helped with the trunk.

"A sister and a brother. My brother's a football player. And what is your name?"

"Kevin—I mean, Cynthia." Everyone laughed, but Virginia couldn't tell if it was good-natured laughter or derision.

Goldilocks found her voice. "And your mom and dad?"

"My mom is a jet pilot and my daddy is a weatherman. I'm not kidding! My dad has been a weatherman all his life—ever since I can remember, that is. He's never wrong with his forecasts. Mom had me and my brother and sister, and after we were big enough, she went back to school and became a pilot. Now she flies the weather plane for my father sometimes."

"What did he do before she learned to fly?"

"He used a weather balloon. Once he even rode in a blimp. He liked the blimp; he said he liked the idea that people on the ground were looking up at him to read the messages flickering on the sides."

"My name's Drango the Dragon," came a voice from the back of the room, "and I'd like to know what your favorite color is."

"I have two: black and white. My best friend's a zebra." They laughed. "Any more questions?"

"Where are you from?"

"From the scrap heap, naturally. And in case any of you should be seized by the uncontrollable desire to write me a letter, my mailing address is 123 Transformation Drive, Lockerbox, USA.

"What about your tall friend?"

Gina looked around, then up. "Oh, you mean Virginia? I'm not sure I'm authorized to divulge that information."

"Aw, come on. Please!"

"Well, I'll have to consult first with the party in question." Virginia and Gina whispered for about half a minute before Gina turned back to the class, dusting off her hands in imitation of a football coach emerging from the huddle.

"Virginia says it's fine if you can guess. I'll give you a hint: it's a medium-big city with lots of industry."

"Cleveland!"

"No, but not far from Cleveland. And not as large; I said a *medium-sized* city. Here's another hint: there used to be an oatmeal factory right in the center of town. The kids used to go downtown once a week and collect free cookies fresh from the assembly line. Any guesses?"

"Columbus?"

"Nope. Anyone else? Well, I'm not gonna tell you."

They groaned. "No, I'm not gonna tell. Ask your parents if they know where there was an oatmeal factory right in the center of town. And that'll be where Virginia was born."

Stopping for a traffic light near her apartment, Virginia spotted a supermarket and decided to stock up. A fish chowder, herb tea—soup weather indeed, this seeping chill and drab sky heavy with the decision whether to release its rain. Back when she and Ernie Jr. were small, Grandma Evans would let them roll out biscuit dough while she chopped carrots and sprinkled okra into the blue pot simmering on the stove. They'd spend all Saturday in the kitchen, devising elaborate games with paper dolls and matchbox trucks on the green-and-white linoleum while Belle and Grandma hovered over cooling cups of coffee. And if they behaved well enough, they got to suck the juices off the wooden spoon.

The store had no fresh seafood, just frozen halibut and fish sticks. And no leeks. She picked up a bundle of green onions and a lonely package of chicken breasts, deciding to switch to Chinese stir-fry. But when she asked for ginger root, the grocery boy at the vegetable scale merely stared. "Sorry," he said, taking in her jeans skirt and dangly earrings, "we don't have much call for that sort of thing here."

What did he mean by *that sort*? And if this was *here*, where was *there*? Virginia cruised the aisles looking for the staples she'd grown accustomed to. No decent herbal tea. No brewer's yeast. One kind of plain yogurt without the active culture needed for making one's own. One brand of soy sauce. No tahina paste, of course. Chastened, she went back through the aisles and bought a hunk of sharp cheddar, two cups of yogurt, eggs and milk, a can of tuna fish, five cans of Campbell's soup. *Things'll pick up when I go to teach at Oberlin High next month. At least there's a good college there—with a conservatory,* she reminded herself as she inspected the plastic-wrapped loaves of bread. The heaviest she could find boasted seven grains, but it was about double the size and half the weight of the bread Colette used to bake back in Wisconsin.

Despite Virginia's efforts in the tiny kitchen, her dinner turned out to be a pitiful affair; somehow the college nostalgia over Campbell's Split Pea with Ham didn't overcome the vague taste of cardboard mixed in milk. Still, she felt a keen pang of pleasure, a strangely cheerful sensation of isolation that sharpened her sense of herself. It had begun to rain; the unbroken tattoo on the roof was a balm rather than an inconvenience, the blank walls a comfort rather than a desolation. Outside, the city where she was born had retreated behind the soft erasure of mist. She felt like a hermit hunched before a successfully lit fire in his inviolate cave. The apartment was a refuge from the clutter and all the talk, the introductions to strangers.

There were no black teachers at Washington Elementary—just like the old times—though now nearly half the pupils were black. And all the teachers were women except for Mr. Jacobs, the music teacher. They seemed to Virginia—in their attitudes and interests, even their conversation and the way they dressed and applied makeup—like creatures from another epoch, "America the Comfortable" come back in a postsixties time warp. In the teachers' lounge they discussed their peonies and their diets, though they must have been chewing over the same diets together for years. No mention of better teaching techniques, new pedagogical theories, not even if they had read a good book lately.

Belle would have called it "chat," spitting the word out like excess phlegm. Belle hated gossip and never stopped to talk, not to a neighbor out watering the lawn or someone she ran into at the supermarket. Virginia's father was even more tight-lipped; he refused to acknowledge the existence of irrelevant banter. After the strict code of utilitarian communication in her parents' house, it had been a relief, at first, to join in the giggly dormitory gab-fests in college, full of gossip and beauty tricks and mean-spirited stories about unpopular core-course professors.

But Virginia had quickly grown out of that period of mindless ramble. Music, theater, Clayton, Puppets & People— the Muse didn't tolerate "gobble-gobble." That's what Parker termed it. Among the troupe members there was a rule: whoever engaged in gobble-gobble for longer than five minutes had to chuck a dollar in the "good times jar," which was used to procure treats like champagne or new records. If you were accused of gobble-gobble but could prove that it had served some grander purpose, the accuser had to deposit fifty cents in the jar. Parker had the best rebuttals, though he rarely committed the indiscretion; instead, he would defend Colette's chatter as "ritualistic behavior intended to establish a communal sense of generalized well-being." The majority didn't always accept that, though, and Colette would laugh and drop her buck into the jar while Parker began to tinker on the piano.

By now the rain had subsided to a pale drizzle that seemed to bloom up from the pavement, like soft explosions in a minefield. Yes, soup weather, harbinger of the cold ahead, all the glacial forces of Canada gathering along the shore of Lake

Erie for the numbing onslaught, dumping their white burden not directly at the border but on the benighted area thirty miles inland, what Cleveland TV meteorologists, clean chins shining above their navy blue ties flecked with diminutive logos, fondly referred to as the snow belt.

No, cello weather. She took the instrument out of its case and began tuning the strings. No wonder she'd chosen this monstrosity, this womanly shape she could wrap herself around after her mother had retreated into unexplained grief and intransigent resentment. Virginia tried the prelude of Bach's Second Suite, but the melodic line sounded as if she had torn a xylophone apart and tossed the keys at random into a sink. So she returned to the First Suite, and in a little while it sounded just as bad.

"Sometimes it happens all at once," Kadinski had said. "You try and try and suddenly it all clicks into place. Didn't I tell you it would?" He had her begin every lesson with deep knee-bends; then she was to twirl the cello like a ballerina and let it fall into her positioned arms. "If it can pirouette, it can sing," he declared. But first she had to make it shriek and wail by sawing the bow across the strings and sliding her fingers up and down the neck until her eardrums threatened to pop; only then, Kadinski said, was the instrument warmed up.

"Okay; here's the passage where you want to stomp your foot like Rumpelstiltskin," he would yell during the Fauré. Debussy was a light on water; Brahms, endless halls filled with mahogany furniture.

And then, in the middle of her junior year, Kadinski handed her a flat package wrapped in shiny blue paper. "You will need this," he said. Back at the dormitory she carefully peeled away the tape and pulled out the book. Above a woodcut of a lyre nested in olive leaves ran the inscription

SIX SUITES
for
UNACCOMPANIED VIOLONCELLO
by
J. S. BACH

She learned to hate that book with all the desperation of being trapped. No matter how much she practiced, it came out like grade-school études, endless bow strokes that left nothing but aching elbows.

At the next lesson, Kadinski gave a little speech on the deceptive simplicity of Bach. "These suites," he expostulated, "will refuse to reveal their beauty unless the performer has a certain—how shall I put it?—comprehension of their soul." And that was the last he had to say.

For several weeks Virginia struggled, with no progress. Try as she might, the notes refused to go together. She listened to recordings, mapped out melodic and bass lines—and still came no closer to making music out of it. Kadinski kept quiet in his straight-back chair, arms and legs crossed, smiling faintly at the air around him. She bit her lip and scraped on, finishing each lesson in a rage: how could he expect her to play this thing if he refused to tell her what it was about?

In her despair, Virginia went to the library and checked out books on Bach, until finally one paragraph from a volume published in 1802, *Johann Sebastian Bach: His Life, Art, and Work*, by Johann Nicolaus Forkel, seemed to shed some light, however mercurial. She copied it into her notebook:

. . . it was an established rule that every union of parts must make a whole and exhaust all the notes necessary to the most complete expression of the contents, so that no deficiency should anywhere be sensible by which another part might be rendered possible. . . . He not only fully satisfied this rule in settings for two, three, and four parts, but attempted also to extend it to a single part. To this attempt we are indebted for six solos for the violoncello, which are without any accompaniment and which absolutely admit of no second singable part set to them. By particular turns in the melody, he has so combined in a single part all the notes required to make the modulation complete that a second part is neither necessary nor possible.

When she returned to the instrument, things seemed to go better, though not well. But during the lesson that followed, Kadinski stopped smiling and spoke.

"You've got the notes," he said. "The notes aren't hard. Now love it, understand? Love. And after you love it, mistreat it."

If he was aware he'd hit a nerve, he gave no indication. Virginia knew he had told Clayton exactly the opposite. Clayton's playing was all passion; the music came out in brilliant sobs, more a conquest of the heart than a display of virtuoso technique. She didn't know where love for the music ended and her feelings for him began, but in those days it didn't matter.

The week before, she had joined him in the practice

room where he was playing Brahms's Sonata in F Major. Five minutes before midnight he had turned off the light and they'd held their breath, waiting for the raspy sound of the janitor's broom to sweep past on its slow traversal of the halls. As she huddled in the dark, she sensed rather than heard Clayton shift positions, stretching his right leg into the center of the room as he leaned back in his chair, the molecules shuffling to accommodate the long spiral of muscle and sinew, and she contemplated the way he must be resting his bow at his side, lightly, his wrist upturned on his knee, the blood thudding serenely through the veins under the delicate sheath of skin. She wished for him to touch her then, but he held still, matching his breathing to hers until the heat from their bodies rose and intertwined near the ceiling. When the janitor's key finally clicked in the back lock, he turned on the light and started the Brahms again, the music of anguish and rapture spilling all around them.

They left around two in the morning. There was something exhilarating about being together in a forbidden place, clothes brushing as they emerged from the narrow stairwell into the murk of the main foyer and stood for a moment in the vapory patterns cast by the mullioned panes. Then they leaned on the dark wooden doors, nudging themselves into the world again, and he said goodnight, pausing at the end of the crosswalk to bow slightly with his Old World formality before setting off for his fraternity house. For that week, it seemed, he had decided once more that their relationship should remain platonic.

Virginia drifted across the quadrangle. She felt as if a mysterious, undiscovered continent lay before her, vast and implacable but slowly relinquishing its secrets. Burning at her back she could sense the desert she had turned from; she could smell the ocean a thousand miles away. If adolescence was the storehouse of fantasy, then this time of her life was a screen upon which the fantasies played.

She loved college for its elusive goals, its fictive freedom. The instant she had set foot on the green quadrangle outside the dormitory, she'd felt a sharp and delicious thrill. Not that her parents had kept her in a cage, not that she hadn't always been encouraged to "exercise her mind" (Dad) and "expand her horizons" (Belle); even before the day she'd brought home her first straight-A report card, she'd felt the unspoken pressure to be The Best. During the stormy years of adolescence the pressure had intensified into her parents' wish that she become a "professional"—a doctor, a lawyer, a dentist or psychologist, even a teacher—some job befitting her "scholastic abilities."

But far away from home on her National Achievement and Minority Advancement scholarships, Virginia had quickly gravitated to the Fine Arts Building, a brick leviathan from the Victorian era. The rooms were cavernous and the halls prone to gloom, even where there were no corners . . . yet the hardwood floors had been sanded and waxed, a few skylights punched through and practice mirrors erected, all of which gave the interior an inspired mix of Gothic dark and classic ethereal.

During her first semester Virginia dutifully took core curriculum courses, but she'd slip over to Fine Arts and wander the halls, breathing in the varnish and glue of the stage sets, listening to the musicians going over scales, standing back to watch the ballerinas glide down the corridors, reed-slim and otherworldly with their slue-footed gait and high, sculpted buttocks, pairs of battered slippers slung over their shoulders.

The second semester of her freshman year Virginia signed up for Introduction to Modern Dance and Theater History I, fulfilling a physical education requirement and a humanities elective. She wanted to do it all—dance, act, play music. But soon the stage was where she felt most alive. By the time Belle noticed anything awry up there in Wisconsin, Virginia had rejected any notions of choosing a career that would, in Belle's words, "advance the race" and had firmly ensconced herself in the drama department.

She spooned the last of the pea soup into her bowl. *And this is where I've ended up—with a rusty car parked on the street, and a carton of books and a cello in a one-room efficiency.* She felt like the hero in *Children of Paradise,* the mime who takes off his white paint and becomes merely ordinary.

Who had told her about that film—Clayton? No, she hadn't known him then. Someone had said, "It's one of the most beautiful films of all time; every drama student should see it." She had gone alone, hardly breathing as Barrault shaped the void with his white-gloved hands, carving love out of the air.

From then on, pantomime was Virginia's passion. She gorged herself on the biographies of Chaplin and Barrault; she found textbooks on mime and tried to follow the exercises. Finally she realized that wasn't enough, so she went to her advisor.

Professor Barks was a large man with strawberry-blond hair. He looked like a cross between Lord Jim and the heads carved on Meerschaum pipes. An unsuccessful playwright who had also failed at directing, he demanded to know, "Whatever gave you the idea to waste your time on mime?"

Virginia said nothing. She despised him.

"Virginia. Already you've taken more than your share of dance courses, and you insist on private cello lessons and, lately, even orchestra. Plus you have your other studies. What would your parents say? Why endanger your progress in order to study a dead art for which there are no jobs?"

Virginia answered in a voice that surprised even her, because for all its calmness it was very angry. "Since I finished the drama prerequisites and became eligible for casting, there have been four major productions. In the same period of time, there have been over a dozen studio productions, ranging from one-acts to full-length. So far I have had one walk-on in a musical and I played the horse in Cocteau's *Orphée* where, if you recall, the determining factors were my experience in dance and the fact that I would wear a horse head. You and I both know how few opportunities there are for black actresses. This university isn't going to write a part just for me, and the members of this faculty aren't ready to cast a black woman opposite a white man. So tell me: what 'progress' am I endangering? I need experience or I won't get a job, anyway. I could become a good mime if you'd stop stalling and suggest the right teacher for me."

Nathan Mannheim was a slight, pale man of indeterminate age. His abundance of white hair grew in thatches; a tuft fell across his forehead, another batch sprouted and fizzled just behind his left ear. His voice was surprisingly modulated and eloquent. "Don't be afraid of the space around you," he used to say. "Take it in your hands. Shape it. Make it come to life."

During the course of the semester Virginia progressed in Mannheim's mime class from abdominal-versus-ribcage breathing and walking the tightrope to deceptively simple movements such as hobbling like a crone. At the flick of a spotlight she could render ten of the more than twenty kinds of laughter classified in Chinese theater: she scoffed, snorted, smirked and sniggered, chortled and chuckled, giggled and tittered, roared and cachinnated. Then, for finals, she spent all week preparing an entire scene. From a list of fifteen, she had chosen a situation she felt was tailor-made. Number six read: *Virtuoso Musician (any instrument except piano).*

That Saturday, Virginia arrived early. She took her place center stage in the magnificent room, head bowed before the straight-back chair, concentrating by calling to mind the countless times she had sat down to play the cello—in the bedroom of her parents, before her music teacher in junior high, at high-school concerts, with Mr. Kadinski in his bright humidified study, on the concert stage with the college orchestra, encumbered by yards of black cloth, once even in the mask of an old woman for the production of a student play called *Shake a Leg for Me, Mrs. Calabash.*

She conjured the cello itself in her hands, in the set of her back and the curve her body made to accommodate it. She tightened the bow, an act she had done so many times that she almost forgot to mimic it, and began to play, not just random bowings and fingerings calculated to simulate playing but an actual piece—the second Gavotte from Bach's Fifth Suite, "The Discordable," suitably flamboyant. Kadinski's favorite.

When she had finished, Nathan Mannheim sat awhile with his arms folded, a faint smile on his face.

"Miss King," he said, and stopped. He was choosing his words.

She felt paralyzed, yet somewhere anger was rising.

"You have made the mistake of knowing your subject too well." He tented his fingers and rested his lips against them. "In most cases if you are asked to walk, you walk—nothing to it. But to walk on a stage—that is a different kind of walking. You understand that; you learned that the first week. You even used this knowledge at the beginning of your piece when you sat down in the chair. That was good. But the instrument . . . you actually *do* play the cello, am I correct?"

Virginia nodded, amazed.

"When you have the instrument in your hands, you may play it very well; but to the uneducated observer—even to me, someone who knows a good deal about classical music— your performance was unconvincing. It was too—how best to say it?—too complicated. That is the proper way to hold the bow?"

Again she nodded.

"Fine; but to my eyes it seems too relaxed. Never mind that that's the way it's done. No one will believe you can get a peep out of such a large box without more of a . . . well, clutch. And your left hand. Too fast."

"Too *fast*?" She had deliberately played the Gavotte more slowly than it should be; it was hard to remember the notes without hearing them. A few times she had forgotten and faltered. And he claimed she was playing too fast?

"Yes. I could barely see your fingers. You may have been hitting actual notes—maybe you can play three times as fast as that—but for the human eye, you played too quickly. Your fingers seemed to be flying up and down a rubber ladder. The neck of the instrument was lost; the wood was no longer solid. It dissolved under your hands. Remember: no one but you can hear the music."

You've got the notes. The notes aren't hard.

"That means you have to make me see it. And that takes different movements than making me hear it. If you want me to see an allegro, or even a presto, you cannot slur the notes together, because I will only see a languid right hand and rather frantic fingerings of the left—everything will seem out of sync. So: exaggerate the long notes. Saw away at the fast ones. Let me see the line of music. To do that, you have to violate some of your principles as a musician, perhaps. But in the art of mime, sometimes you do things false in order that they appear true to the audience."

Virginia's disappointment had evaporated. Instead, she was seized by an excitement that threatened to spill into exuberance. She tried hard to conceal it because she didn't want him to stop talking.

She had been so concerned with the score's harmonic structure, Bach's neat, near-monotonous modulations, that she had failed to hear the musical line. The Prelude to the First Suite, for instance: eight notes to a measure, regular as clockwork; but that didn't mean the phrase ended at the bar or, for that matter, that each eighth note had the same value. The music lurked in this intricate grid of notes; but she had to take a little from her guts and the air and then shape it, make it live. Take the Prelude of the D Minor Suite, operating on phrases of four and five sixteenth notes, the four-note phrases beginning on the first beat of the measure and receiving slightly less value than the more stately five-note descents. Broken up, of course, by descending two-note groupings of sixteenths.

Bach had given himself a narrow construct within which to create music, but within this matrix of rhythm and intonation he had all the freedom he needed. Each arpeggio spilled into the next measure, and yet the counts added up at the end. Give those tones belonging to the melodic line a slightly longer value, the harmonies slightly less, and the whole would hang together by the magic tension between melodic line and the existing bar divisions. It was like jazz, what Ellington meant by *It don't mean a thing if it ain't got that swing.* Playing Bach, she had to put inaccuracy into every note, that supreme inaccuracy—call it mistreatment, call it love—that makes the notes "bend" and become music.

Next cello lesson, when she had finished playing the Prelude to the Second Suite, Mr. Kadinski straddled his chair, spectacles twitching on his tiny nose, and pursed his lips quizzically as he studied her with his gray eyes. Then he nodded. "Good," he said. "Now we can go on."

Seven

The seats in the auditorium were too small and close together for adults to fit comfortably. From the broad arc at the back of the room the rows descended like spokes toward the miniature orchestra pit, where a battered upright piano stood next to a wooden lectern. From this platform the PTA chairwoman would preside over the order of the day—bake sales, field trips and suggestions for fund-raisers would be discussed and countermotioned in utmost sincerity.

Before the board meeting started, Mrs. Woods had introduced Virginia to Mosstooth's mother, a petite brunette in a navy skirt and white blouse closed primly at the neck with a cameo. *It should be an American flag pin,* Virginia thought as she extended her hand, smiling.

The woman crinkled her nose and said, "Puppets? John never mentioned it. Well, that should be a hit with the kids," as if Virginia were offering them cotton candy or an extra recess.

"See?" Mrs. Woods whispered. "These are the concerned parents. Without them we couldn't run this school. And they *are* excited about your presence here at Washington Elementary."

There were murmurs, a scattering of applause, when Virginia stood up and went to the lectern after being introduced as "an artist." She was embarrassed, more for them than for herself. They didn't know what to do with her. Did they expect a show? Okay, she'd give them one.

"Most of you know by now who I am. Your children come home and tell you what 'the Puppet Lady' did in class." She avoided looking at John's mother. "It sounds like a lot of fun, but you're thinking: what can a puppet do that can't be done better by a textbook and the teacher?

"First of all, I'd like to remind you that puppets have been around for a long time. Puppets are universal. There are puppet shows in Japan as well as New York, in Turkey and Mozambique, in Spain and Indonesia. And 'dolls' are nothing more than puppets without a means of movement. Whenever a child pretends that Barbie is about to go on a date with Ken, a small puppet show is taking place. Extend this concept over the course of human history and it becomes logical that the first rock or piece of gnarled wood a cave man used to represent friends or enemies while telling a story was a kind of puppet. So puppets are nearly as old as human beings.

"Let's take some examples from history. When Cortez came to Mexico, he had a puppeteer among his soldiers. American Indian medicine men used marionettes during religious ceremonies to awe the tribe, as did their Egyptian counterparts centuries before. By the tenth century A.D., the Javanese shadow puppets had reached such a level of sophistication that they became the basis for Javanese theater itself. In the seventeenth and eighteenth centuries the puppet theater of Japan— *Joruri,* it was called—rivaled the *Kabuki,* or human theater.

"All fine and good, you say, but most of us grew up on Lamb Chop." *There, that got a laugh. Forge on.*

"How can a puppet, a lifeless object, show a human being how to portray emotion? A Russian actor by the name of Obrazsov was fascinated with this question. He decided that puppets did not imitate people but that they were instruments for pointing out people's odd characteristics. And with this theory came a startling discovery: puppets did not have to look like real people; they did not even have to act like real people. It was enough that they were symbols of the traits of men. Obrazsov became convinced that puppets possessed qualities different from and more effective than those of an actor.

"Puppets don't have the limitations of human beings, and anything they do becomes more forceful by virtue of the fact that they are free from any real feeling. They are indestructible, even immortal—how many times has Punch hit Judy over the head with his club, only to have her reemerge unscathed?

"Put a puppet into a child's hands and she knows all these things instinctively. Have children dramatize a current event or an episode in history, and they will identify with the scene as if they had been there in person. Let a class put on a puppet show written by the students, and I bet you that play will contain the children's private dreams, wishes and fears. Kids can learn and enjoy at the same time—and that's the best of both worlds.

"They say a picture is worth a thousand words. If that's true, puppets are more valuable, since they are moving pictures. I wish I could have given you a puppet show tonight instead of boring you with my words, but I wanted to take this opportunity to share my thoughts with you. I'll let the children take care of the puppet show."

The applause was polite and a bit uncertain, not the thunder she had secretly hoped for. Mrs. Woods was clapping heartily, but when Virginia caught her eye, she beamed just a little too brightly. It occurred to Virginia that she shouldn't have expected applause at all. This was a PTA meeting, not a performance.

She sat down. The order of business ran its course. She was not looking forward to the Open House afterward, when more parents would show up and question her. After all, who believed in puppets? Who took their fables seriously?

The first puppet show she had seen had been in Phoenix over a decade ago. Belle had heard about the show at the YMCA from another mother. Virginia didn't want to go; she was nearly twelve, too old for "kid stuff," and "American Bandstand" was on TV, have a heart! But Belle needed Virginia to help with Claudia, who at two and a half was languishing from "lack of stimulus"; couldn't Virginia learn not to be so selfish?

"Look there, Little Beet, look at the girl in the fluffy dress—isn't she pretty? Like a picture. And the rosy curtains all brocade."

Yecch. Virginia preferred the witch with the poisonous skin, warty and green like the Wicked Witch of the West. She was trying to train her two new cats, Jezebel and Hagatha, how to cast spells. "You are black cats," the Wicked Witch screeched, "and only black cats can activate a spell!" But Hagatha and Jezebel, being the black cats that they were, were too busy fighting to stop and lend their spellbinding stare to the steaming caldron. The witch was beside herself. "You're impossible!" she yelled. "Tonight is Halloween, and some witch or warlock is bound to stop by to rent a few bad-luck props!" The cats hissed, exposing cherry-red jaws—the children gasped, then laughed. The witch kicked both cats out the window, but they popped up again at the sill, singing:

> *Trick or treat, trick or treat,*
> *Black cats land upon their feet!*

"Hush, Claudia, they're only puppets! Look, there's another cat slipping into the kitchen, a pretty yellow one, with blue eyes!"

> WICKED WITCH: Arrgh! A yellow cat! Yellow cats bring good luck! Scat! I'll be ruined if anyone discovers that my black cats have been in the same house as a yellow one.

> YELLOW CAT: I like you.

> WICKED WITCH *(beside herself, running in circles)*: If he leaves right away, the good luck may not have a chance to spread.

Why was Belle shaking her head? Look, the witch was casting a spell on the yellow cat!

> Greedy Czar and bloody cassock,
> Change this cat into a hassock!

Two other witches entered; they were fat with dark blue skin and bright red lipstick. Payne and Crustacia were feeling wonderfully wicked, and they were looking for two very bad black cats—wasn't it dreadful how treacherous the market had gotten lately? Some suppliers would even try to pawn off brown cats for spells. Now brown cats may be mean, but they're not as rock-bottom hateful as black cats!

"Outrageous," Belle whispered. "How could anyone suggest I take my children to this . . . this . . ."

"It's just a puppet show, Mom."

"Just? Young lady, don't you see what they're doing?"

"But black cats are part of Halloween!"

"You're hopeless! Don't you understand anything?"

How the children squealed! Claudia tried to get down; she wanted to stroke the cats. Virginia thrust the squirming bundle into Belle's arms. She was such a know-it-all, she thought; let her handle her own child.

WICKED WITCH: Jezebel and Hagatha will demonstrate their spell-casting stare on the hate potion.

CRUSTACIA: Excellent! That's one of the most difficult spells.

WICKED WITCH:

> Eye of toad and tail of rat,
> Pinch of sulfur, gangster's hat;
> A lock of gray hair from a nag,
> Evilness is just our bag!

JEZEBEL and HAGATHA:

> Arithmetic problems, four schoolbooks,
> All the teachers' dirty looks,
> A robber's loot, a fisher's bait,
> All together, hate hate hate!

WICKED WITCH: All right cats, STARE! (*The yellow cat slips through the window and stares.*)

BLACK CATS:

> Mix our hate stares
> Through and through . . .

YELLOW CAT:
> Love is stronger
> Than both of you!

WICKED WITCH *(ladling up a bit of brew)*:
Mmmmmmmm, that's good! And oh, how I love
everybody! *(She dances around the kitchen, kisses*
CRUSTACIA.*)*

CRUSTACIA: *Yecch!* Look! A yellow cat!

*Jezebel and Hagatha climb onto the edge of the caldron to drink
and fall into the pot. They emerge as handsome yellow cats with
turquoise eyes.*

PAYNE: *Three* yellow cats! Aaaaagh—good luck!
Let's get out of here! *(Both witches stomp off.)*

WICKED WITCH: Oh, I've never been so happy
before in my life. How did it happen? We made a
hate potion.

YELLOW CAT: While you were staring at the caldron and wishing hate, I was staring at it and
wishing love. Everyone knows love is stronger
than hate. I changed your hate potion into a love
potion.

WICKED WITCH: I should be angry, but I feel too
wonderful to care! I think I'll just change my
whole business into a good magic shop. From
now on I'll only train good yellow cats.

JEZEBEL and HAGATHA *(hugging each other)*: Oh, goody!

> Once the world was bleak and dark
> Till the flame of love did spark;
> Hatefulness is such a drag,
> From now on loving *you*'s our bag!

The harsh sunlight outside was blinding, but Belle didn't stop to put on her shades. She sped into the torrid October afternoon and across the parking lot like a tornado, swerving between the rows until she had reached the car and opened all the doors to let the hot air out. Then she stood clutching Claudia to her chest as if an army of Huns were just over the next mesa. Virginia lost a thong in her haste and instinctively tried to hop, but the ball of her foot accidentally touched the searing asphalt and she yowled.

Belle didn't move a limb; when her eyes focused on Virginia, though, the hard expression on her face softened. Virginia retrieved her thong and made toward her mother, exaggerating her limp as she threaded a path between the fiery automobiles.

"Poor baby," Belle said when Virginia caught up with her, rubbing her daughter's cheek with her thumb. "I'm sorry you had to see such trash." Virginia slid into the passenger's seat and reached over for Claudia; Belle slammed the car door and turned the ignition. In Virginia's head another door swung quietly open: a black girl in blue leggings lay spread-eagled in the snow, while the white girl stood above her in yellow boots. *Nigger!* She closed her eyes and tried to stop the memory from coming, but it was too late.

Virginia hesitated outside the auditorium. There were still a few minutes until Open House; with any luck she'd remain invisible. Had she been away from ordinary people so long that she'd forgotten how to adapt? *Smart-ass college graduate,* they were probably thinking.

"Miss King?"

She jumped.

"I'm sorry; I didn't mean to be sneaking up on you."

She had noticed the woman earlier, sitting quietly through the meeting, a young mother with large dark eyes set in a brown, plump face. She was wearing a cardigan, though the evening was warm.

"I just wanted to say I liked your speech. It was very interesting."

"Maybe I talked too much," Virginia muttered. "I guess I was nervous, and wanted to prove to you all that I wasn't just a fly-by-night *artiste.* Instead, I probably came off as an arrogant college graduate lording it over everyone."

"Oh, no, I enjoyed it." The woman put her hand on Virginia's forearm, lightly. "My daughter raves about you. And you're right, puppets are everywhere. Just look at "Sesame Street"—the Muppets are teaching our youngsters how to read."

The Muppets. Why hadn't it occurred to her to mention them? God, she was out of touch.

"My daughter's name's Renee. Renee Butler. You might not remember her. She's kind of quiet."

"Oh, yes, of course I remember Renee." Virginia's heart was pounding. "I remember her very well, in fact."

"You do?" The woman's face lit up, and Virginia saw the resemblance.

"I'm Sarah Butler," the woman continued. "I don't know much about puppets, and I'm not sure I can help much, but I was wondering if you had any plans for involving parents. I'm sure some of us wouldn't mind at all."

"Oh, that would be wonderful!" Virginia was surprised at the intensity of her reply. The missed opportunity of the Muppets haunted her.

"What has to be done?" Sarah Butler asked.

"There are programs to be designed, for example, and costumes to sew, and maybe someone to build a stage—"

"Costumes?"

"The little dresses that fit over the children's hands. The kids are really excited about making their own puppet heads, but I'm afraid they can't handle a needle and thread yet. I brought some ready-made puppets with me, and some that I made; but I thought the children would be happier using puppets they had made themselves."

Sarah Butler nodded. "I know a few mothers who go in for that sort of stuff. Mrs. Lee's got a real knack for drawing, so she'd be good for designing programs. And Mrs. Nettles is always willing to pitch in . . . and since I have a sewing machine, I'll help you with the costumes. But you'll have to supervise."

"Oh, don't worry," Virginia hastened to reassure her. "The patterns are really basic. We could do it in a few hours."

"Come over for coffee. This Saturday, around ten-thirty?" She scribbled her address on the torn-off corner of an envelope.

"Why, I'd love to," Virginia replied, a bit breathless at how easy it had been. "That would be simply perfect."

.   .   .

Under the fluorescent lights, Mrs. Woods's classroom appeared smaller than during the day and more Spartan, almost impersonal. Several wooden tables displaying learning materials, projects and prize essays had been set up along the walls. Virginia quickly glanced at the table piled high with puppets, a green construction paper sign proclaiming EDUCATION AND THE ARTS—THE ARTIST-IN-RESIDENCE PROGRAM. Avoiding it carefully, she walked over to the windows at the back of the room.

Outside, the streetlights came on. Virginia gazed down into the school playground. It looked like an illuminated skating rink; the caked dirt lay glazed under cold blasts of light. The lights at the far periphery assumed a radiance like a false horizon; the sky seemed to begin at street level, inky blue washing to deepest teal where the real horizon began, just above the backyards of the houses opposite, and panning into navy far above the trees.

Parents were still coming in. They cooed at each other and made casual conversation. *I'll have to turn around and join them,* Virginia thought, *but how?* She only knew what not to do again—no more speeches, no more philosophizing, no more slight smiles that could be mistaken for condescension. She should be humble at all costs, listen to Mrs. Woods's chatter about the exalted realm of education and afterward answer all questions put to her and even ask some in return: What is your daughter's name? What's your son's favorite subject?

"Miss King?" Sarah Butler beckoned from the puppet display. Three other women were standing around the table as well, smiling nervously; Sarah had obviously rounded them up. All of them looked a little embarrassed, and each woman nodded eagerly as she was introduced. Ida Lee was diminutive; she was as thin as a teenager, and very dark. She was the hairiest woman Virginia had ever seen—she wore her thick black hair massed about her collar, and her forearms were covered with fine dark strands like peach fuzz. Her eyes were very black, the whites dazzling, the lids prominent and slanted. They were also slightly popped, which made her look constantly surprised. When she announced that she'd like to help print up posters, she seemed amazed at her own offer.

Anne Nettles was a stocky woman with close-cropped blond hair, a Goldilocks in her thirties. "My Marianne loves you," she gushed. "How about if I helped Ida with publicity?"

Then there was Mrs. Parnell, one of those huge women possessing a kind of serene grace; despite her large frame, she moved as if on invisible rollers. Her glowing brown, astonishingly round face displayed delicate features; over this perfect sphere she had snapped on a poodle-cut wig that seemed more ornament than deception.

"I've never seen a puppet show in my life," she admitted, laughing, "but Sammy idolizes you, so it's okay by me. What can I do?"

"Plenty," Virginia was about to reply, but Sammy's mother's attention had already wandered to the display on the table. She grabbed Virginia by the elbow and pointed to the books on puppetry that Mrs. Woods had arranged in a neat half circle.

"Explain this stuff to me," she said in a gruff voice. "I didn't understand half of what you was saying upstairs at the meeting . . . too elevated for me." She pronounced the second syllable of "elevated" with a long e.

More parents joined the group around the puppet table

and were looking on with friendly expressions. Mrs. Parnell, big as a barn and louder than every animal in it, had voiced the hurt feelings of those who had attended the PTA meeting and supplied the needed catharsis; now they felt ready to receive the upstart.

Mrs. Parnell had no specific curiosity, but she unabashedly put herself in the role of moderator, soliciting inquiries from the others with a good-natured pressure technique: "Margaret, I heard you asking earlier if the kids were going to make their own puppets, isn't that right?" Embarrassed, Margaret admitted to the question, and Virginia explained various techniques, like using a light bulb as a base for papier mâché. Sarah quickly enlisted volunteers for sewing costumes. Then Virginia tried to get Mrs. Parnell to put one of the puppets on her hand, but she backed off: "My fingers'll fall all over themselves." None of the other parents seemed inclined to try, either. They gazed wistfully at the cheerful little heads perched on the deflated bodies, but they would not touch.

"Is there much call for this kind of thing?" Ida Lee wanted to know.

"It's limited," Virginia acknowledged. "Except for children's puppet shows. There's not much in the way of marionettes, the Pinocchio type of thing—they're pretty complicated to operate. By the way, I read in the *Beacon Journal* that the University of Akron is hosting a Javanese puppet show Sunday night. It's a traveling troupe, with its own gamelan orchestra and everything."

"What's 'gamlin' . . . a gamelawn orchestra?"

" 'Gamelan' is the name of the musicians. It's mostly gongs and drums. The Javanese puppet show is meant for adults, which is why the university's sponsoring it, I guess."

After a few more questions they had run out of conversational fodder and began drifting away. Virginia excused herself to get a drink of water.

She was barely outside the classroom door when someone came bounding up the stairs and ran full-force into her, sending them both spinning off in opposite directions.

"I'm really sorry," he panted. "Are you all right?"

Virginia had just missed being thrown against the row of gray lockers; she stood with closed eyes for a moment in the middle of the hall, trying to catch her breath.

"I think so."

"You don't know how sorry I am," said the tall, slender black man exuding massive waves of British Sterling aftershave.

"It's all right," she replied, wondering if he shaved in the evening.

He inclined his head, checking her out. "A pretty young thing like you shouldn't be allowed out without protection."

He tried a big fey smile on her, but Virginia wasn't impressed. "I wouldn't need protection if you watched where you were going."

He didn't budge, just stood there staring, his cocky smile slighter now. Virginia stared back. His fawn-colored slacks were beyond immaculate, his shirt a little too close-fitting, though the salmon shade, in a material somewhere between silk and soft cotton that shimmered faintly under the dim hall lights, was crassly appealing. His skin was the tint of pale coffee, he had liquid brown eyes in a face . . . *a face as finely chiseled as an Egyptian mask,* she thought. His Afro was rounded and shining. Even his mustache glittered. He was—as Grandma Evans would say—too good-looking to do good.

"Are you a new teacher's assistant?" he asked.

"Guess again."

"Kevin didn't mention any new kid in the class. You *did* come out of that room, didn't you?"

"I did." She began to enjoy his confusion.

"Then whose mother are you?"

"No one's." She turned toward the water fountain.

"Ah, stupid me." He poked a finger against his forehead. "You're the Puppet Lady!" His grin was dazzling. "Kevin talks about you all the time. But he couldn't remember your name."

"Is Kevin your son?"

"Yes, ma'am." He shook his finger at her, playfully. "But you sidestepped my question, Miss, uh . . ."

"King," she replied, smiling in spite of herself, "Miss King."

"Well, Miss Puppet Lady King . . ." he said, extending his hand.

"Virginia," she laughed, outdone, and continued walking toward the water fountain.

"Virginia King." He dogged her heels the few paces to the fountain and tried it out again, varying the inflection: "Virginia King."

He hesitated as water bubbled on her lips, waiting for her to stand upright, but she hovered over the fountain, oblivious.

"Mine's Terry. Terry Murray. Just your average ordinary guy. I didn't expect the Puppet Lady to be so young."

"I could say the same about you," she said, rising to face him.

"Well, someday I'll tell you the sad and lonely story of my life." His voice dropped a notch as he took a step toward her. "What are you doing after this?"

"I'm busy," she replied, in what she hoped was a cool voice, and crossed in front of him toward the bathroom.

When Virginia returned from the lavatory, she discovered that Mrs. Woods had called the parents together to announce that she would arrange tickets for anyone interested in attending the Javanese puppet show at the university. Dismayed, Virginia watched the people gather around the front desk where the teacher was preparing a sign-up sheet. Javanese puppets! She could predict their reactions: bewilderment, suspicion, indignation. What an idiot she'd been to mention it at all! In her confusion she retreated to her display at the side of the room; too late, she noticed Terry Murray already at the table, playing with the puppets. He pointed to Gina and grinned.

"Is this you?"

"Her name's Gina."

A ringless hand toyed with the tight curls of the steel wool, touched each pearl button.

"Nice." Another caress. "Kevin tells me you do most of your talking through her."

"Kids feel more comfortable talking to a puppet than to a grown-up."

"That a fact? Maybe I better try that myself." He slipped the puppet over his hand. She'd never seen Gina from this angle before; trusting, happy, she leaned against his shirt and smiled up at him.

"Tell me, little Virginia—"

"Her name's Gina."

"Tell me, Gina—why won't your mother give me some

slack? I just want to be her friend. Is that a crime? Would you talk to her for me? I'd like to invite her out tonight."

"Mr. Murray—"

The puppet spoke up. "His name's Terry!"

"This is ridiculous. I don't know you."

"Just say the word and we can change that," he replied, the caress of his voice becoming a full-court press.

Why didn't anyone come over? Virginia cut a glance to the side and saw Ida Lee grinning at her. She wheeled back and looked Terry Murray straight in the eye. "I told you: I'm busy." Turning on her heel—*like a hero in a bad Western,* she couldn't help thinking—she walked off and stationed herself behind Mrs. Woods and the sign-up sheet.

She avoided him the rest of the evening, but she could still picture Gina next to his cheek and almost feel his breath, warm and minty, on her lips.

Eight

Virginia finished the *Prelude* of the Third Suite with a strong C major chord but couldn't bear diving into the elaborate and rather grave *Allemande* right away. Sighing, she put the cello back into its case. The autumn evenings gave less and less light, and it was raining again, but she was too lazy to switch on the lamp; instead, she flopped across the bed and picked up Cocteau's *The Infernal Machine*.

What had Mrs. Woods said? "It'll be the event of the year!" Sure—if she could keep the little monsters in tow.

They'd been eager to write their own play, but she'd insisted they make the puppets first. John, the boy with the mossy teeth, decided to make a football puppet; when Virginia ventured that a football with arms would be hard to maneuver across a stage, he answered, "It won't have arms. Just a mouth." The other boys were designing football teams to go with the talking football while the girls, not to be outdone, were dreaming up some kind of fairy with sequins and pink tulle.

Kevin barely said a word, just stared at her all the time. But whenever she looked at him and smiled, he dropped his eyes. She wondered why his parents had divorced. After her run-in with Terry Murray at Open House, Ida Lee had come up to her and whispered: "Go for him, honey; he's available."

Mrs. Woods had suggested that writing the play could be part of the regular writing workshop, so after recess Virginia turned to the task at hand: herding clumps of boisterous children into corners of the room where they would work on various parts. The boys wanted their football story, the girls a love story; both groups had a hard time imagining puppets could do anything other than play sports or kiss.

But the idea of a talking football was so ridiculous that even the most unimaginative child was inspired to fantasize: if there was a talking football, there could be a fairy godmother to bestow the ball to the lucky person; and if this magic gift was a birthday present, why couldn't the birthday cake have a speaking part, too? A couple of the girls hit upon the idea to create a few majorettes, and the boys insisted on a football coach.

Marianne-Goldilocks graciously declined a speaking part, though no one had asked her. Virginia put her in charge of writing songs for the fairy godmother and the majorettes, and in no time she had rallied a group of other girls, Renee included, who took up camp around the teacher's desk, pencils and notepads poised, while Marianne scribbled lyrics on the blackboard and led the stumbling composition with a self-important voice.

Virginia understood how some of the girls could be attracted to Marianne's flamboyant confidence. The shy yearn to be witty, even garrulous. Silence may be associated with wisdom, but even at their age, they have already seen that the world pays attention to the talkers.

She pulled on an old T-shirt and slid under the covers. Was she shy? Ernie Jr. would have said, *If you have to ask, you aren't.* Belle claimed their father was shy, though to Virginia it seemed more like a deliberate self-containment; he spoke only when there was something to be said. Virginia had never seen him engage a group of listeners with jokes—but then, she couldn't remember a time when she'd seen him in a group of people. How isolated her family had become in Arizona! They rarely had guests for dinner and the phone seldom rang; Virginia and Ernie Jr. had preferred going over to their friends' houses. Even Claudia seemed to have given up trying to break the silence that had settled over their house like a bell jar.

Virginia lay in the dark, listening. The rain had stopped, and there was nothing to hear—no crickets, no groaning compressors in ancient refrigerators, no old wooden joists settling for the night as in Wisconsin. And in Arizona the night was full of the gentle hiss of the swamp cooler and the roar of the cicadas, grating out their death song or courtship rites, she had forgotten which.

Ernie Jr. had been incredulous when she decided to try out for majorettes in the spring of her sophomore year at high school. "What!" he gasped, ducking his head in embarrassment, though at what she didn't know. In fact, she'd been as astonished at his reaction as he seemed to have been at her decision.

"What's wrong with being a majorette? You like football." She said it, though she knew the comparison made no sense.

"But I don't play football!"

"Because you can't. They'd snap you in half like a stick." She backtracked hastily; they rarely fought, and she was frightened at the speed and direction of this unexpected exchange. "Look—the seniors on the squad are giving two weeks of twirling lessons to the girls who want to try out. I've got nimble fingers from playing cello—hey, I got rhythm! Why not?"

But the fingers had very little to do with baton twirling.

Every afternoon Virginia went to the band room with her shiny new baton and rehearsed forward and backward verticals, around-the-worlds, and frontal double-handed spins. They practiced in the cramped amphitheater of the band room, and when more girls showed up on the third day, they moved into the corridor; the seniors didn't want to take them outside where spectators could gawk.

"We don't want anyone to know who tried out, just in case they don't make it," Doris said, hooking a swatch of heavy auburn hair behind her ear. Doris was co-captain of the squad; petite and muscular, she was the best twirler in the group, and rumor had it she had been passed over for head majorette because her father was Mexican.

On the first day of tryouts, right after the head major-ette, a Twiggy blonde, had made a few introductory remarks, Doris immediately zeroed in on Virginia.

"It's all in the wrist," Doris said, demonstrating how far her wrist twisted back on itself (exactly the opposite from playing the cello, where the bow hand swayed gently right and left like a grass skirt, but was never to slosh every which way); this allowed the baton to rotate in the cradle between thumb and forefinger, the white rubber tip swinging back to nearly brush her elbow.

Oh the wonder of spinning! When, on the third day, Virginia managed her first frontal, the slim rod rolling smoothly from one hand to the other, palm over palm so that it spun on its axis, a silver-spoked wheel that seemed to float before her waist—well, she was hooked. There was nothing like this illu-sion, this near-perpetual motion.

The subtle technique of marching was the first order of week two. Knees high, toes pointed toward the earth, chest and chin up, arms swinging in a crisp clockwork motion. Don't switch those hips! Just sway a little bit, a hint of a swing, and the short, flared skirt would do the rest. Two girls quit; that left ten contenders for four openings. Next they began learning routines. The seniors demonstrated several and the novices chose their teacher according to whichever routine they decided to present during auditions. The routines were named after the majorette who had thought them up: *Mandy's* was as flamboyant as the tall junior, all wide-armed sweeps with lots of flare and graceful dance movements but very little twirling. A whole flock of girls clamored around her. *Doris's* was the most difficult routine; it even contained a mini-aerial (only one-and-a-half rotations) connected to a spin around the back.

Doris had two students; halfway through the second week the other girl switched to a different coach (and an easier number), and Virginia and Doris were by themselves. Every evening after supper Virginia would practice aerials in the backyard while Claudia oohed and aahed. Aerials were pure enchantment, a mixture of precision and faith: One tossed the baton with just the right angle, releasing it straight up out of the palm of the hand as if it were being pushed into the air, and it would fall right back where it had left the earth. It was the relationship of skill to magic, confidence to power.

There was no contest, really; Virginia wasn't even nervous. And so she became one of the girls, the only black face and legs on a line of spanking white-and-blue uniforms. In that shimmering outfit she felt the membrane of illusion rise between her and the audience. Her baton spun easily, as though the twirling itself were a breathless silvery web slipping effortlessly from her magic wrists. In the majorette uniform she was a Titan, a fifty-foot woman whose legs stretched high and away, joining together somewhere above a cloud. The princess lines of the bodice, its frog fastenings and brass-buttoned epaulets! The perfect circle of the skirt, cobalt-blue cotton lined with white silk! Tall white boots with blue-and-white pompons (they used one skein of yarn for each boot), the shiny-hard white hats with those outrageous plumes! For the first time in her life Virginia felt not only attractive, but effective—like she knew how to handle what she had and, as they said in the lavatories, "deal that stuff."

The white girls on the squad seemed more blasé about it, though. Most of them came from the other end of the school district, literally the other side of the tracks, and everything about them was different from what Virginia had known— their jokes and mannerisms, the way they acted with boys. She gaped at their dizzying procession of boyfriends and their talk about everything they did with them. Their stomachs were flat and there was a hollow between their thighs. Contrary to the big-hipped women black men ran after, their boys liked them with no hips at all.

They tried to mold their bodies to the *Vogue* standard, glamorous in their long straight hair and sharp noses, their peach-colored chemises and sheer nylons. Whenever they changed into their uniforms for pep assembly, Virginia peeked at their flowered bikini panties and lacy bras. She had never seen such extravagance, and she tried not to stare when they stripped off these very same undergarments after assembly and washed up at the sinks, chatting as if it were the most natural thing in the world.

The Butler residence was a gangling wooden house of the design common in the area, a main gable with a gentler eave to one side. The narrow elevated lot was supported by a low wall of concrete blocks. Three steps up to the lawn, along the concrete walk, then four broad wooden stairs onto an open porch with white railings.

Virginia had once propelled a bicycle up and down a brick driveway like this one, still wobbly on two wheels. Severe winters and scorching summers had made the bricks buckle, creating small valleys and swells so that the dark red surface seemed to be heaving sluggishly.

Renee opened the door. She was in high spirits.

"Mom says I'm supposed to entertain you while she finishes something. Did you bring Gina?"

"No . . ."

"I thought Gina went with you everywhere!"

"I let her take a nap this afternoon. She might get jealous with so many new puppets in the making."

Renee led her to the gray sofa and ran out of the room, returning seconds later with a narrow cardboard box. Inside, on a bed of cotton balls, lay a tiny plastic flute.

Virginia lifted the tonette out of its makeshift cradle and turned it over slowly in her hands. "When I was your age, I used to play one of these. I could never get it to sound like anything."

"Dad says it'd wake up people in China." Renee giggled. "In the spring we get to choose our own instruments. Mr. Jacobs says I'd make a good flute player."

Flute, the feminine instrument. Played by girls in junior high, high school, college, girls in tight skirts, ankles crossed and sleekly stockinged legs slanted to one side, so that the row of seated bodies had all the precision and anonymity of a chorus line.

"I chose the cello," Virginia said. "It was hard at first, but I liked it. I even brought my cello with me to Akron."

"Oh, will you play it for me sometime?"

"Maybe."

"Please?"

"We'll see!" Virginia put the tonette to her lips and blew a few notes, making a face.

Renee laughed again, but took it from her and bedded it down gently. "Why'd you choose cello?" she asked, tucking the box under her arm.

"Well, my brother played the trumpet, so I didn't want to play that, of course—or any other wind instrument, for that matter, so that took care of the flute. And we couldn't afford a piano. And *everyone* played the violin. That left the viola, the cello, stringed bass, and the harp. The harp was too expensive, too."

"What about drums?"

"Drums? You know, I never even considered them."

"So how'd you choose?"

"Cello had the nicest name. It sounded . . . cuddly. And it rhymed with Jell-O."

Renee laughed until she nearly choked. "That's a silly reason," she said finally, looking grave.

"I've done lots of things for silly reasons, sweetheart. For years I refused to eat strawberries, even though I used to love them. Do you know why?"

"Why?"

"Because I was convinced the little seeds would grow in

my stomach. Once I tried to pick out the seeds, but all I had left was red mush."

"Oh, that's not so silly. My brother does the same with grapes." Small cool fingers grabbed Virginia's hand. "Wanna see my room?"

Like an interloper, a clumsy foreigner disrupting other lives, she started up the stairs with Renee.

"I can jump four stairs at once," Renee said. "Wanna see?"

"What do you mean, 'at once'?"

"You know—you stand on the bottom step and jump, and then you go up a stair and jump, and then on and on. It's like flying."

"Isn't that dangerous? I mean, what if you miss?"

Virginia knew that didn't matter. To stand at the top of a flight of stairs and feel your spine stretch to span this arc, the overwhelming urge to turn and run up into safety and the equally pressing need to jump down into that void, the body hurtling so rapidly there seemed no way for the heart to catch up with it. . . . For years she'd had dreams of falling. She would stand on the landing, considering the trajectory, and when she finally jumped, her only fear was that she had not leapt far enough and wouldn't clear the last stair. If it was a good night, she landed as soft and insubstantial as a feather. If it was a bad night, she woke up in the darkness, flat on her aching back.

When Virginia and her brother had learned that the house they would be moving to in Arizona had no basement and no second story, they'd begun jumping down the stairs they would soon lose forever. Three steps at first, then four, five. Dad in the living room with the newspaper. Belle upstairs, where she couldn't hear, or in the kitchen yelling up that they would hurt themselves. Part of the secret was in the knees; the rest was the state of mind you had when you jumped—you couldn't think of falling. You had to float, to let go, let the steps disappear under you. The leap was not just a matter of seconds; it was a morsel of boundless time and perpetual space.

No one could stop them from leaping. They were possessed; come scolding or whipping they would jump, until finally they lay breathless at the foot of the stairs.

"My brother can jump six steps," Renee said. "He's already eleven."

"That's great."

"Yeah. He's playing farmer with Dad today. They went to some place out in the countryside to pick apples for cider."

"I'd like to meet him sometime," Virginia replied. "And your father."

Renee shrugged. "Dad's a dud. Richie's cool, though. Here's my room."

It was very simple and neat—a twin bed against the wall, flowered wallpaper, a white chest of drawers, and a small toy box under the western window where the sun broke from a cloud bank, pouring through the organdy curtains and onto the wooden floor. Renee chattered as she bounded from chest to bed, pulling out dolls, but Virginia only half paid attention, staring, lost in the gleam of the floorboards. The neatness of the room was disturbing. It was not merely clean; it looked cleaned out.

"So you and your brother get along, huh?" she found herself saying.

"Yeah, I guess."

"I have a brother, too. He's two years older than me, just like yours. And I've got a sister nine years younger."

"A little sister?"

"She's not exactly 'little' anymore. Claudia was born right after our family moved to Arizona. I took care of her a lot; when she woke up in the middle of the night, I was there singing a lullaby before my mom had time to stir."

Renee seemed far away.

"I bet you'd like a little sister, wouldn't you?"

Renee didn't answer. She slumped on the bed like a rag doll with the stuffing gone, staring down at the hands in her lap.

Virginia could have slapped herself. "Tell you what," she added quickly. "While we're waiting for your mom, why don't we do something fun? I'll show you how to make a Japanese empress out of that Ping-Pong ball, okay?"

"I don't care," Renee blurted. Just then her mother called them, and she went bounding down the stairs.

Sarah Butler burst through the swinging kitchen door, bearing two cups and a steaming pot of coffee. "Hello, Miss King, sit down! That is, if you can find a clear space."

She put the tray on a side table. The dining room had been converted to a combination family and play area. The television, an assortment of toys scattered on the hardwood floor before it, dominated one corner; in the opposite corner stood a cabinet-style sewing machine.

"I'm sorry I didn't greet you right away, but Renee wanted to show you her room first, and I was cleaning up the mess in the kitchen."

"It smells delicious."

"I was baking some oatmeal igloo cookies. Sit down, sit down!"

Virginia chose an armchair in the sewing corner; as she

sank deeper and deeper into the cushions, Renee clapped her hands and laughed.

"I should have warned you," Sarah said. "That chair's nearly as old as this house. I just couldn't bear to throw it away."

"Cookies are one of my weaknesses." Virginia smiled and surreptitiously adjusted her skirt. "But what are oatmeal igloo cookies?"

Sarah laughed. "That's Renee's name for them. They're made with oatmeal, but they have to be chilled first." She shook her head in amusement.

"There's nothing better in this world than the smell of warm oats," Virginia said, folding her arms and inhaling deeply. It called up memories of breakfast in a small kitchen and the glow of the copper-bottomed pot as it swung over the table delivering a steaming portion to each bowl. As children, she and Ernie Jr. had eaten oatmeal every morning with a kind of local pride. They used the round Quaker cartons for top hats and decorated them with macaroni shells and gold spray paint for Christmas.

The mills ran seven days a week. In good weather Virginia, Ernie Jr. and their friends were allowed to take the bus home from Sunday school; but instead of catching it at the bottom of the hill, they would walk the half mile downtown to the bus lineup. On stifling hot days the chimneys spewed out a thick white smoke that settled in the streets and stuck to the lungs, a syrupy, slightly burnt odor that masked the rubber stink from the tire factories and overwhelmed the truck fumes. They would detour along Mill and Broadway in order to walk by the Quaker Oats silos.

What a joy it was each time to catch the first glimpse

of those giant cylinders, startling in their whiteness, like a monstrous packet of chalk or cigarettes or, of course, gigantic oatmeal cartons! Inside these massive silos the oats were ground, rolled and poured into brightly labeled cardboard cartons. It was a process as mysterious and exalted as another town phenomenon, the zeppelin. Anyone's father who worked in the Quaker Mill was respected as much as an airship engineer or, for that matter, a chemist in the labs at the rubber factories. There they stood beneath the austere pillars to catch a whiff of something that went beyond them, out into the world.

"Renee!" She was perched on Virginia's armrest. "You keep on bouncing on that chair, you're liable to end up with a straight pin in your behind!" Sharp bones, and the evergreen scent of hair pomade—Renee laughed and slid off, plopping into Virginia's lap.

"Get up from Miss King this instant!" More giggling and untangling of legs. "Renee's turned out to be a pack rat, too. See those chairs?" Pushed against the wall behind the kitchen door were two child-size wooden rockers, a rag doll propped in each—black boy, black girl. "The kids outgrew those chairs long ago, but do you think they'd let me give them to the Goodwill? Uh-uh. They put their old dolls in them so I couldn't say they were just standing around taking up space. Renee's worse than Richie; she drags the chairs into the living room so the dolls can watch cartoons. Okay, young lady"— Renee, just in the process of tugging the girl doll and its chair out for inspection, stopped in her tracks—"that will be quite enough. You know what you have to do. Go on, now."

Groaning, she went upstairs. Soon the shrill ladder of a C major scale on the tonette drifted down, sounding like the shrieks of a demented peacock.

Sarah winced, shaking her head. "What we endure for the betterment of our children."

The old-fashioned knee-pedal sewing machine responded to her touch "like a faithful old dog," she said, biting off the thread.

"We're so glad to see Renee excited about the puppet show. Normally, she's very shy—there aren't many kids her age in the neighborhood. Strangers usually make her freeze up entirely. But you've scored a hit with her."

"She's a real sweetheart."

Sarah Butler reached over the sewing machine and plucked a scrap of bright yellow cloth from a basket. "I've been experimenting with puppet bodies. This one's the best so far. Is the neck too wide?"

Virginia inspected the mitten. "I brought a few samples," she said, fitting a pirate head into the neck and fastening it with a rubber band: "Looks good, Sarah." Then: "I'm afraid I might have said something wrong upstairs."

"Oh?"

"We were talking about siblings, and I mentioned my younger sister, and then I asked if she'd like to have a little sister, too."

Sarah stopped the machine in mid-seam. "What did Renee say when you asked?"

"Nothing. She just got very serious and quiet. Then you called us down."

Sarah sighed and pushed the fabric away. "Poor Renee. Last year I got pregnant. Renee was excited; she was convinced it would be a girl, and she made us drag down her old crib from the attic and set it up in her room. My mother was furious when she heard about that crib. She's old-fashioned, superstitious." She turned back to her sewing, absentmindedly finishing the seam. "But she was right this time. In the sixth month the doctor couldn't find the baby's heartbeat anymore, so they operated."

"I'm sorry."

"We've managed. . . . There, that's done." She held up another mitten, this one in red. "Your turn."

Virginia took the cloth body into her lap, thinking *Smaller than a fetus* as she reached for a white cotton hand and pinned it onto the end of one sleeve. At six months her mother had begun to bleed. Would Claudia have survived such a premature birth? "Still a high chance of brain damage," the doctor had worried. "If we can make it to seven . . ." So Belle took to bed for the last three months of her pregnancy. With a patience she had never managed on her own two feet, she lay flat on her back, waiting for her new child to clothe itself completely in brain and muscle tissue, in glands and lungs. The move cross-country and the stress of a new environment must have overtaxed her body, the doctor told Ernest, but Virginia felt that the cause was deeper, like a wound that hadn't healed. What threatened the baby wasn't physical. It was some strange grief, maybe the same grief that paralyzed her father at the kitchen table, his brow bent over his clenched hands long after grace was said, the same grief that turned Belle's gaze inward and made her talk to the unborn child when she thought no one was listening. Maybe it was even the sadness Virginia and Ernie Jr. felt at leaving Akron for a place that looked like the moon.

And into this smoldering sorrow Grandma Evans came. As her daughter waited in the spare room, laid out as if for burial, the older woman dusted corners and vacuumed the new house, combed four heads of hair including her own, ironed five sets of clothes, and got the two kids fed, dressed and off to school each morning.

That was the only time Grandma Evans had ever come out West. She swore she'd never come back to that "pancake griddle," that "sandbox for scorpions and rattlers." When Belle finally had Claudia, just two weeks ahead of term at five and a half pounds, it was Grandma Evans who changed her and bathed her, Grandma who kept Belle from feeding the baby every hour so she wouldn't get the colic, Grandma who told Virginia and Ernie Jr. hair-raising stories about toddlers running in front of speeding cars and sticking their tongues in electric sockets, showing them by example how to care for their little sister before packing her two borrowed suitcases and making Ernest take her to Sky Harbor Airport. No amount of pleading could make her stay a minute longer than the fourteen days her own mother had made her lie in "childbed" after each birth.

"Just remember, Belle," she said, handing the baby over a last time, "you might get to loving this child too much, just 'cause both of you worked so hard to get her here. Now that she's here, let her do her own living."

Nine

Virginia pulled over at the interstate entrance to consult the map. She'd left the Butlers drained and a little shaky from the maze of coincidences, but after a shower and change into jeans and sweater, she felt like her old self. Finally, sunshine! A glorious Saturday afternoon lay before her unopened, the crisp air reviving in her the thrill of freedom, of exploration.

The Ohio printed in red and blue hairlines was different from the Ohio she carried around in her mind. On the map were rivers and state parks she never knew existed, even islands in the middle of Lake Erie! She consulted the AAA tour book: "Kelleys Island, population 175; bicycle and boat rental, deep sea fishing, Indian hieroglyphics. Automobile ferry at Marblehead Peninsula."

The onset of fall in the swampy countryside west of Cleveland had been subdued by the moisture in the air and of the earth. Golds and reds were muted—even the black of the trees and the plowed fields had a warm quality to them. Although visibility was excellent, the light seemed almost misty.

Lake Erie stretched calmly to the north and disappeared in a sheen of haze. On the outskirts of Huron, the white facade of the Pillsbury factory rose so suddenly from the slack horizon that at first Virginia thought the Wedgwood blue insignia was the label on a leviathan sack of flour; then the smokestacks came into focus behind it and destroyed the illusion. She was nearing Cedar Point, the amusement park the whole clan had gone to one summer weekend when she was seven or eight. Grandma Evans had clucked her tongue at the dirty beach, but Virginia had thrilled to the wonder of it, all the millions of particles of rock pulverized from long-vanished cliffs ("the grinding stone of Time," Dad proclaimed) laid out like an ecru wall-to-wall carpet that extended into the water and underneath the lake all the way to the other side, where Canadian families spread out their blankets and warned their children to stay away from the edge. They might have chicken to eat, too, and maybe their own local specialties. Virginia's family nibbled on Salem potato chips and drank Norka soda pop—"Akron" spelled backwards—and Grandma had brought along her "watermelon cake," a deep pink confection stuffed with raisins and covered with bright green frosting.

Aunt Carrie had been there, too, in her old-fashioned straight skirt and funny cloche hat. That must have been one of their last outings together. Aunt Carrie: every time Virginia rattled around among the emotional furniture of her childhood, her short aunt with the big bosom popped up among the artifacts. She seemed to have been pretty much of a fixture in the family. Why hadn't Dad kept in contact with his sister after the move? Virginia resolved to call her as soon as she returned.

To be a child again in the backseat of a station wagon, watching the colorless asphalt surface spill out behind the wheels! You could actually see time go by—the greenhouse passed a minute ago was now just a glint at the end of the road. With every exit ramp they passed, she had tried to imagine the kind of life she might have led had they turned off there.

Except for a couple with matching checkered shirts on bicycles and a few older people with shopping bags, the ferry was nearly empty. Virginia stood at the far rail and watched the water spread before her like a plain, then the green smudge of land growing into trees, houses, a pier. This was the Midwest, too. How calm it was! No human crisis, it seemed, could flourish long in this landscape. The colors elated minimally and offended no sensibility. Everything was artlessly beautiful. It reminded her of something she'd read in a magazine—the laconic reply made by a Plains farmer when asked if he ever yearned for a more dramatic landscape: "Mountains are all right, I guess, but they sure do block the view."

Once off the boat ramp, Virginia turned left, away from the folksy harbor village. She rented a bicycle at the first lean-to by the side of the road. A little farther along she bought two fish cakes at an open stand and a bag of apples. Stuffing them alongside her cardigan in the bike basket, she started down the rutted road along the shore. Deep green foliage of indeterminate species pressed against the edges of the roadway. She pedaled up a slight rise and curved almost immediately into an unscathed world: trees leaning toward the light, strange birdcalls, no cars. She recognized a black chestnut but wasn't sure about the copse of thorny stunted trees—hawthorn, perhaps. Without names, the trees and plants assumed a mute sovereignty. Occasional bicyclists burst from the mottled tapestry and waved in passing, disappearing again as nature swelled to receive them. Virginia tried to imagine the Erie Indians who had lived on this island, later named after a white man, Indians gliding silently along the green-choked shorelines of their lake. "The Indians had the sense to share their world with those creatures who had claimed it before them," her father had said. "The Indians knew that we're living on borrowed ground."

Saguaro. Prickly pear. Creeping devil. Beaver tail. Teddy

bear cholla, Bishop's-cap. Ernest Sr. had recited the names as they trooped through the Desert Botanical Garden near Phoenix, past ranks of cacti as picturesque as their names, unlikely creatures that looked like barrels and hedgehogs and pineapples, rattails and firecrackers.

They'd been in Phoenix less than a year. As usual, Belle had stayed home—Ernest had suggested making it a family trip, but at the thought of trundling her tender cargo through a labyrinth of thorns and spiny plants, Belle had clutched baby Claudia to her chest and stared at the three of them in outraged reproach.

Their father explained how to suck the prickly pear for its juice and break off an aloe leaf to treat a wound. "That's how the Indians persevered," he said.

Ernie Jr. wanted to know if he had ever done those acts himself.

"No, but now I've read up on survival in the desert," their father replied. "The desert teaches you to fall back on your inner resources. My mother used to call it 'making do.' Well, to the Papago and Pima tribes, making do was a way of life."

Virginia and her brother remembered their other grandmother only dimly; she had died when Ernie Jr. was in first grade. What they knew was what Belle had told them, that she'd led the life of a dog with the heart of a saint, which didn't seem a story worth pursuing. Their father hardly ever mentioned his side of the family; he never attempted to create a place for his past in his children's memory.

Virginia shared her father's rapture for the desert, but Ernie Jr. was less reverent; he was twelve and he didn't take anything for granted.

"Sounds like some more of that Hopi junk to me," he said.

"What do you mean, *junk?*" their father demanded.

"They told us in school that the Hopis still believe in thunder gods and pray to idols and stuff," Ernie Jr. countered, uncowed. "It's some primitive religion."

Ernest King, Sr., was furious. The following week he checked out books on kachina dolls and Hopi ceremonial dances from the public library, and the very next Saturday piled them into the car at six in the morning for the five-hour drive to Second Mesa. Belle had refused to get up that early; they had a breakfast of milk and Cheerios.

They drove north out of the Valley of the Sun, up the curving road that crossed the yellowish desert hills toward Flagstaff. Their father lectured them incessantly.

"The Hopis have an intimate relationship with the earth and the spirits that govern nature. They believe a man should never leave the land he was born on, lest his roots shrivel and die."

These were the kind of drives their father loved, treks long enough for him to construct an interpretation of the cultures described in those borrowed books, spinning out his compulsive version of the rules for leading a sweet and contented life, with not much else for the captive passengers to do but daydream, staring out at the passing unfamiliar void. Virginia and Ernie Jr. fell asleep before they reached the Mogollon Rim and didn't wake up until the car turned off Route 89 well inside the Navajo Reservation. Navaho Nation encircled Hopi Land entirely; on the map it looked like a stranglehold.

Ernie Jr. harrumphed through the trading post outside Oraibi while Virginia admired the feathers and silver jewelry, the rugs and baskets; she rummaged through bins of cheap rocks: pyrite and Apache tears and blood-streaked jasper. Best of all were the kachina dolls, brightly painted wooden figures carrying a spear or a sheath of corn, with horns or plumes sprouting from animal heads. The Hopi woman behind the counter explained that the smaller ones were for children, though they weren't toys. She was squat, broad-faced and the color of buckskin, dressed in a long, gathered skirt and blouse, both purple. Her black hair, streaked with gray, was pulled into a bun. Virginia was as intrigued by the smooth plains of her face and faintly oriental black eyes as she was by her manner: instead of the exasperated politeness most adults dispensed to inquisitive children, the Hopi woman spoke to Virginia as if it were a child's place to ask questions, and hers to answer—no patronizing sweetness but a patient matter-of-factness.

She let Virginia touch a feather. "Hopi parents hang kachinas up on the walls so that their children learn to recognize their gods," she explained, and added that there were more than two hundred of them, some with human features and others whose eyes and mouths were rectangles or triangles. "On feast days the men in the village dress up as kachinas and perform the ritual dances. White people are not permitted to see these rituals."

"Hey," Ernie Jr. exclaimed, "that means *we* can see them, right?"

The Hopi woman looked embarrassed, but their father merely laughed. "When a Hopi man puts on a kachina mask," he told them later, standing in the parking lot overlooking the cracked and crevassed landscape, "his troubles disappear. He forgets his name. He no longer has a wife or a family. He is no longer the person who put on the mask but has received the spirit of the god represented by the mask. He walks and talks differently, because he has become Thunder Maker or Yellow Corn Maiden."

On the drive back Ernie Jr. leaned over to Virginia. "Listen," he whispered, his words muffled by the hum of the engine. "Henceforth, let him of the wise and wondrous words be known by his true name: Rubber Smoke from the Far Hills Kachina." And both children hid their faces behind the back of the seat, choking from silent laughter.

A smaller road beckoned toward the lake, where Virginia found a sad beach, closed for the season, stretching along the remains of a glacier, a stone outcrop whose surface was swirled like pulled taffy. Backtracking, she made her way up the main roadway past a cemetery and stopped to read the stone monuments: SEMMISH, O'HARA, HIMMELEIN, MARTIN, and KASPAR.

Virginia followed the sign to Inscription Rock, which turned out to be a boulder marked with rather ordinary pictographs, not nearly as mysterious as the ruins of the Anasazi Indians in the Southwest, a people who had disappeared without a trace sometime during the thirteenth century. Ernie Jr. had scoffed at first: "No one just disappears," he said. "They must have died off or been slaughtered by the Apaches." To him the Apaches were the only interesting Indians.

But there was no evidence of forcible takeover, their father explained, and no indication that they had abandoned their villages in search of better land. They simply ceased to exist. All they left, it seemed, were petroglyphs scratched into the steep red-and-gray rock, pictorial stories of antelope and rivers and arrowheads and corn.

"No one knows what happened, but there are theories." They had already clambered over the excavation site, and while they made their way up the cliff where the caves had been found, their father rolled out the possibilities: starvation, volcanic eruption, earthquake, disease, and the most far-fetched theory of all—UFOs. Visitors from outer space. Ernie Jr. dropped the stick he'd been dragging in the dirt, rigid with excitement. Virginia held onto the rickety guardrail, dizzy with fear; she kept her eyes pinned to the pictures on the rock face less than a foot away, where the line of broad-chested stick men appeared to waver, wobbling in the monotonous gait of the dancers at the powwow she'd seen on the White Mountain Apache Reservation the year before.

In time, Ernie Jr. had taken an increasing interest in their excursions and instead of merely trotting along had begun to develop obsessions of his own. For a while he was fascinated by old mining towns. He scoured the public library for books on Jerome and Tombstone in their heyday and was especially smitten by the pitiful fates of those abandoned ventures whose short-lived glory was reflected in their names: Nugget, Gunsight, Paradise, Total Wreck. Whenever they went on another trip, he would comb the road map for possible side trips. But their father found these ghost towns distasteful, the ill-conceived dreams of white men who believed the earth was theirs to be plundered.

How different was she from her father? He seemed to drift through daily life as though he were following some inner urging, some long-range interior decree. Increasingly, he would take off and let the pieces fall where they pleased, like their madcap trips to Canyon de Chelly and the Hopi mesas.

But were the Arizona expeditions so different from the Sunday drives in Akron? He'd push back his dinner plate saying, "Let's take a spin," and off they'd go, cruising the desultory neighborhoods until they ended up at the factory as if by accident. And once (she must have been five or six) the family had just finished up their coconut cream pie on a Friday evening when he crumpled his napkin and said, "Let's drive to Niagara Falls"—so they stacked the dishes in the sink, piled into the car, and drove five hours to the Canadian border.

Weird snatches of memory remained—the smell of warmed vinyl and car-radio static, changing into their pajamas at a gas station, exhausted yet exhilarated, stumbling behind their dad along a sidewalk lined with streetlamps disguised as gas lanterns and Belle saying "It's midnight!" With every step, miniature Daisy Ducks rose and fell across the sea-green flannel of Virginia's jammies ("Who cares if they're in their pajamas, Belle? They're kids, for chrissakes!"); flecks of mica glittered up from the concrete as the light struck the pavement. Then the back-lit panorama of millions of gallons of water plunging toward the earth (if there truly was an earth down there; they could only see mist). When Virginia woke up, she was in her own bed with the sun pouring through the curtains. Her father slept until noon.

The photographs turned out to be disappointing. Arrested in mid-plunge, the cascading water was a solid wall of froth, frozen under powerful spotlights. And there was nothing to compare them to for size; cooped up on these glossy squares of paper, the almighty falls looked like a molded vanilla pudding.

· · ·

A little farther down the road leading back to the harbor stood a brick school building, set away from the street, and then wooden houses in need of repair but with firewood piled up under the porches, motorboats propped on blocks and on the mailboxes the names from the cemetery: THE SEMMISH FAMILY, THE MARTINS, HERE LIVE THE HIMMELEINS.

Virginia shoved the front tire into the slot of the bicycle rack. "We're living on borrowed ground," her father had claimed; but then he would mention the Hopis, who believed a man cut off from his roots would wither. What was her father's home—the desert, or the company? What had he been reaching for, and what had he left behind?

"Off-season rates now, just twelve dollars." The white-haired woman at the inn stamped her receipt vigorously and led the way upstairs. "Clean and bright," she rasped like a parrot, rattling the key before throwing open the door.

"Is it always like this?" Virginia asked. "The light, I mean; is it always so brilliant?"

"Summer we get a mist comes up landside and boomerangs back in on us. That'll burn off usually by midday. Winter's too dull. In my opinion, now's the best time—clear sky from six to six. But you can't tell tourists nothing." She looked at Virginia with more of a grimace than a smile, and shuttled back down the hall.

It was immaculate, with that illusory brightness of rooms by the sea. The single window was luminous with reflected light, as were the white pitcher on the bed table and the two water glasses, the varnished surface of the small desk, the brass handles on the chest of drawers, the mirror next to the door. But the air was somehow dim and sad.

Poor Dad. Running away never did anybody any good. Suddenly, Virginia felt very tired. Opening the window to let in the last of the afternoon light, she threw herself across the bed.

At first she dreamed she was lying in a field of grass, her skin the temperature of the cool earth underneath. Then the light changed, and she was back in Akron; her father was boarding a train. She had followed him, down a tunnel slowly widening into a cavern with phosphorous lakes, and stepped into the last compartment just as the train was pulling out. There were black women in head rags clutching cord-wrapped bundles and children wailing at their skirts; old black men with rusty knuckles and cracked shoes, young men who looked old, stooped and bleary-eyed.

Someone had chalked a game of hopscotch on the gangway and she couldn't resist skipping through its squares, taking care not to step on the lines: two, three, then four steps at a time, she jumped down to a lower deck; in the infirmary Belle was stretched out on a white table, a nurse checking her temperature. "The baby's dead," she said. Virginia wondered at her calm, but she couldn't wait; she ran off, along the dim corridor. By the time she reached the duty-free shop, she was nine years old. The woman behind the counter asked her what she wanted.

"That," Virginia said, pointing to a Spanish dancer whose nipples lit up when a switch in her back was flipped.

Yes, it all began at nine. The day after the midnight trip to Niagara Falls, she'd lifted her skirt behind the neighbor's garage and made the little boy from the corner kiss her there. He was four and he had big lips so then she made him kiss the scab on her foot. When he told his mother, she said he was a lying little pip-squeak. He had lips like a duck, and everyone called him Rinky Dink.

Virginia woke up late and ate a gigantic breakfast—eggs, link sausages, hash browns, an English muffin smothered in blackberry jam. The waitress cocked a tweezed eyebrow. "Someone's hungry this morning," she observed dryly, and refilled the coffee cup for the third time.

"It's the good air," Virginia replied, but she was ready to board the ferry and leave this floating carousel of memories.

Again a gorgeous day. Since it was on the way, she decided to stop off at Oberlin and get a sneak preview of the next station assigned by the Arts Council; she'd move there in less than two weeks.

She drove southeast, along two-lane county roads that wound through picture-postcard towns with improbable names like Milan and Berlinville and Florence, past stately facades adorned like pastel wedding cakes poised on expanses of luxuriant green. Bells were tolling as freshly waxed family cars headed home from church parking lots.

As she rolled into Oberlin, she began to relax. Students were everywhere, students and bicycles, and both came in various colorful states of disrepair—men in ink-stained windbreakers pedaling balloon-tire bikes, women in long peasant skirts wheeling by on ten-speeds. One girl's jeans were bedecked with patchwork as elaborate as a prize quilt at the county fair.

Virginia pulled in front of the Ben Franklin drugstore. A little walk would do her good, then a soda (she hoped they had an old-fashioned soda fountain) and back to Akron.

Heading down the sidewalk toward her were three black guys. They slowed up: two looked older than the third, in their mid-twenties; one wore a brown leather jacket and carried a briefcase, the other had a trim mustache and a trenchcoat slung over his shoulders. But it was the one in the middle, a short round-faced guy of eighteen or nineteen, who spoke.

"Hey, sister, what's happ'nin'?"

Virginia had to smile. "Nothing much," she replied.

He brought the trio to a halt. "Sister, I can't say I've seen you around. What's your name?"

"Gina."

"Gina? Nice. My name's Jerry, and he's Mark, and this here's Floyd." Floyd put his briefcase under his arm and nodded, slightly embarrassed.

"Like I said, I ain't seen you around. Are you new on campus?"

"I don't go to school here. Just visiting."

"My buddies here are visiting, too. Detroit's the home base. Floyd's an Oberlin alum." Floyd held out his hand.

"I'm from the East," Virginia lied, shaking his hand. "Upstate New York."

But Jerry was not about to leave a stone unturned. "Can I be of assistance, Gina?"

"As a matter of fact, yes," she said quickly. "How do I get to the library?"

Floyd broke into a grin; even Mark forgot to be cool and smiled. Vaguely aware that some indignity had been committed, Jerry hesitated, at a loss; then he affected a mock-serious face.

"That's heavy, sister, very heavy." He nodded his head. "A beautiful Sunday, and you're heading for the temple of wisdom. How about having lunch with us instead?"

"Come on, now," Virginia sputtered; Jerry laughed and held up his hands in mock defense.

"Sorry, sister. You can't blame me for trying, though. Now, if you insist, I'll tell you the best way: Go through that arch, cross the street, and then just keep straight. You can't miss it."

"Thank you."

"You can't miss it," he repeated, "but if you do," and he grinned—"just whistle and I'll come running!"

Virginia had intended to seek out the music conservatory, but now felt obliged to follow Floyd's directions. She cut through the town square, a grassy area the size of a city block and shaded by elms. Students were sitting cross-legged or had spread themselves out on blankets, in pairs; a few loners were reading, backs propped up against trees. The sun filtering through the elms in feathery blotches streaked them a shade brighter here and there, like frosted hair. As she moved slowly through the chirping, luminous academic Eden, she felt curiously old.

"Could you tell me where the conservatory is?" she asked the reference librarian, a lanky man with sandy hair that kept falling over his wire-rim spectacles.

"Conservatory?" He seemed astonished by the question.

"Yes. The Conservatory of Music."

"Why, right here, Ma'am."

Ma'am! What did he think she was? She glanced down at her jeans—they were clean, even pressed, and without a single patch—and sighed. "I thought this was the library," she replied.

"Yes, Ma'am, that's right. Oh—you must be from out of town." He seemed relieved to have found an explanation and grinned, then pulled out a campus map and circled the Conservatory of Music with a red Flair pen. It was on the other side of the lawn; she'd missed it by cutting through the square.

The interior of the conservatory was a network of light and air, blond wood and white linoleum hallways. At the end of each corridor was a little seating area of upholstered chairs and low tables tucked into the alcove, potted ficus and hanging ferns dripping their spidery green down the windows that peered out into a windblown courtyard, so that the boundaries between outside and inside seemed to evaporate. At every turn in the labyrinth more light poured in golden shafts from the little square windows in studio doors, and interlaced with this luminosity strains of music—a clarinet afloat on the comic-sad suspensions of Mozart, the thunk of a double bass, a sprinkle of piano, even a harpsichord—how intimate a microcosm, how familiar this profusion of sounds! Virginia found herself humming along with scraps of melody until she passed another door and a new motif sprang up to supersede it.

On the bulletin board she read that there was a recital going on that very minute, a mezzo-soprano performing the usual student program designed to show range and versatility: assorted French and Italian arias, a few Schubert Lieder, wrapping up with a spattering of modern selections: Charles Ives, Gershwin, a young American composer Virginia didn't recognize. The concert hall wasn't hard to find; she waited outside until she heard the applause between pieces, then slipped in, taking a seat in the last row.

The amphitheater rose gently away from the stage, where a robust young woman stood resplendent, her caramel-colored skin glowing against the emerald green of her dress. Virginia caught her breath. The singer held her pose until the

rustling in the audience subsided, then, with a barely perceptible nod, signaled the pianist that she was ready for the Schubert, seven chords and a pause, then twelve, each measured
cluster of notes a leaf shaken of the last rain before the voice
unscrolled like a sheath of dark silk: *Ihr lieben Mauern hold und
traut, / Die ihr mich kühl umschließt.*

Wasn't this where she belonged—in music? Virginia
doubted she had the single-mindedness to become a professional musician: the long hours alone in the studio, then the
ritualized presentation of years of solitary struggle, all the joys
and griefs of private experience translated into a wordless ecstasy of sound, the performer all but invisible in his or her
formal attire, the preordained gestures of the concert stage. She
preferred the stage as a platform for discovery, for interpreting
experience; for even though the prescribed words might be recited a dozen times the same way, the thirteenth time they
could be magically transformed by the actor's inspired hesitation as the hand reached for the fallen rose.

When Virginia had finished college, she hadn't even
imagined going on to graduate school. She had been eager to
get into the "real world," since she felt she hadn't ever really
lived. But what was the real world—working as a secretary
typing letters to names that would never grow faces? Living
hand-to-mouth in a ramshackle farmhouse with a bunch of
wonderful weirdos? Teaching kids to tell fairy tales with hand
puppets?

"The hands and the eyes are the most important features on a
puppet," Nigel had said. "We watch the eyes and feed our own
emotions into them, so they must shine, they must be large
and capable of depth—unless the puppet is not to be pitied, in

which case opaque beads will serve perfectly. And the hands should be well-defined. Not too intricate, lest they appear spidery and diabolical. Defined. Articulate. They must make up for the musculature we lose in the baggy arms of the puppet. They must channel all the energy of the voice."

Virginia had bent over the workbench for a closer look: these hands were cramped into a gesture of terror. "Chile," Parker replied to her silent question. "These are the hands of Chile."

"But we aren't doing anything on Chile," she protested.

He just looked up at her, silent—disappointed?—she couldn't tell. Finally, the ghost of a smile drifted into his gaze, which became a shade more electric; he grinned and went back to his whittling.

Parker was in charge of designing all the hands. If the puppet was to be outfitted with cloth hands, Colette and Virginia did the cutting out and sewing according to his patterns; then he would specify where stuffing should be added in the heel of the palm or the pad of the thumb joint, and Colette did the trapunto with the smallest crewel needle in her basket. When the character called for wooden hands, though, Parker holed up in the far corner near the French doors, where the light poured over his left shoulder, and patiently whittled and filed and sanded until he was satisfied, down to the little fingernail. Such fanatical precision wasn't really necessary. Nigel would smile and say, "Nobody will see that fingernail, but we'll know it's there. More importantly, Parker will know it's there. Leave him be."

Sometimes he just started up without instigation and began to carve a pair of hands he had dreamed of or seen on someone. Sometimes the idea for an entire puppet show would grow out of a pair of Parker's hands.

He had twisted a bandana into a narrow strip and tied it around his forehead. Virginia stood watching him work for a moment, fighting the impulse to touch his hair, to run her fingers through it like in the movies. Oh, she knew what White hair felt like—she'd fastened barrettes and put in hair clips for the girls on the majorette squad, while they told her how much they envied her for having hair that kept a curl (what a laugh!) and stayed put in rain. After making the mistake of explaining hot combs to them (their eyes widened in horror, though they would lay out their hair on ironing boards without batting an eyelash), she decided not to disabuse them of these notions and took care not to let them see her tugging out the kinks after marching in drizzle.

Afros changed all that. Still, after a whole year with Puppets & People, no one but Parker had ever seen Virginia braid her hair for the night.

"I like your headband," she finally said, and walked away.

The only other guy she had known who had worn a headband was her brother's friend, David Goldstein. David and Ernie Jr. had been in the same accelerated math class since seventh grade, and they would spend hours after school hunched over the dining-room table, plotting parabolas and tossing around multisyllabic formulas that sounded to Virginia like incantations.

Then, in their senior year, David flipped out. He began wearing thin leather-thonged sandals, even in winter—buffalo sandals which came from India and were treated with buffalo urine; you were supposed to soak them in the bathtub and put them on wet so they would dry to the contours of your feet. He rejected all clothes except blue jeans, peasant shirts, and fringed vests; he wore beads strung from apple seeds and did his own patchwork.

One day Virginia came home from majorette try-outs and found both of them in the living room, David sitting cross-legged on the sofa, pulling at a brown-black strand of hair as they speculated on the draft lottery. He was wearing a head-band, a strip of turquoise cloth knotted over his left ear with the ends dangling just short of his collar-length hair. Virginia was awestruck. He seemed like Jimi Hendrix come down from the heavenly stage, so outrageously *serene,* so confident that his message was the banner of the dawning age.

Belle was horrified. She tried to embarrass him with her withering asides, but David wasn't fazed. She forbade him to sit cross-legged on any of her furniture, even with his sandals off, since the soles of his feet were, in her words, "filthy" and "simply disgusting." "That's cool," he said, and sat on the carpet, bringing along an embroidered cloth he called his prayer mat to place under his patchworked haunches. Claudia thought he was pretty weird, but played up to him just to infuriate Belle.

"I can imitate any inanimate object," he claimed once. "My specialties are round things. Go ahead, name something round."

He curled himself into a watermelon, a pumpkin, a boulder, a basketball; then he did bacon sizzling and butter sliding across the pan. When Claudia requested a dodo egg, he stayed so long balled up on the carpet that they got frightened and tried to shake him out of it. After three or four minutes of frantic jostling, he groaned and slowly unfolded.

"Man, that was some trip," he murmured, spread-eagled on the rug, a beatific smile on his face. "That was nirvana."

Parker had been a sixties radical, an A student storming the Stanford administration building. He'd done drugs, flipped out and was selling handmade marionettes on the street when Nigel found him and put him to work. The troupe had just started up then, an odd collection of ex-engineering and ex-drama students with a mission to bring art to the masses. Politico and radical intellectual though he was, Parker loved to flirt. He was also a pretty fair dancer and once had swung Virginia into a searing tango in front of the entire troupe, finishing with the requisite back-breaking dip, his lips millimeters away from hers, in his eyes a flicker of arousal and fear.

"Have you ever done anything impulsive, Virginia?"

Parker's gaze held—no, entered her. He had never looked at her that steadily before.

"Does compulsive behavior count?"

"No, it doesn't."

The troupe had grown accustomed to Parker's midnight ramblings. He'd wander into a bedroom to engage his sleepy victim in a philosophical inquiry, then break off midsentence and go off elsewhere, maybe play a few measures on the piano, maybe go back to the kitchen for something more to drink. Sometimes he didn't go to bed at all; in the morning they would find him laid out cold on the davenport or curled up on a window seat; several times Virginia found him snoring outside her door. But the night of the tango was the first time he had dared to enter her room.

Impulsive. What had she ever done on the spur of the

moment, unpremeditated? Nothing, really. She was amazed, and disturbed. Then she brushed it off. Parker, after all, was a drunk, and drunks occasionally say profound things.

"I quit my job and joined this ship of fools. I'd say that was a major impulsive action."

He shook his head. "No good. You studied this stuff in school. You were programmed to do something like this."

"I studied *this*—puppets and madness? As far as I can remember, I completed a degree in the dramatic arts. Tell me where this stuff was on the course list."

"There's a bigger word for what we do here."

Still the gaze, neither judgmental nor searching, merely waiting. *I'm not playing straight man to his ludicrous badgering,* she thought, meeting his eyes in belligerent silence. After a hairsbreadth of a pause, he stood up to leave. Virginia released an inaudible sigh, watching his slim shoulders, his hunched, self-conscious gait. She felt a blaze of shame, then, and regret: he'd only been trying to *communicate,* as they used to say. He'd tried to open another lane of thought, and she'd thrown up a roadblock. Just as she considered calling him back, he stopped at the door and turned, his hoarse voice trailing to a whisper as he lifted his arms for the oratory: " 'Two gates for ghostly dreams there are: one gateway of honest horn, and one of ivory. Issuing by the ivory gate are dreams of glimmering illusion, fantasies, but those that come through solid polished horn may be borne out, if mortals only know them.' "

"Homer. *The Odyssey.* Right?"

"Illusion, Virginia. Glimmering illusion. That's all we're doing. We're playing with shadows, pretending they'll come to life with the first rays of the full moon. And we learn to do it so well that other people believe in the shadows. But do you know what? To the others, the shadows *are* real. Only to us they're not."

He was gone. Virginia plopped back on the pillow but knew she wouldn't be able to sleep. Had she ever been impulsive? It was one of those questions asked in the touchy-feely encounter groups they'd toyed with in college, after-dinner sessions where you took turns telling one positive thing about the person next to you, or experiments in trust like standing in the center of a circle of friends, arms folded over your chest and eyes closed, and then letting yourself fall backward knowing someone would catch you.

Scented candles and sealing wax had been the same kind of hocus-pocus. Even during the summer she'd turned seventeen, when she read everything she could find in the public library on Taoism, sitting cross-legged for hours in her darkened bedroom listening to a scratched recording of gongs and Buddhist monks chanting mantras, her longing had not been inspired by any impulse. No: its roots were not in spontaneous desire but a compulsion toward the opposite, the wish to control her urgings.

Months after that first nighttime incident, Parker visited Virginia's room again.

"Tell me what you think of me," he wanted to know.

Earlier that evening he had helped her with one of her puppets. She had been trying to carve the head of a young black woman, but her whittling was too crude. Parker had studied the knob of wood for a moment, then bent to work: nose and lips blossomed under his meticulous knife, the eyes rising eerily from the refined cups of their lids.

Now here he was in the middle of the night, swaying at the threshold to Virginia's bedroom.

"I think you're crazy to crash in here," she said.

Parker grinned and leaned against the doorjamb, then held on to it with both hands as if he were drowning.

"Look, Parker, give me a second to wake up and I'll help you to your room." With a little coddling he would go back and pass out.

"I don't want my room. You think I'm so whacked I don't know where I am, don't you?"

"I don't think anything."

"That's always been you landlubbers' problem." He chuckled. "Pretty good, eh? Landlubbers. Two feet safely planted on the ground. You've stood on the rolling breast of the sea with nothing between you and death but a rotting piece of wood . . ."

Virginia kept quiet.

"Where was I? Oh, landlubbers. That's you landlubbers' problem. Reading Malcolm Lowry to me, thinking it'll inspire fear in my soul. What do you know about it? That man knows what it's like. If you're high all the time, the world assumes a special sort of logic. You should try it. Let go!"

"Parker, you're spaced out of your mind."

"More like spaced into it. James Joyce was a space cadet, too, you know. 'O! the lowness of him was beneath all up to that sunk to! No likedbylike firewater or firstserved first-shot or gulletburn gin or honest brewbarrett beer either.' True, true—no kick to it. And how about: 'O who shall deliver me whole' / From bonds of this Tyrannic Soul?' Andrew Marvell. Can you do that?"

"No, I can't."

"A smile! Do I see a smile cross those fulsome lips? Doth my lady deign to grace me with her favor? Her arm laid bare upon the silken coverlet, the moon silvering the pillow whereon lies her head, the mirror and the chamberpot—"

"Parker—"

"—in the honeyed middle of the night, baby. I enter on tiptoe and falter, dazed by her beauty. Is she dreaming of me, I wonder? No, you're awake and staring at me like a bloody frog. Where's the azure-lidded sleep of my lady? The perfumed light, the thick velvet cushion upon which to rest my love-befuddled noggin?" He cocked his head expectantly. "What willed me here? You did, Virginia. You bade me come tonight."

"You were stumbling through the house in a barbiturate haze and bumped into my door is what willed you here."

"Barbiturate! Isn't that a wonderful word? Isn't the *sound* of it lovely?" Suddenly he slumped to the floor and assumed the posture of Buddha. Beneath the dark cap of hair the angular planes of his face were white as bone.

"I like you, Gina. Let me call you Gina, will you? Just tonight. The first time I saw you, Gina, in those funny little shoes, I said to myself, 'She's okay.' And do you know why? You have an intelligent beauty. Intelligence shines all over those features. It's almost scary. Have you ever seen your profile? No, of course not—but if you *could* see your profile, you'd know what I mean. It's noble. You have a great head. I loved carving that puppet tonight—you did recognize her, didn't you? It's the kind of head people want to take in their hands—no bumps, no irregularities, just sleek, unadulterated curve. I would love to wake up next to that head."

"That's enough, Parker." Virginia made a move to get out of bed, remembered her nightie, and thought better of it.

"Don't worry, I play by the rules. But you know what the funniest thing is? Years from now everyone will think we lived in a commune here. Nobody'll believe the Spartan dignity in which we thrived. Oh dear, I see you're outraged. My Lady of the Immaculate Name, don't you ever get tired of being outraged? It's bad for the heart, you know. A man looks at you and you bristle till he scuttles off. Boy oh boy, if some man were to stand his ground . . . if he were to walk over to you and place his hands on either side of your pillow so that any movement you made to escape would only throw you into his arms . . . if he held your warm sleepy body against his cool vigilant one and kissed—why, you'd go like a waterfall. Wouldn't that be nice? Don't worry, I won't touch you. After all, I'm the Great White Coward."

"Parker . . ."

"Yes, milady?"

"How long are you going to keep this up? You're young, you're smart, you know what's happening to you. Don't you want to stop it? Or can't you? I mean, what do you imagine your life will be like? Do you have plans? Hopes?"

Parker was staring at his toes.

"Look," Virginia said, "that was stupid. Forget it." She was about to apologize again when he lifted his head and looked her straight in the eye.

"Which *Peanuts* character do you think I am?"

"I—I've never really thought about it," she replied, taken by surprise.

"Come on, take a guess."

"Oh, right now, you mean? Hmmmm . . . Charlie Brown? Snoopy?"

A low-pitched laugh gurgled up; his body wobbled from side to side. "No, no, no. Come on, look at me! Can't you tell?"

"Sorry."

"Linus! Linus in the pumpkin patch, waiting for the Great Pumpkin." Abruptly, as if someone had flipped a switch, Parker resumed his Buddha posture. He shrugged. "Sure, I have plans. Sure, I want to stop it. But I'm waiting for a Sign —voices, angels appearing in my dreams. *El momento de la verdad.* I figure if the Sign comes, it means someone thinks I'm worth saving." He got to his feet. "Look, Gina; tomorrow I won't remember anything I said tonight. Do me a favor, will you? Don't remind me."

Ten

The trip from Oberlin to Akron took just an hour, a leisurely drive over two-lane roads winding through clapboard towns and the burnished flatlands of Great Lakes country. Again Virginia was struck by the similarity to Wisconsin: a little browner, perhaps, the light a bit more eastern; but the feeling of déjà vu was so mixed up with the recent and the distant past, she wasn't sure whether she was coming home or leaving again.

She made it back in time for a take-out pizza before the Javanese puppet show. A grand total of eight had signed up and were to meet at seven forty-five in the lobby of the small concert hall. Virginia recognized them immediately. They were in full regalia—high heels and suits, even ties—standing in the middle of the lobby like a circle of mother yaks protecting their young from cold and attack. Blue-jeaned students shuffled past, some engrossed in discussion but most of them alone, heads tucked in their collarbones as they studied the program notes. Untouched by the world around them, they skirted the little group of adults with imperturbable disregard. Virginia caught sight of Ida Lee and Sarah Butler.

Now Mrs. Woods saw her, too, and waved her arm like a born tour guide. "There you are, Miss King! We were beginning to fret."

Virginia glanced at her watch. "It's quarter to. Or did I misunderstand . . ."

159

"Oh, no," Mrs. Woods hastened to reassure her. "You're right on time. We were a bit early, that's all." She introduced the others, people Virginia least expected to be interested in such things, especially on a Sunday night—a salesman for Amity wallets and his housebound wife, a factory worker whose plump spouse wore red doubleknit polyester.

"We need you to give us a little introduction to tonight's performance. That is, if you don't mind doing overtime." Polite laughter.

"Well, I don't know exactly what to tell you. The play you'll see is a version of the *Wayang Purwa,* which is the story of the Great War between nobles. It's very stylized; but there's everything in it, love and scandal and blood and betrayal . . . just like soap opera. In Indonesia a single *Wayang* performance lasts nine hours and takes place in the open, under the night skies, and traditionally they use oil lamps to cast the shadows on the screen. I have no idea what kind of lighting they'll use tonight, with the fire codes and all. I can't imagine what it will look like if they use light bulbs—you see, an oil lamp flickers, which makes the puppets' shadows tremble almost as if they were breathing."

Should she explain that *Wayang* was a semireligious ceremony? That the solo puppeteer, the Dalang, was a sort of high priest? *Wayang Purwa* dealt with holy myths every Javanese knew by heart and lived with daily, almost like farmers live by the almanac.

"The Javanese shadow play is a community event," Nigel had explained, unpacking box after box of intricate, gold-embossed figures, tissue paper billowing out of the cartons and wafting to the floor. The puppets were cut from thin leather and perched on the slimmest of bamboo poles. "Somewhat like a block party. Children can watch, play among themselves, or imitate what is happening on-screen; people come and go as nature calls."

They filed into the theater, Virginia turning toward Mrs. Woods in such a way that everyone in their tight group could hear her. "In Indonesia, the men are behind the screen with the puppeteer and the orchestra, while the women sit in front and only see the play of shadows against the flickering surface. But tonight I don't think we'll have to sit apart."

Everybody laughed. Virginia had quoted Nigel verbatim. She felt a rush of nostalgia: sitting under the stars, a bedsheet pinned to the washline and all the candles they could find lined up behind the makeshift screen, until the flickering light gave the puppets an energy all their own.

Here they sat in clap-down wooden seats, waiting to view what was probably a freeze-dried, vacuum-sealed production intended as a cultural exchange, a mini-ceremony packed up in a few shipping trunks and carted across America on one-night stands, an intellectual's kiddie circus.

Most people in the hall were students. Virginia looked down the row; Mrs. Woods and the parents were flipping through the program notes, frowning. She wanted to lean over and tell them not to worry about the plot, because in Indonesia the spectators knew the story already; that what was important was style and beauty. But she kept quiet.

"Well, well. Good evening."

She looked up, startled. He had come into the row from the other side. Before she could think of how to respond, he had taken the seat next to her, crossed one elegantly clad leg over the other and leaned over the armrest in an ostentatious display of curiosity.

"Do you have an extra?" he asked, flicking the corner of her program. A heavy gold chain dangled from his wrist, clinking lightly. From the corner of her eye she saw Ida Lee nudge Sarah.

"Take this one," she replied, tossing it into his lap.

The gamelan orchestra filed into the room from the back and down the aisles, small-boned men whose skin had a sheen like finely grained wood. Some carried small flutes and tapping sticks; others mounted the stage empty-handed and took their places behind diminishing rows of gongs, inverted brass cylinders dangling from threads, drums and zithers. They struck up a bright, stately music, the house lights dimmed and the curtain slowly pulled apart.

The screen was stretched between bamboo stalks and occupied nearly the width of the stage; silhouetted in the center of the luminous panel was Kajon, the Tree of Life. It was more the idea of a tree than a tree itself: like Magritte's stylized cypresses, it was a perfect, inverted teardrop, with lacy cutout foliage and two serpents intertwined around the trunk. The Kajon was flanked by a tiger and a bull, who kept watch over a gate.

Three taps with a stick, and then the Dalang intoned, a syncopated chant (it took seconds before Virginia realized she understood him, his English was so thickly accented) in which he thanked the gods and implored their continued blessing as he undertook the arduous task of relating this tale, a tale of extreme beauty and a tale of warning, a tale suffused with perfume and death. The Great War had begun, signaling the destruction of every worthy being. It was the seventh day. Kajon, the Tree of Life, inclined slowly to the right. . . .

It was a magic moment, the tipping of the fulcrum as

the puppets seemed to glide across the glowing scrim and the gamelan ensemble started up the gongs and bells, sharp as mountain air and clear as threads of spun glass, the reedy strums of the zither and the sweetly piercing brass. The puppets took their positions: Arjuna the shining warrior; his older half-brother Karna, who suffers from an excess of pride; the fighting princess Srikandi, Arjuna's beloved, with her exquisite bearing and unerring skill at archery. But just as good and evil exist side by side, always in equal proportion, in balance, so each of these noble personages has two sides: though he is known as the dazzling defender of all things good and righteous, Arjuna himself is lacking in human sympathy; Karna is overly proud but also bold in battle and love.

Virginia looked over at Terry; to her surprise he was gazing raptly at the screen. He was wearing a different cologne tonight. Feeling her glance, he smiled, his eyes still focused on the stage.

Bold Karna had suffered humiliation at the hands of the princess, who sent her arrow to shave off one side of his mustache. He must repay shame with shame; his arrow ran through Srikandi's dress, causing it to drop to her feet seconds before she fell to her knees, weeping. Now Arjuna had no choice but to avenge his lover.

Elegant shadows moved across the field of light like delicate ghosts from the past, threatening to evaporate. Finally, the two warriors met. Arjuna moved through the Battle of the Flowers with a supernatural grace, his arms flicking so fast they seemed almost invisible. Vain Karna, with his fragile frame and eyes shaped like rice kernels, was an equally great hero, his hair curled up onto his nape in the *shrimp's tong,* a sign of nobility. Arjuna drew back his invincible arrow, Pasopatif—and there

Prince Karna stood, still upright in his chariot, blood streaming from his neck where the arrow had pierced it!

Nearly imperceptively the light behind the screen began to flicker, causing the puppets to fill with shivery breath. The screen had become transformed into a membrane, the mutable tissue of life itself. Now the shadows seemed not ghosts from the past but manifestations of the soul of a people Virginia knew she could not hope to comprehend. She longed to possess what she couldn't have, the next dawn, the next foreign port. On the gangway, the pier was veiled in mist and faintly roseate at the edges where it tipped into the sea, the last exhausted light winked. A few final clear blasts from the gamelan orchestra: *Come ashore!* The house lights came up.

And so she went ashore, disappointed, for nothing could quench the chill that coiled inside her, the cage of wonder in which she burned. A tap on her arm aroused her from her trance.

"A drink?"

"I have my car here," she said, still rather muddled.

"I know a place right around the corner." They squeezed into the aisle, where Ida Lee was trying to organize a get-together and discussion at Joe's Pub.

"How about it, Miss King? Ready to give us a little lecture on this here shadow show?"

"Sounds like a good idea," Virginia said, seizing the chance, "though I'm not sure I'll be much help. And please call me Virginia."

"I found it very interesting," Mrs. Woods said, a bit pompously, "but I have to excuse myself. My husband should be home now from a conference in Columbus."

"We'd like to come, but I got the morning shift," said

the factory man, extending his hand in an old-fashioned hand-shake.

The wife of the Amity wallet man also demurred. "Our baby-sitter is only thirteen. This was nice. Something . . . different."

"Well, Kevin's in bed and the lady next door is watching 'Perry Mason' reruns on my TV, so I'm at your service," Terry said, smoothing his shirtfront.

Ida's smile widened. "In that case we'd best be moving along, then," she said, taking Sarah's arm.

"But you're the one who suggested the discussion; you can't back out now!"

"Oh, I was just trying to be sociable. Come to think of it, the laundry's still in the washer; if I don't get on the ball, the kids won't have a thing to wear tomorrow! You two just go on and enjoy the rest of the evening."

She'd been set up. Sarah Butler stood by, smiling as if all this were the most innocent transaction imaginable. "I better be getting along, too," she said. "Thanks for this evening. I didn't understand everything, but it was truly something else."

It was cool, and Virginia drew her shoulders together under the cotton jacket. "What a deep blue! And not a single star!"

"Pollution on both counts. The sky never gets black in the city." Terry switched sides to be next to the curb, touching her shoulder lightly in transit. "Where have you been, on a farm?"

"How did you guess! For the past year I lived in a farmhouse. I worked with a troupe of puppeteers in Wisconsin."

"Wisconsin!" He rolled the word in his mouth as if it were an exotic new flavor of sherbet. "What's a sister like you doing with puppets on a farm in Wisconsin?"

Why not? she was tempted to ask. Or why not Laramie, or Boise? You could just as well ask what business did a black girl have with a cello, or studying German or eating French fries.

"I went to school in Madison," was all she said.

"College, right?"

"Right."

"What were you in?"

"I studied the dramatic arts—acting and mime. My minor was music—cello."

"Wow. Cello, mime, and Indonesian puppet theater in Wisconsin—heavy, sister."

"Not really," she replied, gritting her teeth.

"Where were you before Wisconsin?"

"Arizona."

The sherbet had grown claws and spikes, and he spit it out: "Arizona!"

"Arizona *is* a real place. I can testify to it: I grew up there."

"I thought you grew up *here.*"

Now how did he know that?

"Kevin told me," he answered, divining her expression.

"That little devil!"

"No sweat; he's been called worse. How'd the little devil earn his name this time?"

"I used a puppet made to look like me—"

"Yeah, Gina."

"Well, Gina had the kids guess what town I'd been

born in, and when they couldn't guess, she told them to ask their parents where the Quaker oatmeal factory had been and that would be the place. Sarah Butler said her daughter had asked her, but she never mentioned it in class, either. Why didn't they speak up?"

His shoulders bunched into silent laughter. "Girl, these are nine-year-olds, and they haven't grown up in Arizona or Wisconsin. They know more than you probably care to hear. And here," steering her deftly under a white-and-green awning and through a white door, "we are."

It was not the kind of place she had expected. A sandwich bar ran the length of the back wall, a counter where you could watch the tomatoes being sliced and the lettuce shredded. Booths on either side, each with its own mini-jukebox and checkered napkins and standard candle in the Chianti bottle. The clientele was pretty varied: young lovebirds and gloomy businessmen, older couples laughing over full-course meals and preoccupied college students slurping coffee.

"My favorite downtown pit stop," Terry explained, zeroing in on an empty table. A waitress slapped down two menus in plastic envelopes. "You can get anything here from a cocktail to veal scaloppine to cappuccino and Black Bottom pie. The waitresses are mean mamas, but they're fast, and they don't get huffy if you only order coffee. What are you smiling about?"

"When you said 'How about a drink?' I never thought you'd take me someplace like this."

"You pictured blue lights and a booth in the corner, huh?"

She nodded, smiling genuinely at him for the first time.

"I see I've got some backtracking to do. I must have made a pretty bad impression the other night."

"It's improving."

"Yeah? Next time the corner booth."

Virginia laughed. "And I'll bring a flashlight."

"What would you like?"

"I think I'll stick to a drink."

"Gin tonic?"

"I'll have a scotch and water."

"That's quite a drink for a woman."

"The women in this town must be timid. Scotch is the only liquor with a soul. I once knew an alcoholic who drank only the best scotch. He said if he was doomed to drink, he might as well have an executioner born of royal blood."

("*Corazón*," Parker had whispered. "What the Spanish call 'the heart' is actually the chest, for it isn't just the heart that aches, it's the whole fucking ribcage. And you, dear scotch, bring out the hairs on mine.")

"Spoken like a true drunkard. But with water? Spoils the taste."

"That's what he used to say, too." The waitress chose that moment to come for the order; but Terry wouldn't let it ride.

"I think I'm jealous," he said.

"Come off it!" She managed to sound perky. "I'd say you'd have the right to be jealous if, one: you were my man, which you are not; two, there were something to be jealous about, which there isn't, and three . . ." she paused.

"What's number three?"

"Hmmmm. If you were the jealous type, which I don't believe you are."

He regarded her quietly, then turned to survey the room. For an instant she saw in him the sad and gentle gaze of his son.

He turned back as the waitress plopped down their drinks and a basket of pretzels, caught Virginia's look and leaned forward, curling his lips into what was supposed to pass for a sexy smirk. He reached out to touch her hand, but she stiffened and drew back, nearly upsetting her scotch. Without a hitch, he switched directions and stroked the sweating glass instead, then held one wet finger aloft as if testing for wind.

"What's buzzing around in that fine head of yours?"

"Nothing that concerns you."

He reached for her hand again, gently. "Oh, I'm not sure about that."

She folded her hands in her lap. "Okay. If you really want to know, I was thinking about a story I read in a German class, about a handsome young man who wanted to be a dancer. Nobody knew if he had talent, but he had natural grace and was totally unaware of his own beauty. One day a famous dancer came to town, was introduced to the boy, and invited him to the Turkish baths. He was planning a seduction. In the baths the boy got a splinter in his heel. He lifted his foot and leaned sideways to inspect the wound, and the older man said, 'You look like a Greek sculpture!' The boy lifted his foot again, trying to imitate his action, but it was no longer spontaneous and graceful. The more he tried, the more awkward he looked. The boy began to spend hours in front of the mirror. The more he looked, the more self-conscious he became—his smile grew forced, he would pinch his eyes into a squint he thought provocative, and his lilting walk became a calculated jaunt. Weeks later, when the older dancer ran into him again, he didn't recognize him. The boy waving from the other side of the street was no different from the swarm of other teenagers heading downtown."

Terry stared ferociously into his drink. "So I'm stuck

on myself—John Shaft loving the ladies and leaving them panting?"

"I didn't mean it that way," she protested, realizing she meant precisely that, waiting for him to retaliate and call her a stuck-up college bitch. She reached for her glass.

A slight frown formed on his face, as if something had just settled into place. "I get it," he said. "Let's take it slow."

"Have you lived in Akron all your life?"

"No way. I'm from Youngstown."

"You sound as if being from Akron is a crime."

"We did kinda look down on Akron—'Nothing but rubber bands over there,' we used to say when we were kids. Youngstown was steel. We were tough as steel, too. Akron kids would come to our parties and end up drunk under the tables." He shifted his weight forward, leaning on both elbows. "Not that Youngstown was any great shakes; we just needed to make it seem like it. And you know what? I don't go back much at all, even though it's just fifty miles. There's nothing there. Nothing here either, for that matter—except a job." He closed his eyes and leaned his chin on his clasped hands.

Virginia wanted to ask him what his job was but, afraid to break his train of thought, she merely said, "Not that there's anything anywhere."

"Hey"—his eyes opened to gaze into hers—"a man's got to keep on looking. You know when I first realized I had to get out of Youngstown? The fall after high school I went to the Turkey Game at the Rubber Bowl. We were a bunch of guys driving over on Thanksgiving to freeze our butts off. I was working in a sports shop at the time, and I thought I was cool, you know: I had a tie on and a pressed shirt, shooting the bull

with the girls who wandered in from the mall. Most of the guys
I used to hang around with had gotten jobs in the steel factory.
They didn't even try to say it was temporary work until something better came along—they just moved right into their fa-
thers' shoes, took up the levers and kept on truckin' the same
rut. So I thought I was cool, but I didn't say nothing about
that when I was with the guys because we still had a good time
together." He fingered the checkered napkin lining the pretzel
basket.

"So we went to the game, and when we got there we
ran into Bernard Jackson—great basketball player, played center for East High a few years back, when we'd all been freshmen
or sophomores. Voted most valuable player, made the All-State
team. I still remember the semifinals where he showed his stuff.
The game had gone into overtime; East High, behind by one
point, gets the ball out with two seconds to play. Bernard
catches the pass in mid-court, stops, turns—and just throws
it. From mid-court, right there in the center circle. Buzzer goes
off while the ball's still arcing, and the whole gymnasium's quiet
as an international chess match cause we're all just watching
that ball soar up, then down, down and *swish!* right through
the hoop. Man, East High's side went loop-de-loop! That boy
could play some ball.

"So that was Bernard Jackson at his height, and here
he was, three or four years later, at his worst—a drunk and a
doper, couldn't keep any kind of job because he was always
jumping off to work up a game with dudes at the Y or something. He didn't have the grades for college, and even though
he was an amazing player, he was too short for the pros—I
guess you could say he wasn't good enough to compensate for
his lack of height, and he wasn't smart enough, bookwise, for

schools to take a risk on him. Hell, he barely scraped through high school. All he thought about was playing ball. And when there wasn't anywhere for him to play anymore, he started drinking and doping, and then it got so he couldn't even face off with the local dudes down at the Y. He could still hit the hoop from across the court, but he couldn't hold on to the ball; he'd forget which way he was supposed to dribble, sorry stuff like that.

"Anyway, we said hi to Bernard standing there, snuffling a little bit with a bottle wrapped up in one of those sad brown paper sacks, you know, and we went on about our business. Round about halftime there was some ruckus up behind me, but I don't pay it any mind because I'm concentrating on the game. Suddenly, I hear bursts of laughter and a few little shrieks, and then something thuds up against my back. First thing I think is, *Shit, someone's lost their thermos and now I gotta sit here wet for the rest of the game,* but I'm cool so I act like someone had just tapped me on the shoulder and turn around real nonchalant. And what did I see? Bernard Jackson, curled up like a baby, out cold. And way up at the top of the bleachers, a line of guys bent over, laughing their guts out."

"What happened?" Virginia asked, appalled. For an instant she envisioned Parker pretending to be Linus in the pumpkin patch, and her brother's friend David Goldstein imitating a watermelon.

"Aw, someone had called Bernard over and was teasing him, nudging him in the ribs and stuff like that, and he said, 'Hey, Bernard, gimme five!' and when Bernard went to slap his palm, the guy drew his hand back and that was enough to send Bernard tumbling." Terry shook his head, leaned back in his chair and hooked his fingers in his belt. "That's when I said to myself, 'Terrence, you've got to get out of this town. You gotta book it, man.' "

Back in her studio apartment, too agitated to think about sleep, Virginia reached for the cello. Why was she so skittish with Terry? He'd been perfectly courteous; after he'd finished his story, she felt it only fair to offer a few anecdotes from her majorette days. An hour and two drinks later she found herself behind the wheel of the Plymouth, her cheek still hot where he had quickly kissed it: "Bye, Gina! See you soon, I hope."

She'd never been very good at "managing" romantic advances; the maneuvers and subterfuges practiced by her girlfriends seemed to her obvious and silly, although they appeared to work. Even joining majorettes hadn't changed her luck. All the other majorettes either had steadies or a steady stream of boyfriends.

"Comes with the territory," Mandy had drawled.

But Virginia's phone had stayed silent. Sure, there were flirtatious exchanges; the Chicano boys talked a sweet line, but they were eventually yanked away by their Hispanic girlfriends, while the white guys never dared more than a surreptitious stare and a blush when they were caught in the act. Half the football team was black, but those guys were slaves to the coach, too busy trying to win the games. Besides, according to Belle, they were "beneath our station," though there was never a chance to test that claim, since the players themselves seemed to be in silent agreement with Virginia's mother: they would smile back whenever Virginia greeted them in the hall, but they never crossed the line to ask her for a date.

That left the boys at church. Most of them were either stiff-necked mama's boys, or hopelessly delinquent. News of her majorettedom wouldn't reach them until their school played her school; then the phone would ring during the week and she'd thrill to the sound of a male voice on the other end, eagerly enduring these halting conversations until they heard about her grade-point average, or Belle would check into their family, or something else would go wrong—she'd say something that went over their heads, for instance.

Once it was just a word: "Don't worry," she'd said on the phone, "you'll surely be exempt from the draft. After all, you're taking college prep."

There was a long silence on the other end and then his voice, curiously flat. "What was that word?"

"I said you'd be exempt because—"

" 'Exempt.' That word. Just what does that mean, exactly?"

She tried to ignore the sinking feeling as she explained, making her definition as casual as possible and finally babbling in desperation: "I guess I learned it from my dad. He used it all the time when we were worried about my brother's number for the lottery; but Ernie came up three hundred forty-seven, so he's safe."

" 'Exempt.' " That faded voice again. "It sounds like a very useful word. Thank you for the lesson." Then he explained that, as chance would have it, *his* brother had to use the phone, and hung up.

And Todd—what a failure *he* had been! It embarrassed Virginia even to think back on that episode. In the fall of her last school year, Arizona State University had held a recruiting weekend. Interested high school seniors were bused across the valley to Tempe, and shunted around all Saturday.

In the evening the Alpha Phi Alpha fraternity threw a dance for the minority students. Except for black lights burning along the disc jockey's box and occasional strobes, the room was pretty dark; on the dance floor Virginia could just make out the legs and arms of the dancers.

"Don't stand around! Get out there and *move!*" Their chaperone, a hefty girl who was president of the fledgling black sorority, hurled herself into the fray. None of the college students waited to be asked to dance; girls even danced with girls.

So this was what college life was like! No more agonized anticipation along the sideline, praying some guy would come up, any guy as long as it wasn't Elton, who ground his hips into his victims, or Richard Lee, who did splits and back flips while the girl bobbed in one place, feeling like a fool.

Virginia spun onto the dance floor as if she were on the field twirling her baton. No way anyone could keep still with the Jackson Five's beat pushing. Besides, it was so dark no one was able to see how well the others danced anyway, and soon Virginia was doing the African Twist with the wildest of the crowd. She didn't even realize she was singing along until someone yelled in her ear, "Go 'head on, lady, sing that stuff!"

She looked up, startled. Grinning at her as he nodded his head to the beat was one of the cutest guys she had ever laid eyes on. Tall, dark and handsome like the saying (though the saying certainly didn't mean *that* kind of dark), with dimples and the kind of long curly lashes Belle liked to say were too good to waste on a man.

When the Delfonics began to croon of everlasting love,

he pulled her into his arms. Oh, God. He had on after-shave! And his cheek was so soft and he held her so gently, like a bouquet of long-stemmed roses. She prayed she wouldn't step on his toes.

"I've seen you," he said.

"Where?" She couldn't imagine why a college man would notice a high-school girl.

"On the football field. South Mountain High against Central. You shore looked good out there."

"What were you doing at a high-school game?"

"I go to South Mountain High. Class of 'seventy."

Now she *did* step on his foot. "Sorry! I—well, I just assumed you went to ASU."

"Are you sorry I don't?" he whispered, brushing her ear with his lips.

"Oh, no. I was just asking." A high-school junior! "I didn't get your name," she stammered.

"I didn't give it. Todd. Todd Williams. I know yours already." He swirled her around and pulled her close again, holding her hand to his shirt, right above his heart. "And before you ask, my sister's a sophomore at the U; she told me about this dance. I'm glad she did."

Virginia kept his leg from insinuating itself any higher than her knee; still, from hip to shoulder they were one, with just a film of electricity where their clothes pressed or slid.

She didn't know how long they spent kissing under the date palm in the backyard of the fraternity house; all she knew was that they went back inside just before the dance let out. And oh, could he kiss! He had a way of nibbling her lower lip and drawing it in between his lips that reduced her to cream and sparks inside. Still, he was a gentleman—not that he didn't try to get under her blouse, just that he stopped after the first couple of rebuffs.

He called the next day, Sunday afternoon. Belle picked up the phone and was so charmed by his manners that she handed the receiver over with a delighted look.

Virginia didn't tell her parents that he was younger than she, and a student at South Mountain High to boot. They talked on the phone every day, all week long. He promised to come to the football game that Saturday, and she spent more time trying to find an eyeshadow that wouldn't melt in the sun than she did practicing her routines. She hated the Minnie Mouse gloves they had to wear this time of year, since the batons heated up from lying in the sun between the pregame show and halftime; the only time they took the gloves off was when they did a dance number with pompons, and then the crepe-paper dye would come off on their skin. Virginia was mortified to think that he'd see her with blue dye halfway up her arms, so she slipped a few foil towelette packets into her boots for a quick washup.

Halfway through the first quarter one of the girls came back from the concession stand with a note. "I think your Prince Charming is waiting for you," she said, grinning. Virginia tore open the envelope:

Deer Virginia,

I'm here, wating at the consesshun stand. You have been in my thots all week. Prety lady bring those fine legs down outta those bleachers and come see bout me.

Love,
Todd

"What's he say? Come on, Virginia, read it to us!" The girls crowded around to get a peek; she quickly folded the note. "Aw, don't be a prude! We tell you all our secrets. I bet he's a smooth operator." They looked so happy for her! Finally, she'd landed a beau worthy of the squad—tall, handsome and best of all, romantic. Slowly, she unfolded the piece of paper again and read it aloud, with corrections, taking care to shield the page from their eyes.

"C'mon, let us see his handwriting. There was an article in *Glamour* magazine that shows you how to analyze people's handwriting. We could put his to the test," said Jacqueline, reaching for the note. Virginia quickly stuffed it into her bra.

"Let me enjoy it for a little while longer, guys," she said. "Just for a while. I want to savor this." Then she excused herself and climbed down from the stands.

Why did it matter so much? When she looked back on the whole "affair," she recalled that his diction was perfectly proper (even her mother was fooled), and they never lacked for things to talk about. He treated her like a queen, and all the girls melted when he glanced over the crowd, seeking her out. They went together for three weeks, but she never again felt cream and sparks when they kissed; in fact, from the moment she read the note her passion fizzled, though she practiced on him, trying out her power so sweetly that he never suspected how numb she was inside.

It wasn't that she thought him "beneath her station"; hell, he was even beneath her age, and that hadn't bothered her. But how could someone mix up the animal *deer* with the salutation *dear*? Children memorized that rule in third grade. And how could anyone who'd gotten beyond the eighth grade misspell *pretty*? Maybe "thots" was just a shortcut, like *nite* and *thru,* but "bleechers"?

When Belle got after her about chasing away that "nice young man," Virginia showed her his note. As she read, Belle sucked in her tongue, then her outrage dimmed and a cold, set look took its place. She handed the piece of paper back with a shrug.

"It's going to be a problem, you know."

Virginia merely stared, struck clean of words. Her mother shrugged again.

"How many black boys are in your high school? Fifty? And how many black male students does Arizona State have—twenty, thirty? Half of those head for white girls first chance they get. Oh, Sweet Beet"—she swept her frozen daughter into a hug—"it's simple arithmetic. The more education you get, the fewer black men you'll meet on the way. But don't you worry. You'll find him."

"You're doing *Bach?*" Clayton's bow struck the music stand, but he barely noticed—and this from a man who gave his instrument a rubdown every evening after practice. Amazed, she forgot his question and stared at the bow quivering in his lax fingers.

Clayton. It had seemed so perfect—the music, of course, but also his lack of jive. He treated her as an intellectual comrade . . . and then, when he discovered Kadinski had assigned her the Suites, as a spiritual companion as well.

"The *Six Unaccompanied?*" As if there could be any other suites. "And Kadinski *gave* you the music?"

She had never heard him address their teacher as anything other than *Mister* Kadinski. Boy, was he upset.

"I don't know if he *gave* it to me. He had it there waiting. Maybe it was a promotional copy or something."

Clayton snorted, disgusted.

"They sound like scales, anyway. He probably thinks I need the practice."

"Scales? Virginia, you can't be serious. Scales! Those suites contain everything—melody, harmony, counterpoint, percussion—*everything*. I'd been itching to study them ever since I heard Starker's recording in twelfth grade. Did you know that Bach wrote them in one swoop? And the cello wasn't even considered a respectable instrument in those times. Not a melodic instrument, that is—and most certainly not for virtuoso solo work. Bach changed all that with one blow."

Give me a break, she thought, as he continued explaining the eighteenth-century patronage system in German city-states, explicating the political problems of secular posts versus sacred appointments, portraying the composer as friend and supplier of entertainment for noble musical dilettantes.

"The Suites are unparalleled. If a cellist were stranded on a desert island, all he would need are his instrument and the Suites—no piano, no trio, no orchestral backup. The Suites are entirely self-sufficient. They can sustain you for a lifetime."

She had just plowed her way through the first two movements of the First Suite and couldn't imagine the chord progressions as exciting, much less sustaining.

"Give it a rest, Clayton," she said.

From that afternoon on, he kept tabs on her progress with the Suites. He'd peek into the practice rooms, hoping to overhear, but Virginia practiced when she knew he was otherwise occupied, either in music theory class (which he hated) or his own private hour with Kadinski. Only after things began to click, after the plaintive strains of the D Minor Sarabande emerged in spite of her sawings, did she begin preparing sections for Clayton to hear. He would listen to them and then pick them apart, more and more gently, she thought, until they were both enthralled by Bach's ability to sing of pain and make it beautiful, to induce heartbreak and then burst out with a triumphal major arpeggio.

They began meeting on Tuesday nights (after her Acting Methods Workshop and his Chamber Ensemble) at the Downtown Bakery, which stayed open until the baker came in to make the next day's bread. After 10 P.M. leftover baked goods went on sale at half price; the later it got, the cheaper the donuts and muffins became. The night clientele was a faithful group, mostly students with limited funds who had changed their sleeping habits, napping through the afternoon and evening and getting up so that they could eat breakfast at one or two in the morning before studying all night. Virginia recognized them by their cheesy pallor, the way they hunched over the coffee mugs or stared off into space, powdered sugar speckling their textbooks.

The bakery was loud and disorganized, all stainless steel and linoleum with a glassed-in display counter as brightly lit as a surgical amphitheater. It was an unlikely place for a relationship to grow. Whoever arrived first waited over a cup of tea for the other before descending on the counter and its array of moldering goodies.

What did they talk about through that winter, Virginia wondered. Then, she would have said, *We talked about everything*. Now, she could only remember the time their conversation had turned personal. They had carried their mugs from the counter to the little round table, not yet sure where their friendship would take them.

"My dad's a real character," she said. "He's always

going off on historical expeditions; he used to take me and my brother along."

"What kind of expeditions?"

"Oh, educational trips. After we moved to Arizona, he took it upon himself to investigate every inch of the desert. We did a lot of Indian ruins. Belle called them wild-goose chases."

"Who's Belle?"

"My mother. She'd kill me if she knew I called her by her name."

"So why do you do it?"

"Oh, you disapprove! Look, my mother and I have what is commonly called a 'difficult relationship.' What about you? You and your mother get along all right?"

"We do."

"And your father?"

"Dead."

"I'm sorry. I didn't know."

"Of course you didn't. It's all right; it happened a long time ago."

"How old were you?"

"Five. Actually, five and a half. The week before I was to go into first grade. I knew I was going to learn how to read and I couldn't wait. That year was a blur. I remember throwing a fit whenever we had free days like Columbus Day and fall break, because school was the place I went to forget."

"Do you have brothers and sisters?"

"Two older sisters. My mother's a nurse. She's worked a night shift ever since I can remember. She'd make sure we were asleep before she left for work, and she'd have a neighbor look in around midnight. We had her phone number at the hospital and the neighbor's number, so we weren't really alone. And every morning she'd have a hot breakfast for us. After we left for school, she went to bed. The neighbor took me in with her two boys on school holidays, and my sisters baby-sat after school until Mother woke up and fixed dinner."

"How did your father die?"

"I'm not sure."

"You're not *sure*? Do you mean the circumstances were mysterious—"

"Oh, no. I'm sure it was natural; I suspect it was from overwork. He hung wallpaper. But he did odd jobs on the side, and everybody in the neighborhood and all his relations were always asking him to 'just take a look' whenever a pipe clogged up or the porch steps started to sag. My mother knew the details, but she never told us. I think she just wanted to spare us."

"But you never *asked*?"

"Do you think that's odd? If you knew my mother, you'd understand. We never wanted to cause her pain. Every evening when she tucked me into bed, I could almost see her life dragging her down; I knew she was thinking about having to go into the hospital and cope with all that suffering. And in the morning she'd look as if she'd just emerged from the gates of Hades, as if she'd been given a reprieve, like Eurydice, but knew she would have to return. That was enough sadness in one family."

"Do you think . . . well, did you ever think that it might have helped her to talk? I mean, now that you're grown and can handle it, maybe it would be a little like sharing the grief."

"I don't know if I actually remember him or if it's just

the photographs." He stood up abruptly. "We'd better be going; it's getting late."

"Actually, it's getting earlier by the minute. After midnight, time runs backward."

"And all cats are gray. Or is that only in Paris? Anyway, I've got to get some sleep. I've signed up for a practice room at ten."

"Why in the world did you do that?"

"The cadenza to the Dvořák's giving me a hard time. I thought I'd slip a little practice session in before music theory drains me of all my musical instinct. By the way, how's the Bach coming?"

"The C Major's been laid to rest. On to the Fourth."

"E-flat Major." Almost a whisper. "That's a lovely one. Airy, but warm, too. And peaceful. Companionable. Play it well, Virginia. Play it for me."

Sawdust, peanuts, nougat smell: spring carnival rides taken on a dare, college girls trying to be as reckless as children. And why not? Only five more weeks of classes before going back to parents and menial summer jobs, back to the heat and grit of hometown stupor—but Clayton had asked her to the Greek fling the next evening, so for now the world was an assault of primary colors, with music grinding out of gaily painted boxes and turning wheels of lights.

"You gotta make sure you get him to take you to his crib," her roommate Kelly had counseled. "Start thinking about it now. Get in an argument over some musical shit, anything to get him to take you to that room! If that doesn't give him the hint, just attack!"

The carnival at the lakefront was full of what Belle

would call riffraff—men with tattoos entwining their biceps like ivy who sold hot dogs and cotton candy; dirty blondes in skin-tight pink pants calling out the winners at the game booths. The young white men who ran the rides were the most unpleasant, rubbing their crotches and winking as they leaned into the car to fasten the seatbelts; Virginia stiffened in self-righteousness and tried to ignore them.

After her second ride on the Mad Mouse, a miniature roller coaster with more twists and turns than plummets, she glimpsed the candied-apple stand and rushed over. Oh, the gooey sweetness and the tart meat when the teeth crushed in! She looked over the red shell across the midway and met the dull yellowish eyes of a black man. He was just sitting there on the ground next to the last booth, dressed in overalls and a jeans jacket, a grimy Mao cap jammed over his matted, un-washed kinks. He stared at her, expressionless, then shifted his gaze so that he was looking *through* her. She stood there, mouth stuck on the cinnamon-sweet glaze, and her stomach soured. She threw the apple away.

And then nausea all the next day, suffering for the dares and double dares. Leaning against the closet for support while Kelly, straight pins between her lips, sewed her into a chartreuse sarong guaranteed to unwind with one well-planned tug. If only the dizziness would stop. A knock; Kelly, cursing, went to answer the door and came back with a pot of yellow mums and a card: *Du bist wie eine Blume, / So hold und schön und rein.* No corsage; mums didn't even have a smell. Virginia thought of him struggling through German 202. Kelly threw the card on the floor: "I can't believe it! The idiot sends a funeral urn!"

All her well-laid plans ruined by a carnival! Virginia

sank into a chair and spooned up a gob of strained carrots, trying not to gag. "You gotta eat," Kelly had said. She'd gone all the way downtown in the rain to buy a sackful of baby food —Gerber's mixed vegetables and applesauce, strained pears and carrots. Disgusting, but at least Virginia could keep it down.

Kelly was a small-town white girl from southern Wisconsin, close to the Illinois border. She was tiny, with red hair worn in a shaggy-dog bob that made her look like Peter Pan. Despite her size, she had the biggest and most unabashed mouth Virginia had ever heard. "I'm used to calling the cows home," she joked. Their very first day together (after her parents had stacked her stuff along her side of the room and gone), Kelly had shut the door and cheerfully admitted to Virginia that she'd never been alone with a black person before.

"I never even talked to one, 'cept in the stores at the mall or in a . . . practical capacity like that," she said. "I'm not scared of you, but I think my parents near about shit a brick. I bet you anything they'll be calling up first thing they get back home to see if I've been stabbed or something." She chuckled.

Her candor had had a calming effect on the strained situation. She was also willing to learn, and as the first weeks of communal living went by, Virginia found herself submitting to a barrage of outrageous questions: Do you carry a razor? What's that stuff you're putting on your hair? Do you tan? Can blacks get embarrassed?

"What the hell is *that* supposed to mean?"

"Well, you all can't blush, so I thought—"

"We *do* blush. You just can't see it."

After a month Virginia admitted to herself that she liked Kelly. The only problem was that Kelly liked her, too— so much, in fact, that she imagined they were nearly sisters and, like a sister, felt she had the right to go wherever Virginia went. On Saturday afternoons when the black girls would gather—seven from their building, and three or four dropping in from the other dorms—Kelly wanted to tag along.

"You all are segregating yourselves!" she cried out, hurt, when Virginia tried to dissuade her. "How do you expect us to work for integration when you don't want it either?"

How to explain that they needed these once-a-week sessions, needed to be among themselves, to touch base? That if you were scattered like raisins among the white swirls of coeds during the week, it made you feel better if you could complain about being caught out in the rain, knowing the others understood how disastrous that was, all the kinks to comb out? How could they laugh about getting ash if they had to explain it to a white girl?

"What's ash?" Kelly wanted to know.

Virginia sighed. "Dry skin. On darker complexions, dry and flaky skin looks gray. Like ash."

"Oh." Then: "Now, that didn't take much effort, did it?"

Virginia sighed again. "Kelly, you're just being stubborn. You refuse to understand. They're my friends. You're my friend, too; but they're in a different subset. Remember new math? Sometimes subsets intersect—the circles overlap, and the shared area is a new subset. In this case, the circles don't overlap."

"That's ridiculous. It depends on how you define it. We have lots in common. We all take core courses. We're all women. We're all alive on a Saturday afternoon, for heaven's sake! Why do you have to define it according to race?"

"I don't define things racially all the time. Just on

Saturday afternoons. The rest of the week I'm a student or a woman. On Saturday afternoons, I like to be black."

"You're making fun of me."

"I'm sorry. What I mean is, there are some things I can talk to them about that I don't need to explain. Like being the only black in Chemistry 101, in that huge lecture hall where the professor could never know who was absent except me—all he has to do is look for the black spot. Now, I have to explain that to you. With Yvonne and them I don't need to. I can say, 'Yvonne, you owe me a favor; take my place in Chemistry on Monday morning,' and everyone would howl."

They usually congregated at Yvonne and Yolande's, the twins from Chicago, since they were the only blacks who shared a room. The administration had tried to break them up, but they had protested they were inseparable and what was this anyway, the Middle Passage?—so they were allowed to stay together.

They were full of confused energy and exhilarating ideals. Politics had swept into their lives; they tended their Afros like prize roses but renewed their subscriptions to *Mademoiselle* and *Glamour*; they condemned frivolity and threw themselves into leftist rhetoric, but dancing to Marvin Gaye was a different story.

At last Virginia was securely tucked into her dress, her evening bag stuffed with lipstick, Kleenex, two plastic spoons, one jar of baby carrots and one of applesauce, and contraceptive foam. Kelly had fastened a green silk rose in her hair, at the temple, shades of Lady Day.

Clayton was waiting in the lobby, oddly elegant in his white dinner jacket, and as soon as Virginia saw him, her stom-

ach unclenched. Sometime around midnight she grew used to
feeling his arms around her and her adrenaline leveled out; by
twelve-thirty they managed to get into an argument over an
obscure theme in Brahms's E minor Sonata for Cello and
Piano, and after the dance they went over to his fraternity to
hear the record.

Although she had been in the house before, this was
the first time she'd been upstairs. His room was not as she had
imagined it. She'd expected austerity, a single bed under the
window—and though a sagging bed stood under the window,
on the other side of the room was a set of bunk beds, the kind
of sturdy construction designed to mimic Early American.

It was a mess, really. Clayton dashed in first, pushing
shoes and books into the corners with his foot before turning
on the desk light. A minuscule area rug, more gray than any
other color, lay between the beds, as self-important as a postage
stamp, snagged and pocked where the end pin of his cello had
rested. The gaudy drapes must have been left behind several
owners back, and the hunting wallpaper (geese and wild sedge)
as well. Crammed against the back wall was a desk littered with
notebooks and musical scores in precarious piles, the top sheets
cascading silently to the floor.

He placed the needle on the spinning disc and they sat
on the edge of the bunk until the music reached the disputed
section.

"There!" he said, pointing. "The countermelody. I
knew there was no major third—"

She leaned over and kissed him. No response. She
pulled back, embarrassed. "I'm sorry. That was pretty bold."

"That's all right. I mean, this is the scene, isn't it?"

"Clayton . . ."

"I'm sorry." He reached for her hand, but instead of pulling her closer he held her at arm's length. "I like you very much," he added.

"Then what's wrong?"

"Why can't we leave things as they are?"

Kelly's voice came to her: "He's probably worried about your virtue or some such thing. Just attack."

"Come on, it's easy. First your arms around me, like this . . ."

His mouth wouldn't open. When her tongue struck the barrier of his teeth, he began to moan, like a dam in high water when the current struggles against it.

"It's all right, just relax."

"It is *not* all right." He pulled violently away but remained seated where he was, two inches separating them on the bunk.

"Haven't you ever been kissed?"

He just sat.

"Clayton, it's no big deal. What did you do with your adolescence, anyway?"

"I played the cello."

"I know that. You mean, that's all?"

"Virginia. Virginia, I was immersed in music. I came straight home from school, did my homework, and practiced. There were rehearsals twice a week for the city youth orchestra. On the weekends I went to the symphony. I'd arrive half an hour beforehand and stand outside; season-ticket holders who couldn't attend that evening would send someone to give away their tickets, so I usually got a pretty good seat. The doctors and lawyers I sat next to liked talking to me; they said it was gratifying to see young people interested in good music." He hesitated, weighing his options.

"Then one night the man sitting next to me asked if I'd like to go backstage with him afterward. We had talked a lot during intermission. He was an architect and an amateur opera buff and that evening's concert featured Shirley Verrett singing Händel; it was close to Christmas. I said yes, of course, and he introduced me to the principal cellist and a flutist, and even the concertmaster. He knew them all, and they were extremely cordial to me. They all went out for a drink and they asked me to come, too. Are you listening?"

"Yes."

"Then he asked me if I'd like to see some of the sketches he was doing for a new arts administration building. And I said yes again. Don't you see yet? He . . . a fourth of the orchestra was gay."

The Brahms droned on, mournful and effusive. She heard her voice ask: "So why did you talk to me, Clayton? Why did you meet me every Tuesday at the bakery and ask me to this dance and buy me flowers? What did you think I would think?"

"But I like you, Virginia. It's . . . this is confusing for me, too. I guess I'm just scared is all."

"What does that mean? First you tell me about that man and now . . . I don't get it."

"You're the only woman I've ever cared for, Virginia. I feel closer to you than I've felt with anyone." He let her hand go, then took her carefully into his arms.

The kisses were wonderful; but it wasn't until early morning, when he awoke to the warm pressure of her hips curved against him, that things took their course. And though she liked lying in his arms most, this moment of opening to him—the vacillation between *exposure* and *revelation*—filled her with ripples of sheer pleasure.

191

In the weeks that followed they tried everything they could think of. And everything worked, inside and out of the room; it even seemed that the less time they spent on assignments, the more positive the results. Clayton returned from his lessons with a grin on his face, the Dvořák as good as conquered; he hadn't even exerted himself. Virginia got an A for the scene she'd prepared from Tennessee Williams's *Camino Real*. Each night after rehearsals she would walk the eight blocks to his place, slip in the side door, past the motley assortment of boots and umbrellas and up the narrow stairs smelling faintly of beer and tennis shoes, halt at the landing like an explorer on the brink of a new world, and wait to feel her heart take its rightful place. Between the silken tones of the Delfonics and the niggling underdrone of a television somewhere, she heard, as if overhearing, his music from the end of the hall. For a moment she stood in the familiar world, then moved down the corridor and into the darkened room where all was allowed but sight and speech, where truth was to be grasped in darkness and silence. And if she laid herself down, fully clothed, next to where she imagined him to be, he was there by the mere strength of her desire.

They were like two people in a kayak, two torsos but one body, lap-deep in the sea. The sense of peril never left them. When she was lying on top of him and felt his heart through the layers of clothing and skin, when he finally undressed her and they lay still a little longer, listening to Brahms or Hindemith or Elgar, it was with a sense of terrible risk and yet privilege that they took this moment of pause. When she stopped by his practice room and waited a moment outside the door listening, she felt him and he, inside practicing, felt her as well. They moved with caution, a slow exploration. Once her unexpected visit made him so happy that he dragged her to the floor just inside his room, in the middle of the afternoon. Day by day, the disorder of the room became a map of their complex emotions—the cello case open and the air full of sunlight, or the shades drawn and the bed unmade, the twisted sheets mimicking their convolutions.

One night, a few days before his graduation, he wasn't there. The room wasn't darkened, the desk lamp had been turned to the dimmest setting. She went in anyway, lay down on the bed, and listened to Johann Sebastian's Fourth Suite.

The Fourth Suite is a question of ear. Like the trapeze artist who executes a perfect somersault: time stops for the spectator, and the artist appears to be suspended in air. But—Kadinski had clapped his hands triumphantly—*during the execution of this feat the artist has actually propelled himself forward, so that at a precisely predetermined instant he and the bar of the trapeze meet. Now—what makes this act so stupendous? The tremendous space traveled in between!*

All of a sudden he was standing in the door. She must have fallen asleep. For seconds they stared at each other, both dazed at the abruptness of the confrontation.

"Don't ask me anything. I've been with a man."

She couldn't think of anything to ask. The room unchanged, buttery early morning light seeping over scattered music and books, the cello case open in the corner. Six-fifteen. She sat upright, and smoothed down her blouse. The bed hadn't been made in days.

"It just happened. You can't expect me to . . ." He was roaming the room, his left hand compulsively practicing fingerings in midair. "I can't . . . I can't restrict myself to . . . I just can't do it. It's not normal."

"Normal!" she screeched, spitting the word into his face. All she felt was overwhelming shame. Shame that she could be so naive, shame that she had loved him, shame that she loved him still.

Clayton. So much time had passed, and he still occupied her thoughts. Virginia loosened the bow and put the cello away, then poured herself a scotch. But when she finally slid under the coverlet, she couldn't fall asleep. *I've got to call Aunt Carrie,* she thought. *I'll get her number from Grandma tomorrow.*

After graduation, Clayton had gone to Chicago to seek his luck. She clung to the slim thread of his letters, which came irregularly, though often enough to keep hope from unraveling. She'd grown used to his meandering style, his sloping script full of the politics of job hunting among professional symphonic groups and the myriad fly-by-night musical gigs in the Windy City.

Clayton never communicated anything *too* obvious. Never a word about *them,* never an "I miss you" or even "I love you, in my fashion." If he was lonely, a lyrical paragraph would materialize, without warning or utilitarian value. When the mercury plummeted below zero for the first time, in sailed a three-page rhapsody to winter memories: "Hot chocolate, red plaids, nostrils crackling from the cold, lower lip stuck to the frosted windowpane; sniffles and aspirin, hot cider and acorn squash, pine needles shriveling on a burning log. . . ."

Once he quoted Saint-Exupéry: "The secret of the desert is that somewhere there is a well"; and she remembered scoffing in high school at *The Little Prince,* that blond-haired waif in his pseudo-desert with his stilted pretensions to wisdom; had Clayton fallen to that?

Virginia tailored her letters to match, filling them with gossipy news and startling tidbits like the taste of walnut soup, or scraps of dialogue from Derek Walcott's *Dream on Monkey Mountain.* She spent her last semester trying to convince the theater department that there were enough qualified black actors to warrant a staging of the play; but to the white professors in charge, the notion of a Caribbean tragedy was more radical and risky, apparently, than a production of a play by a neofascist sympathizer: Ionesco's *The Chairs.*

Maybe she even preferred this oblique method of communication—no pain at least, no terrible change. Though she'd dated others, she hadn't slept with anyone since he went off; it didn't seem much of a sacrifice.

That day when she pried open yet another precious tan envelope (he was the only man she had ever known who used stationery), she was apprehensive as usual, unsure whether gold dust would trickle out, or a scorpion. How surprised she was to find just one paragraph: "Why don't you come for a visit before the weather gets too nasty? It's still not that cold that you have to step out into the street with three layers of fur. We could go to the Art Institute, maybe a concert. (Unfortunately, not one with me playing in it—still no luck.)"

Kelly lent her her battered green Duster and didn't seem worried by Virginia's confession that she'd never driven in such a busy city. "There's nothing to it," Kelly replied. "It's not like you've suddenly decided to swim the English Channel or something. Just don't panic when you hit the traffic outside Chicago. Most of those clowns whiz along like cartoon characters, but it ain't Manhattan."

Kelly had been in New York over the summer on an internship with an advertising agency and had come back convinced that the whole place should be condemned: "Just pull out the stopper and let it go down the drain," she'd hooted.

The drive through the countryside was beautiful, farmland unrolling around her, distance making itself palpable as it retreated before the windshield. Although these rich brown and chestnut fields looked nothing like the crimson and gold austerity of the desert, there was a similar sense of space, and with that space an air of possibility, born out of bittersweet loneliness. She loved watching an autumn storm come boiling over the fields; she loved the square white houses and the barns painted red over the wood rot, and she liked wondering who had done the painting and how long it had taken to fill in the exposed edges, and what they had been thinking about as they worked.

ILLINOIS WELCOMES YOU, read the sign. What was Clayton doing while she was driving toward him? Was he straightening up the apartment, humming as his mind worked through the fingering of a difficult passage? Would he prepare supper, or would they go out? And then—what then? She had tried not to think that far.

The traffic into Chicago was nightmarish—automobiles swooping in from all directions, it seemed. The steering wheel grew slippery under Virginia's clenched hands; she fought the temptation to cling to the incandescent white lines dashing past like stabs of a knife.

She pulled into his street just after nightfall, an urban neighborhood quieter than some, even a few scarred trees. A familiar voice floated out over the scrubby lawn: "I was beginning to worry." She moved toward the voice, wading through the ancient weeds to receive two dry kisses, one for each cheek.

She followed him up the dim stairs, the landing lit by a lurid fifties-style sconce, then down the tiny hall to a brown door like all the others, except for the incongruous sight of his name done in calligraphy above the doorbell. The interior was a copy of his old college room, made a little more elegant by a twelve-foot ceiling and faded finery from gangster days—dark woodwork and a marble fireplace, chipped scrollwork framing the recessed shelves. His bed sagged against the wall to her right.

"I thought you'd be tired after your drive, so I've arranged to bring the concert here." He grinned and tossed her bag onto the bed. "Yes, a private concert—Elliot!"

Through the doorway across from the kitchen Virginia heard a book being shut and a chair pushed back. *What's this?* she had time to think before Elliot strode into the room smiling, his hand outstretched. He was slight and pale, with curly hair and horn-rimmed glasses.

"Virginia, this is Elliot Stern."

She went on automatic pilot, smiling back as she took his hand; it was warm and dry, like Clayton's perfunctory greeting kisses.

"Elliot's a harpsichordist. He's been introducing me to the rarefied air of Renaissance and Baroque music. And Elliot, this is Virginia King: a cellist at heart, but she's been deluded into thinking she was born for the stage."

Elliot lifted an eyebrow, but it was all too rehearsed, too civil. *Cut the crap,* Virginia thought, enduring his bemusement with polite fury.

"So you're a harpsichordist? Where are you hiding it?"

He chuckled. "I'm not in the habit of carrying it around."

"Elliot lives here. In this building, I mean." Clayton

had the grace to lower his eyes. "That's how I got this place. When Elliot heard that the couple below him was moving out, he let me know and I rushed over. Apartment hunting in Chicago is a trip."

"Clayton thinks I did him a favor, but believe me, it was a purely selfish gesture. With another musician in the apartment under mine, I could be sure no one would complain to the landlord about my practicing at odd hours."

"How convenient."

"He may be a shining example of the self-centered musician, but he's a better cook than I am, and that's what counts right now," Clayton said. "How about some supper?"

Virginia could not recall what they ate, just the colors —rosy brown meat and pale green puree—but she would remember the translucent flicker of candles reflected off the glasses of wine lifted over and over again in mock tribute, ironic toasts presented to cover the excruciating awkwardness of the situation. *This is awful,* she thought but asked aloud, "What's on the program tonight?"

"Johann Sebastian Bach's Sonata for Viola da Gamba and Harpsichord, played on original instruments," said Clayton.

"But not," Elliot added, laughing, "by the original musicians."

"Nor on the original chairs."

Virginia joined in the laughter, her automatic pilot performing at top capacity. "Since when have you played viola do—"

"Viola da gamba," Clayton corrected her gently. "It belongs to a family of early string instruments—there's a treble viol, a tenor viol and the bass viol, which corresponds in pitch

and size to the violoncello. But they're not the forerunners of
the modern string family; the two groups existed side-by-side
during the fifteenth and sixteenth centuries and the violin, viola
and cello finally won out."

"Survival of the fittest," she murmured.

"Or the loudest," Elliot countered.

Clayton continued the lecture. "The gambas are fretted
with catgut. Even the strings are catgut instead of wrapped steel
filament. That makes for a lighter, reedier sound—similar to
the difference between a flute and a recorder."

Virginia took in Clayton's animated expression as he
extolled the neglected merits of this musical dinosaur. Was this
the Clayton of Villa-Lobos and Brahms, all heart and flailing
technique, what Kadinski, with a smirk, had called "impas-
sioned"?

But once they had gone upstairs and she was tucked
into Elliot's spongy bright red sofa ("My bleeding heart," he
joked), she had to admit that the music was glorious—translucent even, the harpsichord's thistly arpeggios and riffling
chords literally plucked out of thin air. Add to this the thick-
bellied gamba, bowed underhand with no vibrato (the piteous
tremor of the soul), and the Bach sonata seemed music for
angels, wiped clean of misery and desire.

He's distilled his very existence, she thought. *He used to
want to fit in; now he's decided to make that impossible.* But as
she listened, Virginia was struck by the composure in Clayton's
playing, a newly found balance. She looked up, and the pleasure
in both their faces—Elliot's thrown back, ecstatic, Clayton's
eyes closed and his very being suspended on the thread of the
rhapsodic phrase—gave her the answer she'd been dreading all
those months of tan letters.

In the theater, the curtain would have fallen just then, with the two musicians upstage right, encapsulated in a silver-blue spot, and the woman downstage left, drenched in the warmth of a yellow gel. But in the real world she had to listen on to the end, struggling to keep her composure among the lumps of the red couch, which made her feel mortal and messy.

Eleven

The day after the gamelan show, Mrs. Woods took Virginia aside before class. "Mr. Murray has volunteered his services for heavy work," she said. She gave Virginia a note Kevin had brought to school.

Miss King:

I told Ida Lee and Mrs. Woods that I was building a puppet stage for the show, which I will do, next Saturday. Could you supervise? I promise, no funny stuff. (Though you *are* a foxy lady.)

Terry Murray

"This is the first time we've been able to get him involved with the school community. It must be your doing," Mrs. Woods whispered, eyes twinkling.

After class Virginia drew Kevin aside. "Would you give this to your father?" she said, handing him a folded piece of paper upon which she had hastily written: "Thanks for the offer. I'll send a book with diagrams home tomorrow with Kevin. They might give you some ideas. Saturday at one?"

She watched the boy tuck the note in his knapsack, eyes lowered, and leave the room. There was no real need for more than a curtain, strung at head level; she could rig that up herself. But now she'd set the ritual into motion; she fought the urge to run after Kevin, to change the note. The coward in her was so strong that she had to hold her breath. Deliberately turning back to the desk, she set to packing up her red trunk.

When she looked up, Renee was standing right under her elbow. "Careful, honey," she said, surprised. "I could have knocked you in the eye!"

"Can I talk to you, Miss King?"

"Of course, Renee. What's up?"

"When are you going to play your cello for me?"

"Well . . ." Mr. Jacobs, the music teacher, had discovered that Virginia was musically inclined and asked if she would mind demonstrating the cello to his instrumental students.

"Last week you said you might play the cello for me!"

"I'll play it for you tomorrow at Instrumental Music!"

"But . . . I thought just for me. . . ." The child looked down at her hands. "I thought we could do it today."

"I'm sorry, Renee, but there's so much to do, and you'll hear me in music class—I mean, don't you want your friends to hear it, too?"

Virginia knew that wasn't the point, and she felt a little guilty, using such a cheap appeal to Girl Scout honor in order to silence the child. She sighed. "Don't you have a school bus to catch?"

Renee shrugged. "I think it's already gone."

"Oh, Renee," Virginia said, shaking her head. "I guess we better make sure. Come on."

As they left the building, the last bus was just pulling out of its space. "That's not my bus, anyway," Renee said. "I think it's Kevin's."

Virginia shot her a glance. Although Renee bore her starched collar and pigtails with the stoicism of an obedient child who still believed the world would live up to its promises, she didn't seem reluctant to help those promises along. There was a certain resolve in her gaze, a penetrating attention.

Virginia decided a walk might do her good. They set off across the dusty playground with its patches of caked dirt. Renee was kicking a pebble; her bulky red pullover reminded Virginia of her favorite sweater when she was that age: a hand-me-down, she remembered with a shock, from Aunt Carrie, too large for a child but she wore it anyway, from October on through the winter. The scratchy luxuriance and peculiar smell —she would go sulk in the corner of her bed on a rainy after-noon, tucking her chin under the cowl neck in order to breathe the comforting scent of a lady who had worn one toilet water all her life, mixed in with her own puppy-dog smell. Years of Woolite and mothballs had not driven out the odors of mud and vinegar, fish and molasses.

Renee chattered beside her, skipping in time to a song the children had learned in music class. Virginia wanted to say something that wouldn't sound dumb, some praise that didn't gush. Just one word, softly spoken. That was the irresistible thing about music—it needed no intermediary of the mind; it was a direct infusion, straight to the bowels.

"You've got a nice voice," she said when Renee had finished. "Did you know some African tribes believe that the mark of a healthy soul is its ability to sing? And the French have a wonderful expression—*méchant*—which means 'wicked' but comes from two other words meaning 'no song' or 'bad song.' " She went on about the glorious gift of making music, talking over the girl's head, but she didn't care. She'd under-stand it later.

The streets were deserted; a few ashen-colored leaves

scuttled along the gutters. Everyone seemed to be cuddled up inside the houses with the curtains drawn, waiting for the predicted rain. Virginia realized that she'd have to hurry back to the school parking lot before the weather changed.

"What do you normally do after school?"

"I dunno. Eat a snack. Go outside and play till Daddy gets home."

A faint scent of bergamot wafted from Renee's neatly plaited head. Virginia could visualize the glass jar of hair pomade, its teal-blue contents. She'd seen a bergamot flower once and had bent over its red blossom to sniff the same unmistakable scent. How could anything that red smell so blue?

"What are you going to be for Halloween?" Virginia asked.

"Peter Pan."

"Peter Pan! He was one of my heroes, too. He never grew up—no wonder he could fly. Your mom's making your costume, I bet."

"Uh-huh."

All the kids were obsessed with Halloween, getting more and more involved in what Parker had once called "the October experience": ironing leaves between sheets of wax paper, writing autumn poems, assembling trail mix from dried apples, nuts and raisins, cutting out construction-paper bats and witches.

"You're lucky to have a mom who can sew," Virginia said. The stores were crammed with Halloween costumes: peaked witches' hats and bright plastic jack-o'-lanterns for lugging candy, racks of ready-to-wear gowns and pantaloons with necklaces and belts already printed on their cheap plastic, brittle masks with identical blank expressions—Mickey Mouse and

Snow White, Dracula and the Roadrunner, blank eyeholes waiting to be filled.

She walked Renee to the door. Sarah Butler answered the bell on the first ring.

"I was packing up supplies and when I finished, she was waiting," Virginia explained. "So I thought it best to walk with her. I hope you weren't worried."

Sarah had clamped one hand over Renee's shoulder and ushered her firmly into the house. "Scoot, young lady! I'll deal with you in a minute." She turned back to Virginia.

"I was getting worried. When I saw the school bus go by and Renee didn't come, I called the school, and they said they didn't know what had happened."

"I'm sorry," Virginia said. "I should've informed the office."

Sarah smiled, a little grimly. "Renee does tend to fixate on people. Why don't you come in?"

"I can only stay a moment." They went into the sewing room and Virginia eased herself into the flowered armchair, recognizing the gloomy sound track of "Dark Shadows" on TV.

"That's such a stupid program," Sarah mumbled, turning down the volume. "So how's the puppet show coming along?"

"Oh, everything's fine, thanks to your costumes and all the help the other parents have offered."

"I heard Terry Murray is going to build a stage," Sarah said, smiling.

"But I only just found that out today!" Virginia protested.

"The grapevine always works fastest," Sarah replied.

"You know that. Ida phoned me with the news. I do believe he's interested." She lifted an eyebrow. "Good-looking, smart —he's a supervisor with the County, after all."

Virginia didn't say anything, astonished how quickly her private doings had become a community event.

Sarah tilted her head. "He's a divorcee, you know. From all reports the wife was no good—didn't even want custody. Any mother who doesn't want her own child is crazy for sure. But he's done fine with that boy." She studied Virginia calmly. "What a dreary day! Why don't I warm you up with some hot cider, and when Ed gets here he can drive you to your car? He'll be home in an hour."

So that you can get me to confide in you and you can bear the juicy tidbits to Ida, who'll get on the phone and spread all my business around? No thank you! Virginia stood up. "Thank you, but I really should be going. If you could lend me an umbrella, I'll be fine."

"All right, if that's what you want." Sarah dipped into the next room and reappeared with a large black umbrella. "The Butlers' finest."

Halfway to the corner the rain began, a chilling drizzle that drifted under the umbrella, coating her sweater with a glaze of pearly mist, like a long cool drink for one's pores. The return of unpleasant weather exhilarated her. Leaden skies and shortened days were perfect for indulging anxieties; it was the time of year for unshackling skeletons in the closets, for lying awake in the dark as invisible wings whispered by the shuttered windows.

What kind of future awaited a girl like Renee? Wife and mother, Kroger's cashier or Sears clerk, teacher or secretary or data processor; maybe even lawyer or doctor. But what about her inquisitive heart? How would she nurture it in a town whose only theater performed superficial musical comedies, where the major entertainment was television and the weekend cabaret?

As she turned into the school driveway, Virginia shifted the umbrella, lodging it between ear and shoulder while she rummaged in her purse for her keys. She glanced around, recognized Jean Gilroy's yellow Volkswagen and the janitor's Camaro; otherwise the parking lot was deserted.

The next morning's weather looked much the same. Booker T. stood his hallowed ground among the piles of fallen leaves, his stone face streaked with dark rivulets where the rain had trickled down. Without much foliage left to soften its edges, the school building ruptured the view, a brooding clot in the milky tissue of inclement weather. After struggling to push its way over the horizon, the sun seemed to have given up the fight: the midmorning sky was a surly pewter color. It was as if someone had peeked out from the heavens and, with a disgusted snort, clamped a lid down on the whole mess.

Virginia locked the car door. Not since her arrival two weeks ago had the school yard seemed so bereft—no children swinging, or racing across the playground, or screeching through a game of tag.

She sighed and drew her scarf up to her earlobes as Mrs. Peck came out of the building and walked toward her car.

"Off to the superintendent," she explained as Virginia greeted her. "By the way, there's a letter waiting for you in the office."

The cream-colored envelope was edged with tiny blue flowers and in the very center, also in blue, a crabbed hand had written:

Miss Virginia King
Washington Elementary School
Akron Ohio

The sheet of stationery inside was also ornamented:

Dear Virginia,

You may not remember me, your being away from Akron and home folks so long and all, but I am your Aunt Carrie. I used to baby-sit you when you was small and was at your house on the average once a week until right before you moved to Arizona. Well I was talking to Mrs. Evans the other day and she said you was by to see her. I was going to call you then and there but then I didn't know if you wanted to hear from an old woman like me so I thought better not.

   I don't know what your parents told you about me, or if you remember me at all. Everyone in the family call me Crazie Carrie behind my back and maybe you know me as that too. But I have always been interested in the Arts and it did my heart proud to hear you was doing so well. It reminded me of my dear brother your father.

   Now to the point of this. I want to see you and thought I could come up by the school sometime, after school was over so I wouldn't disturb your teaching. Maybe we could have a little talk. Please don't get mad at a crazie old woman, you'll understand it when you are old like me.

Your Aunt Carrie

Aunt Carrie! Beaten to the punch. Trust Grandma Evans not to leave things up to chance.

The tiny voice on the other end of the line seemed unaccustomed to speaking on the phone. "Yes?" she asked, as if the only persons who could know her number would be bill collectors or sales sharks.

"Aunt Carrie, this is Virginia. I got your letter. How are you?"

"Virginia?" The voice cracked on the second syllable; there was a pause and a muffled cough, then she returned, slightly stronger. "Is that truly you?"

Is that truly you? In a flash, Virginia could see the diminutive, dark-skinned woman standing in the middle of their living room, arms folded across her ample bosom as she looked down on the pencil drawing Virginia had just finished: "Is that truly your daddy? Well, there might be a resemblance."

The words poured out of Virginia now as she apologized for not calling sooner, explaining how busy she'd been at the school. "What about Sunday?" she asked. "May I come over for a visit—say, around three?"

"Honey, you don't need no appointment with me. Just come on over. I'm here."

Virginia paid for her dinner at the Chinese restaurant around the corner and drove back to her apartment. Something Aunt Carrie had said on the phone kept bugging her: "You know where Furnace Street is, near where the old train station used to be? You got to remember that old station; that's where I last

laid eyes on you"—and instantly Virginia recalled the scene as
she had dreamed it but with Aunt Carrie beamed into the
picture: dark, stout Aunt Carrie in the funny cloche hat Virginia had imagined her wearing at Cedar Point.

She propped the Bach Suites up against the cushions
on the daybed. Which one next? Ah yes, the Fifth. "The
Discordable": The A string had to be tuned a whole step down
to G, subduing the tone and making the harmonies more forlorn, more compressed, as in church hymns. She kept missing
notes and had to fudge a bit to get the chords in tune, but
beneath the slippage was the true music that gripped and made
pride bow down before the monumental sadness of being alive,
music that required no explication, no translation: dissonant,
unresolved, the music of a human being probing the darker
corridors of the unachieved. The chords were so tightly knit
they seemed to bend, like blue notes in jazz, or a train whistle
in the dead of night, scrawling its grief across the darkened
landscape.

The darkness had a grayish sheen but it was completely still, a
gray without movement. Virginia awoke: she had touched
something, some recollection, but it was gone. What had
pricked it? She closed her eyes again. It was a roar: a roar in the
dark rushing toward her and her brother and her mother on the
platform—then suddenly it funneled into a spoke of bright
light. For an instant she had seen the scene vividly: placards
peeling from the walls, the concrete platform, the blue rails
gleaming in the dim light as the roar of the train filled the
station.

The train! The train station with its iron and glass! It
came. Still invisible but roaring it came, and the roar grew
louder. It roared, it rumbled, it growled like some wild thing. It

must be something much more terrible than anything she had ever experienced before. And as it roared out of the dark direction of Pittsburgh, Virginia knew that she had always thought of Pittsburgh as something dark and roaring, though she had never been there.

She was in her first train station. She couldn't understand why Aunt Carrie was there. Belle said Aunt Carrie had come along for the ride. Why then didn't Mom speak to her? Aunt Carrie of the dark and wrinkled countenance. Aunt Carrie who no one believed was only six years older than Belle. Aunt Carrie: bloodshot eyes, the smile with a missing tooth, the slight leer Belle said came from always smelling her own upper lip. She shouldn't be sticking her mouth where it didn't belong, Belle said. Virginia felt sorry for Aunt Carrie. She wore lots of lipstick to make herself look pretty but she wasn't—her face drooped.

How come Aunt Carrie had not recognized her drawing? Her father had a mustache ever since she could remember. It was thin and curved, like two rattails. Maybe the lines were a little shaky and his mouth crooked, but it was him, no mistake about it; she had drawn him from memory.

"Your father doesn't have a mustache," Aunt Carrie had said. Of course he had! What kind of aunt was she?

A garbled announcement came over the loudspeaker. The train was rolling into the station. And that train carried Virginia's daddy.

"It's time to go," said Belle in a strained voice.

They descended to the platform. There the cool stale air swept upward like the breath of the underworld; funny it was cool. Scraps of brightly colored paper, ripped faces from a billboard staring, a conglomerate of carnival lust and idiocy.

Aunt Carrie had taken out a hanky and was twisting it

—that looked funny. They waited on the platform for the train to come—and it came and it was not like the long and awful sound that had come before it. It was like the movies when the light shines cheerily from its one eye and the squeal of the brakes is exciting, and the people pour off and into other people's outstretched arms.

Virginia fell into her father's arms. "What did you bring me, Daddy, what did you bring me?" she screamed, because he seemed too terribly still, too far from her to kiss. She needed some souvenir, some proof that he had actually come from Pittsburgh. He gave her his name tag. ERNEST KING, GOODYEAR, it said. His shoulder smelled of pipe smoke, whiskey, cologne, hair pomade and faintly, the train.

"Your lovely sister's here, too," Belle said, and Virginia thought she sounded even stranger than before, her belly poking out against her white blouse. Aunt Carrie stood a little to the side, her coat still buttoned. Virginia could barely see her. Ernie Jr. was running up and down the platform, kicking an empty Coke bottle.

Belle hissed something about a letter, then said in the strangest voice: "So I thought it only proper that she come, too."

Her father tightened and then pushed Virginia away—gently, but it was still a push. They were going to have an argument again, except this time it looked like Daddy was going to cry, and she couldn't stand that. No one moved. Aunt Carrie was pulling on that hanky for all it was worth and then she was crying. It wasn't nice for Belle to call her lovely when she wasn't. That must be what they were going to argue about. Virginia had a pain in her stomach. She wanted to go home.

Twelve

What should she wear? She felt ridiculous—after all, she didn't have a "date" with Terry Murray, just an informal meeting to build a puppet stage, parent-teacher business. In a fit of petulance, she pulled on a pair of jeans and topped them off with her baggy purple sweater.

But she caught herself humming as she walked out to the car. Fall had a lot to do with it, she reasoned—this feeling of expansiveness, this affection she felt like heaping on the world. The air exuded an odor of sensuality, of glut and decay, of smoke, boot polish, apples.

On an impulse she stopped at K Mart and bought a bag each of butterscotch balls, nonpareils, and Starlight peppermints; then she swung by Saferstein Towers and knocked on Grandma Evans's door.

"Something for your sweet tooth!" she announced, piling the bags of candy into the old woman's arms.

"Chile, when will you ever learn to call before you come? I might a been entertaining." Grandma Evans displayed a stern countenance, but Virginia could tell she was tickled. "Well, now that you're here, come on in and set a spell."

"I can't stay, Grandma. I've got a—an appointment that I'm late for. School business. I was on my way when I thought of you."

"Hmmph!" was all the older woman said, crossing her arms and cocking her head to take in the blue jeans and slouchy sweater.

"Really, Grandma." Virginia insisted, realizing how crazy it sounded. Why *had* she done it?

"Some school business *that* must be. Well, at least your Aunt Carrie tells me you'll be seeing her soon. I'm so glad; you don't know what it means for her." Grandma Evans's face grew solemn momentarily; then she smiled again. "Run along now, and don't you dare come back without planning to give me a proper visit." She held out her cheek for a kiss; Virginia leaned over and hugged her swiftly.

"Well!" the older woman exclaimed, smoothing her hair. "Get a move on, chile; you don't want to be too late. Though I got to say"—her eyes twinkled conspiratorially— "I'm glad you know how to keep him waiting!" Before Virginia had a chance to protest, her grandmother had shooed her out and closed the door.

Crisp yet sunny, autumn in its leaf-strewn splendor! Virginia liked cruising along the regimental array of lawns, some crewcut-sparse with neatly trimmed hedges, some slightly overgrown. The streets and sidewalks were splattered with gold and rust, people with rakes were piling up the stuff, beautiful dead matter to be shoveled quickly into plastic bags before the next gust. She rolled down all four car windows and the fresh air rushed in, no whiff of pollution; she tried to imagine the scent of apples and nutmeg over the chill edge of wind. There had been a string of days like this one the autumn she met Clayton, the sun blazing in a corner of the ice-blue firmament. "Brain weather," he called it. How naive she had been! And how she wished she could have stayed that naive a bit longer.

Terry's house was one in a row of modest single-story homes, all right angles and no personality. A spindly tree struggled upward from the curbside grass—she remembered calling it "devilstrip" when she was a child, but nobody she'd ever met outside of Ohio knew it by that name. As she pulled into the driveway behind a spanking red MG, Terry stepped out of the front door.

"Hi. Any problems finding it?" Tight jeans and lilac skinny-rib knit top. *We look like the Bobbsey twins,* she thought.

"Not a one." She leaned over to unlatch the door. Terry's roadster couldn't transport much more than its owner and one passenger, so she had offered to carry both him and the lumber in her Fury. "Nice neighborhood," she added.

"Tell me about it." He slid in, immediately saturating the car's interior with the heavenly scent of British Sterling. "Let's roll."

She backed out of the driveway and headed down the street. "Great day," he said, flinging his arm along the back of the seat. "Reminds me of when I was a kid."

"I know what you mean." God, he smelled incredible. At the stop sign she sneaked a look; his right hand reached out the window and drummed the roof as he whistled to himself. The book she'd lent him lay on his lap. There was really nothing like tight jeans on a long-legged man.

"Your book came in handy," he said, catching her glance, "but the model you marked is way too flimsy. I think we should go for the all-time one-and-only supreme deluxe stage."

"The traveling box theater? That's too much work!" The stage he was referring to operated on the principle of a folding screen, with a framework of poles hinged together and burlap stretched over them. Just looking at the diagrams made Virginia dizzy, but she had drooled at the final illustration: a portable scaffold fitted with shelves for extra puppets and an arched proscenium just like an old-fashioned cinema.

"I'm telling you, it's cheesecake if you happen to know

a little about woodworking, which I do." He grinned and stretched his left arm farther along the seatback, not quite touching her. "The way I figure it, we might as well do it right. And it'll be easy to set up. There's no curtain to fool with, and the backdrop's just a piece of plywood. The kids won't even have to kneel. They can stand and hold the puppets over their heads. And the best part is that the whole getup's no bigger than a bag of golf clubs when it's folded. Like an accordion. It'll fit on the backseat of your car."

"And since when have you been such a hotshot carpenter?"

"Me?"

She cast him a flirtatious glance, knowing he just wanted to lift those fine eyebrows and get her to look at him looking innocent.

"Hey, I've been dealing with trees since high-school shop. Just never got out of the habit. Now I'm a regular woodworking whiz. Turn in here."

Carter's Cash-n-Carry had no glittering window displays or fancy setup, just rows and rows of hardware opening onto wider aisles that accommodated the doors and sinks and toilet bowls and lumber piled into cantilevered stacks. She watched Terry move along, kicking the wood shavings scattered on the cement floor, whistling no melody in particular as he consulted his list and pointed out what he wanted to an orange-smocked employee. He seemed utterly content, thumbs hooked in his pockets as he waited for the clerk to pull down the fragrant slabs and boards.

Virginia felt out of place, although the nutty smell of sawdust, cut by the sharp tang of resin, was comforting. Was there no way to clock the evolution of desire? It could pounce like Terry at the Open House, or come sauntering up the walk behind an armful of flowers; it could hide behind belligerence or mask itself as a jack-o'-lantern. It could appear as solicitude, and solicitude could swallow desire; or it could be recognized immediately as the first step in a tortuously slow courtship culminating not when the wedding bells ring but when a proud woman puts down a rifle and takes her flawed hero back into her bed. It could waver and die like a flame, or fade and reappear over and again in a parody of the resurgence of the seasons.

A slight sweetening of the air gave Virginia warning; she turned in time to catch Terry about to tickle her ribs.

"Damn! I almost had you!"

"No chance. I have ESP."

"ESP's no match for the Murray brand of magic." This flirting was so easy. When she was a teenager, she had dreamed of a man with eyes like his—warm cocoa ringed in black, thick lashes.

"Well, I've got it all," he said. "Let's get back and slap it together."

He had her pull up to the side door but then insisted on walking around to the front of his house. "My mama taught me never to let a first-time guest come through the back door; it's bad luck for the relationship. And this is one relationship I don't wanna jinx."

The living room was a model of geometric elegance, almost perversely bland. Under the glass coffee table, a small Persian-type rug provided the only color, muted rose and teal arabesques. How, she thought, could anyone feel comfortable in so much beige?

"I know," Terry said. "The little man's dream—

white-collar job, money in the bank, matching table lamps."
He touched her elbow and guided her across the plush carpet
and through the formal dining room, all brass and glass.

"Everything in this house is my ex-wife's idea. If I had
the money for a new crib, I'd dump it all on the curb tomorrow."

His bitterness surprised her. *Why didn't she take it with
her,* she was about to ask, but remembered that he had custody
of Kevin, and kept quiet.

"I'm not trying to give you a tour," he said, "but this
happens to be the way to the basement," leading her through a
kitchen as impersonal as a dentist's office, yellow Formica and
polished chrome flashing from the Amana refrigerator and
double steel sinks, the utensils dangling from racks.

"It's all so clean. I mean, it's *spotless!*" So different
from the kitchen at Clayton's fraternity house, with its clutter
and spilled juice and conflicting smells.

"Not all men are slobs. But the basement might make
you change your high opinion of my housekeeping. Don't
worry—there are no rats or snakes, but watch out for spiders."

"I think I can handle a spider or two," she replied,
dipping to avoid contact as he held open the door to the narrow
stairs leading down. His cologne rose with his body heat, mixing
with the tingling pine scent of pomade.

It was a typical unfinished basement, a concrete box
filled with odds and ends—cartons of discarded toys, galoshes
and work overalls, a washer and dryer. A workbench backed by
a pegboard ran across the far wall; in the center of the room a
large table saw stood under a naked light bulb. The tools were
arranged as neatly as the kitchen utensils. Terry freed a webbed
garden chair from the stack of summer equipment and set it
up, dusting it off with his hand.

"Have a seat," he said. "I'll bring the wood in."

Virginia had hated not having a basement in Arizona —no basement and no attic. "Who needs them?" her father said. "No tornadoes, no floods and no earthquakes. We don't need to dig in for protection." But to Virginia it had seemed that because they did not dig in, they had made no mark on the earth; they merely lived on its crust. Cellars were for memory, attics for dreaming. How could anyone live without memories and dreams?

"Where do we start?" she asked.

Terry stacked the lumber neatly. "We? You don't need to worry about this. I wouldn't want you to break a fingernail or something."

Her mouth dropped open. "I refuse to sit here and be treated like—" she protested; then she saw his grin.

"Oh, but when I was lugging wood down those narrow stairs, you didn't refuse that chair, did you? Not even a polite offer to help."

"You didn't ask for help," she replied, but he was right; she had enjoyed watching him work. "Touché. But now I'm ready to lend my feeble assistance."

"Okay, you can measure. That is, if you can read a diagram." He pretended to defend himself from a karate attack. "To start with, we need eight 24-inch one-by-twos for the horizontal bars. Measure the distance from top and bottom for the hinges according to the book and then mark where the screws are supposed to go." Next he showed her how to use the buffer, and as he sawed along her penciled lines, drilled holes and cut notches for the shelves, she took the prepared lengths of wood and planed them to a smooth finish.

Sawdust shot from the steel wheel, powdering the floor and filling Virginia's nostrils with a gingery sweetness. How old was he—early thirties? With a nine-year-old son. Virginia had not yet felt the desire for children of her own; the idea of seeing herself reduced, diluted and blended with another person frightened her.

The saw bit into a fresh piece of wood; the jolting screech set her teeth on edge, and she swallowed tightly. Finally, he cut the last lath and slapped the shavings off his jeans.

"Where's Kevin?"

"What?" He turned off the saw. Bits of sawdust clung to his eyebrows and sideburns.

"Where's Kevin? I didn't see him around."

"He's at his mother's for the weekend." Terry positioned a hinge and set the screwdriver carefully into the slot on the head, frowning as the screw chewed slowly into the wood. "She gets him twice a month." He picked up the drill to bore a line of holes along the top of each slat.

"Have you been divorced for long?"

"A couple of years."

"You must've been pretty young when you got married."

"Yeah, right—a dumb kid. We met when I was in army training at Fort Bragg. She's from North Carolina."

"You were in the army?"

"Like I said, a dumb kid. I bet your college friends all got around the draft some way."

Virginia considered; it was true. No one close to her had been to Vietnam except Jim, but he never talked about it, not even when he and Parker had been filling baskets with Popsicle-stick soldiers for their Watergate play. A few of the older boys in her neighborhood in Phoenix had gone, but she'd never had much contact with them.

She hesitated while Terry aimed the drill at another slat. "Did you go to Vietnam?" she asked, finally.

Terry laughed, but it wasn't his usual easy laughter. "Nope. I lucked out. My stint was up right before they started to ship American soldiers over in droves. 'Nam and I never had the pleasure of a personal acquaintance."

He laid the drill on the workbench. "Now let's see if these things fit together," he said, picking up two slats. "What's this play about, anyway? Kevin pretends it's a secret."

"It's the kids' idea. Mrs. Woods suggested a Halloween play, but the boys wanted to make goblins and vampires and stuff like that, and the girls protested. Then they came up with their own story. The hero wants to become a football player in order to impress a girl, but he's too small to make the team. When he sees the girl next day at school, he's so ashamed he runs away."

Terry looked up from the hinge. "These kids made this up?"

Virginia nodded. "The puppets turned out really nice. There's a mother and a father, the boy of course, and the girl who laughs at him. Then there's a fairy godmother and a fairy godfather who are always arguing about how to help, and a talking football . . . "

"A *talking* football?"

"Don't laugh. That's your son."

"No way!"

"Oh, yes. He didn't tell you?"

"All he said was that he had a speaking part."

"Oh, the football has a nice, jagged mouth! It's not as crazy as it sounds: the fairy godfather has put a spell on the football, which was a birthday present from the parents, and the football coaches the boy by telling him how to throw a lateral pass—whatever you call it—and how to run downfield and look over his shoulder to make the catch and score. Stuff like that."

"Sounds crazy."

"That's just the beginning. Each football team is one group puppet—"

"What?"

"A group puppet. You draw a couple rows of heads and shoulders on cardboard, cut out the silhouette, and mount the whole thing on a stick. All the two teams do is bounce up and down and grunt in unison."

"So what else is new?" Terry snorted, shaking his head.

"The girls wanted cheerleaders, but the boys insisted that the cheerleaders be a group puppet, too. So all they do is jump up and down and yell 'Rah-rah-rah.' Same with the majorettes. Then the kids from Instrumental Music came up with the idea of a marching band."

"Oh, man."

"Yeah, they really got into it. The boys claimed no fairy god*mother* would know how to make a boy into a football hero, it had to be a fairy god*father*. So finally they agreed on both a godfather and a godmother: the godfather tries to make the boy into a jock, and the fairy godmother keeps telling him he should talk with the girl instead of trying to impress her."

"What happens at the end?"

"Come now, Terry. If you know the ending, you might not want to see the show!"

"When exactly is this show, anyway?"

"Wednesday. I thought Mrs. Woods had told you. Problem is, we can't get the gymnasium until Tuesday, for the dress rehearsal. I don't know what that'll do to the kids. Some of them have trouble remembering their lines as it is."

"It's gonna be part of the fall program, right?"

"Yeah."

"Then you got nothing to worry about. That thing's always terrible—little kids with sheets over their heads reciting poems about pumpkins and stuff. The puppets are bound to be a hit."

"I don't know if that's a compliment or not," she replied.

"When it comes to you, everything I say's a compliment."

It was such an unexpected moment—*like catching a glimpse of yourself in a store window and liking what you see before you realize who it is,* Virginia thought, returning his smile.

"Listen," Terry went on, "I've got a deal for you; if you'll have dinner with me tonight, I'll come to the show."

"You'll come to the show because Kevin is the talking football; besides, you want to see your stage in action, don't you?"

"Builder's pride, huh?" He laughed. "True, true, but I'm not done trying. How about dinner in *spite* of the fact that I'm coming to the show?"

"Now *that's* a deal." She smiled back, suddenly at ease. "So what's next?"

"Right now there's nothing for you to do but sit back and relax. No, hold up a minute! You're an actress, right? And a storyteller, too, judging from the tales Kevin brings home. Why don't you tell me a story while I screw this together? Talk to me."

"What do you want to hear?"

"The story of your life. What brings you back to Akron?"

"That part's easy. I got a job here."

"But what's with the puppets? At the risk of having you throw up a force field like you did the other night, I got to say that puppets aren't exactly your run-of-the-mill occupation."

"It wasn't puppets at first. First it was music. I've played the cello since I was nine or ten, but by the time I graduated from high school I realized I didn't want to spend half my waking hours practicing arpeggios. So I switched to drama in college and did mime on the side. After graduation I couldn't find work as an actress, so I did the secretarial bit for a short while . . ."

"That's when you got into Puppets and People, right?"

"How did you know the name?"

"The monthly PTA newsletter, where else?"

"Oh, yeah: 'Puppets and People, the Total Experience.' Well, we wrote the plays and made the puppets right on the premises; we did the music and the lighting and staged pageants for special days like the summer solstice and All Hallow's Eve, too."

"A commune, like?"

"No, not what you think." Her voice went stony. "An artistic community. There was no funny stuff."

Terry looked up, realizing his mistake. "I didn't mean it *that* way. Lemme start over." He took a deep breath. "I just meant that you must have been leading an interesting life up there. No nine-to-five, just art and inspiration all day long." He paused. "Akron probably looks pretty hick to you."

"You forget I was born here."

"That doesn't mean it can't still look hick. When did you move, anyway?"

"Early 1961. The upside-down year."

Terry looked quizzical.

"You know—the numbers read the same even when you turn it on its head. I felt like I'd been turned on my head, too."

"Change is rough on a kid," he agreed. "But why Arizona?"

"My dad got a job offer in Phoenix, so up we packed and away we went. Simple as that."

He shook his head. "What kind of job could a black man get in Phoenix?"

"Same as in Akron. See, he had started out as a lab technician. But he had gone on and learned how to do everything an analytical chemist does; all that was missing was the degree, so he couldn't advance. When Goodyear expanded its operations in Arizona, anyone who could do the work and was willing to transfer was welcome; they didn't care whether you had a degree or not. The factory was actually in a little town called Litchfield Park, named after one of the company's founders. Dad wanted to move out there, but my mother put her foot down. She said she wasn't about to move into the middle of the desert with the scorpions and the coyotes. So he had a forty-minute commute from Phoenix and back."

"The pay must have been good."

Virginia shrugged. "I have no idea. I was a kid; kids don't think about things like salary."

"Well, the bread had to be decent for him to take his whole family to a place no black person's ever even seen."

"Oh, that's not true," she replied, chuckling. "There

are lots of blacks in Arizona. Well, not lots, but more than a few."

In Wisconsin she'd gotten used to people cocking an eyebrow whenever they learned she was from Arizona. Older black folks would sometimes remark: "Fort Huachuca, right?" Fort Huachuca had been one of the major bases for black soldiers in World War II, a parched, scorpion-infested and segregated encampment near the Mexican border.

When they moved to Phoenix, their neighborhood had already been integrated. There were white kids whose parents clucked their tongues because they were "wild as young Indians." There were a couple of black kids who spoke just like the white kids, and some kids who spoke Spanish at home and had skin like dark honey and cascades of black hair. *Surf City,* they'd sing, gyrating inside their Hula-Hoops, though there wasn't an ocean anywhere. But there was *Summertime, summertime, sum-sum summer summer* all year long, no falling maple leaves or nippy breezes, no warm apple cider in October when the pumpkins showed their true colors. It had been hard to learn to cope with sunlight that flattened perspective and seemed to leach the puny dye from her dresses; under that relentless blaze the only colors that prevailed were the furious blue of the sky and the burnt cinnamon crags of the mountains ringing the valley.

"I think my dad got a kick out of pulling up stakes and moving west like the pioneers—sort of a personal variation on the American Dream."

"A visionary, eh? Maybe that's where your creativity comes from."

"There is something visionary about him, yes," she replied, surprised at his perception. "He dragged us all over the state."

"Who's us?"

"My brother and me. Once we went to Tombstone to watch the reenactment of the shoot-out at the OK Corral, which was a kind of primitive summer theater for tourists. But his favorite places were the Indian reservations—the Navajo Nation and Monument Valley, the Hopi mesas. He wanted us to know there were high civilizations long before white men came to massacre them, before Jefferson wrote the preamble to the American Constitution."

"A pretty spectacular education."

"With him it's not enough to read about something; he wants to dig his hands into it, to experience it. Of course, he's mellowed over the years. But for a while the desert was like a laboratory to him."

"And your mom?"

"She came along when we went to the Grand Canyon, but that was pretty much it. She had to stay home with the baby, she said. It was a good excuse."

Shopping for history, Belle had characterized the excursions. The first thing she always did when they returned was plop them into the tub and scrub off the dust and grime, muttering at their fresh suntans and complaining that they were getting to be as black and shiny as a pair of Japanese beetles.

Belle had refused to enter into any closer relationship with her new surroundings. Whereas Virginia's father went out to meet nature, accepting the prickly and poisonous land on its own terms and introducing his children to its dangers and its magic, Belle spent her days inside. She ventured onto the patio only during the cool hours, after the sun had dropped below the skyline and the asphalt had steamed off; for years she wouldn't let Claudia play outside during the heat of the day.

Whenever she had to go anywhere, to the grocery store or the post office, she dressed against the heat as if girding her loins for battle, donning broad-brimmed hats and dark glasses, vaselining her lips and taking along a thermos of ice water in case the car broke down.

"She complained all the time about the heat. Claimed the sidewalks burned through the soles of her sandals, stuff like that. Once she swore she was walking across a parking lot and her neck and earlobes began to burn: the sun had heated up her earclips and the silver chain of her lavaliere."

"That's some serious solar power."

"She's pretty hysterical about most things." Terry looked at her oddly, but Virginia didn't notice. "Not a day went by without her warning us to watch out for black widow spiders and rattlesnakes."

"Sounds reasonable."

"Black widows are very shy and won't bite unless you stick your hand in their mouth. And rattlesnakes don't like to hang around neighborhoods—too many speeding cars and too many people. Besides, everyone knew what to do if you heard *that* sound: freeze, then back off, slowly."

"Did you ever meet a rattler?"

"Nope."

"So it's easy for you to say." They both laughed. "I have to side with your mother, though," Terry went on. "It's hard to see your kids grow up too big for you to watch them every second. Just wait until you're a mother yourself."

"Right," Virginia replied, smirking to cover her confusion.

What she had said was not quite true. Sometimes she and Ernie Jr. had dreaded the heat—especially around late July when the monsoon season began and the air, already like a furnace, became intolerably thick with increased humidity. They never got used to opening the door at night and stepping into a dark hot wind, and they were frightened when the skies crackled with dry lightning. But they never let on to Belle, since to admit disquiet would have given her the advantage.

The only one who seemed not to mind the heat was Claudia. She could walk on the hot concrete drive in her bare feet, and she scorned the bonnets her mother tried to tie on her. Poor Belle! Stuck at home with a small child who had the conditioning of a roadrunner while her husband and two older children were out in the wilderness somewhere, exploring the very countryside she was so terrified of.

"You're a strange lady," Terry said.

"What do you mean?"

He shook his head. "I don't know for sure. One minute you're talking about magic footballs, then, before I can blink, we're into alien landscapes. I kinda like that. But just now, you were gone."

"Gone?"

"Yeah; you were somewhere else. I don't mean daydreaming—whenever someone daydreams, there's a little goofy smile to signal that they're out to lunch temporarily. No, you were gone. Poof! Beamed up."

Terry suggested that he change for dinner first and then follow her home so she could leave her car at her place. Virginia demurred; her apartment was too small to have him come up and wait while she showered and changed, and she couldn't bear the thought of him parked under her window in his purring little red machine while she tried to decide how to dress.

So she drove back to her apartment alone. Alone, she could think; alone, she considered the possibility that dinner might become more than dinner, and with the coolheadedness of a prop manager organized her materials—a deep red skirt and matching velour blouse that buttoned down the back, a large purse packed providentially. When she pulled into his driveway again, Terry was already on the front stoop, all in blue.

"Girl, you look better than my MG, and that's saying a lot," he joked, and helped her slide into the leather-lined cockpit.

Iacomini's was the typical setting for the special evening out; there was cordon bleu, wild rice, and white wine, lots of it. And of course, chitchat: the latest movies and the Watergate tapes and Richard Pryor, the fading fame of the Supremes and whether Muhammad Ali had mellowed. Talk and more talk, intended to test, and mask, their deepening attraction, for they were beyond the awkward quips and innuendoes of mere flirtation. When the bill finally came, they both stopped talking. Terry paid with a flourish and propelled her gently out of the restaurant.

He didn't return to his place as she expected, nor did he take her home. Instead, she found herself being driven through an unfamiliar part of town, over railroad tracks, past an old stone bridge and into a neighborhood that was undergoing "deyelopment": block after block of apartment complexes, neat and self-sufficient as small villages—Hazel Court, Summerhill, Riverwood, Eden Terraces.

"Where are we going?" she asked finally.

"Gig called the Odyssey. It's the best place in town if you want to dance without bumping into all the teenies." He curved into a parking lot behind a squat, windowless building.

As Virginia's eyes adjusted to the smoke and gloom

inside, she saw that the dance floor was elevated—a type of pavilion with a low banister around it. The ceiling over the dancing area was hung with a complicated system of strobes, red, blue, and black lights, as well as standard spots. The lower level surrounding the pavilion lay in near darkness; there couples sat in silence at small tables, rebuilding their energy as they watched the dancers bobbing in rhythm with the strobe: *Dissipation. Race relations. Consolation. Segregation. Dispensation. Isolation. Exploitation. Mutilation. Mutation. Miscreation. Confirmation.* Soul music gave them the words of passage.

They found a free table and Terry went off for drinks. Virginia studied the dancers; they flaunted silk pantsuits and gangster hats, voluminous sleeves that flared softly in time with the music, earrings made of peacock feathers, even a pair of shoes with a goldfish suspended in each glass heel. *Proclamation,* sang the amplified voice. *Race relations. Consolation. Integration. Fabrication. Revelation. Acclimation. Salvation. Vibration. Emulation. Confirmation.*

Terry returned and they sat without speaking, sipping their drinks. This kind of dancing had nothing in common with the hopping around at the parties she had gone to over the past year, parties given by white artists and intellectuals where no one paid much attention to the art of body movement, where the art of conversation was more important. Even while dancing, speech was sovereign; and if a debate grew too involved, the couple simply stopped in the middle of the dance floor, arguing a salient point.

As Terry led her up to the phosphorescent arena and they swung into a hand dance, Virginia remembered that "serious dancing" was a marriage of body and will. Elegance was the rule, exuberance the telltale sign of an amateur. The music swirled around the couples, each moving in a strict pattern, with only milliseconds between steps for improvisation. But the milliseconds distinguished the good from the merely adequate. Time enough for a spin or a half turn, a dip—and there should still be a moment left to smile before hands touched and moved apart again. "They called it 'off-timing' in our parents' day," Clayton had explained at the fraternity dance, "because the Lindy three-step is imposed on a four-four rhythm."

Terry reached out for her again, his body buoyed by the exultant wash of strings, tethered by the beat. *Transmutation.* He swung her into his arms, and they moved without break into a slow song: saxophones and a hundred strings, blue-cool eunuchs harmonizing *It feels so good.* She had forgotten how it felt to be touched and found desirable, to want with a will not one's own.

A man and a woman relieved of the weight of speech watched light slide from the windshield, the outside air offering no resistance, the car easing forward with barely a tremor. Earlier this evening, seduction had been verbal—words teased, provoked. Now, immersed in the familiar world of his scent, talk was no longer an issue.

He draped an arm over her shoulder as they walked toward his house, and her arm slipped around his waist. Then his tiny grunt of satisfaction, the key in the lock, the dark vestibule, hands slipping under her blouse, his lips. Her exposed skin chilled, the unexpected heat from his palms. She gasped as he sucked her tongue into him.

Down the hallway she held his hand like a lost waif, neither of them daring to speak. The bedroom door creaked, one dim lamp gave light enough to see that the sheets were blue, a bachelor's detail, marine-blue, a waiting ocean. When he touched her again their bodies merged into one long, yearning curve, and the sea rose up to meet them.

Thirteen

She stirred at the aroma of coffee, the comforting cluck of percolation. *It smells so brown,* she thought, stretching, then snapped awake as she remembered where she was, the deep blue sheets and (she slowly opened her eyes) the peach-and-white-striped wallpaper. She jumped out of bed, headed for the shower, then decided against it. Instead, she splashed water on her face, rubbed along her teeth with a finger full of Crest, and scooted into her clothes. A quick pick through her Afro, and she walked into the kitchen.

"Up already? And here I was planning to spoil you: breakfast in bed with all the trimmings, down to the rose." Arrayed on the tray were plate and napkin, a glass of orange juice, two pats of butter on a saucer, and a rose the color of coral in a crystal vase. Terry was at the sink pouring milk into a creamer, freshly showered and drenched in some exotic scent, clad in one of those white terry-cloth robes Virginia had seen only in the movies.

"Breakfast is served." He held out her chair and she felt warmth radiating from him as he pushed her gently up to the table, then the moisture of his lips on the back of her neck. "My Lord, I've found an angel," he whispered, and slid into the chair to her right.

She had rarely felt less angelic, unwashed and unflossed, with her rumpled blouse and her hair full of lint. If there was anyone who looked beatific it was this gorgeous man calmly sprinkling pepper over his scrambled eggs.

He looked up, smiling. "I've been thinking, princess. There's got to be more schools around here that have room for a Puppet Lady. You should try to get another gig as soon as this one's finished."

"I do have another 'gig,' " she replied.

"You do? Why didn't you tell me?"

"You never asked."

"Liar."

"Okay. You asked, but I didn't know you well enough yet. I *still* don't know you well enough—"

"Oh, no," he said, and they both laughed.

"But I'll tell you anyway," she continued. "I'm doing a month at the high school in Oberlin."

He frowned slightly. "Oberlin? Where's that?"

"Fifty miles from here, silly! Near Elyria." Then, to smooth over his ignorance: "It's a tiny place. Six thousand people, two or three thousand college students."

"Oh, yeah—that radical hippy college, right? Lots of rich cultural-type families from New York send their kids there."

"Not just rich kids—smart kids. And I don't know what you mean by radical, unless you call being the first college to admit blacks and women radical."

"Whoa, whoa!" He lifted his hands, waving his napkin in mock surrender. "Look, I was out of line. More coffee?"

She nodded.

"Anyway, I shouldn't talk about things I don't know firsthand. Which I'll soon remedy. But I do know I like the idea of you being in the neighborhood." He deposited another kiss, this time on her forehead, and suddenly Virginia felt panic. The prospect of last night repeated over and over during the next month and more—to lean across a dinner table to kiss and exchange stories from the past, all the little intimacies of new lovers—the thought both enraptured and terrified her.

"But I won't be in the neighborhood," she stammered. "Not really."

He looked at her with amusement. Then he tried to convince her to stay at his house for the day—"a lazy Sunday" was how he put it—but Virginia needed breathing space.

"I can't," she said. "I've promised to visit an aunt this afternoon whom I haven't seen since I was nine."

"You won't spend all day with her, will you? To-night—"

"Listen, Terry, I've got class preparations. I also have to plan my opening sessions for Oberlin. That starts up first thing the week after next, and it's a totally different bag."

"We can plan them together."

She smiled, and leaned over to him to kiss his chin. "Oh no we can't. If I stay, we'd get zero done, that's for certain."

"Well, lady, since you're calling the shots . . . will you call me?" He leaned back, studying her expression. "You know"—she saw him swallow hard—"I'm in this for the distance. I mean it."

No. 118 Furnace. Ruts and crabgrass, acrid air, the horizon smeared with the lurid sediment of pollution. Hugging herself against the chill, Virginia trudged across the street, up the sunken steps, onto the sagging porch. The door of the small house opened, and she was swallowed in that massive bosom, spongy and instantly comforting, redolent with the mingled disclosures of sweet cologne, mothballs and wool warmed on the skin. Then she was bustled in, her coat peeled off and in a flurry of exclamations and questions —"My, my, what a sight for sore eyes you are! Tea or coffee? Water's on, sit down; I'll be with you in a minute"—she found herself alone in the room.

She sat down on the sofa, pale gold brocade kept immaculate by a plastic slipcover that clung to the backs of her thighs; she scooted forward, finally settling for a ladylike perch on the edge of the cushion. The coffee table, maple-veneered and from another decade, carried several months' worth of *Ebony* and *Jet* magazines; the pale green wall-to-wall carpet had probably been extolled by the salesclerk as "sea mist" or "mint frost" but here, with daylight filtering weakly through heavy yellow drapes, it exuded the melancholia of hospital waiting rooms.

She had the feeling she'd come back to something, like a sleepwalker. The modest yearning this room represented, this acceptance of one's vulnerability toward the exigencies of life— she had denied it and now, through a stroke of good luck or bad, the Arts Council had accepted her application for artist-in-residence and she had reason to return, back to the sulfurous skies and camphorated rooms where she first drew breath. Running and getting nowhere, round and round and faster and faster like Sambo until everything melted down to the antimacassars and hidden peppermints and tasseled pillows, the white leather-bound Bible on a doily and the table in the corner with its phalanx of yellowed family photographs framed and propped up under oval mats. . . .

"My, my, will you look at that. The spittin' image."

Aunt Carrie stood in the doorway to the kitchen, teacups in one hand and a plate of cookies in the other. She shook her head slowly as she clucked her tongue. "Same eyes, same long neck and that way of holding yourself like someone attached a string to the top of your head and pulled it tight. Ernest must be proud enough to bust." She set the dishes down.

Virginia smiled. And Grandma Evans said her eyes were like Belle's.

Aunt Carrie was wearing a navy blue straight skirt and matching V-neck sweater stretched so tightly across the prow of her bosom that two ghostly circles of white shone through where her brassiere strained against the weave. It was an unusual outfit for a woman at home; Virginia had expected a muumuu or one of those loose shirtwaist dresses and a dun-colored cardigan with the sleeves pushed midway to elbow and two buttons buttoned at the top—instead, this attempt at sophistication. The effect was startling: from the wrappings of a legal secretary rose a vaguely gourd-shaped, jowled face whose pendulous lower lip revealed a crescent of deep pink mucous membrane whenever she smiled—as she did now, showing a row of uneven and widely spaced teeth. Her large eyes drooped slightly at the corners and seemed constantly on the point of tearing, giving her the appearance of a chocolate-brown beagle.

Virginia realized she had been staring; quickly, she reached for the teapot. *Why, she looks just like I thought she would. I remembered her all along.*

"Here, let me pour," she offered. "What do you take in yours, Aunt Carrie?"

"The same as you, dear. I don't take much to tea usually—never had occasion to, I guess."

"Oh, I'm sorry! I would have drunk coffee as well."

Aunt Carrie chuckled. "You must have learned that in the university."

"Learned what?"

"Having tea in the middle of the day. Anyway, I ain't so old I can't pick up a new habit. It's good to see you, sugar. Mrs. Evans said you was here, said you was bound to call."

"Aunt Carrie, I want to apologize for not getting in touch with you. I've been so busy . . ."

"Don't go apologizing to me. I'm not one for apologies, makes me blush. You young people got all that life ahead of you, it's no wonder you're busy. We may talk a lot about you not coming round to see us often as we'd like, but we know how it is."

She took a thin white handkerchief from her waistband and dabbed at her eyelids. There was a pink rose embroidered in one corner. "I remember baby-sitting you and your brother, how you liked to draw. You drew up every piece of paper you could get your hands on. Your dad had to lock his desk." She wrapped the hanky around her right index finger, pulled it straight, then started in again with the left index finger.

"May I ask you something, Aunt Carrie? I don't know if it means anything, really."

"What, dear?"

"Well, you mentioned the old station the other day, and then I dreamed that night—I mean, I had a dream about it—not a very pleasant dream, I'm afraid. But you were in it, and me, and my mother. I don't know if you can help me or not. I've always wondered why we had to move to Arizona in such a hurry. I don't remember anyone being too happy about it."

"Your father got a good job offer—"

"I know. But there *has* to be something else." She stared at the old woman's hands twisting the handkerchief; sometimes the rose could be seen among the coiled ends of the cotton, a delicate blemish. "One day, not long after Claudia was born, I overheard my parents arguing. It must have been late spring or early summer, because it was hot enough to turn the evaporative cooler on, and all the windows were open to let the air through. I was playing in the aloes under the kitchen window, and I wasn't supposed to be there, which is why I didn't stand up when I heard them. Their voices carried loud and clear. 'Here I packed up my entire life,' he was yelling, 'left my job and my home for the sake of our marriage, and you *still* can't put bygones behind'—then he walked over to shoo a fly out the window and saw me kneeling there. He didn't say another word, just shut the window."

Virginia folded her hands around her teacup, but didn't take a sip. "I never dared ask anyone," she went on. "Not him nor, Heaven forbid, Mom." She looked up at her aunt.

"You said you last laid eyes on me at the train station. And now I remember Mom not being very nice to you that evening. That's where it all started, wasn't it?"

The squat figure in the corner of the sofa became a little more erect; the hanky stopped twisting.

"It's hard," she whispered. A sigh, barely audible, escaped from her lips and hung like dry scent in the air. Straightening her back a bit more, she placed her hands in her lap and like a schoolgirl reciting her lessons began to speak, her voice trembling at first but gaining strength.

"I thought about it a lot. Not when it happened. When it happened, I didn't think about nothing at all. But afterward, I thought about it. If you remembered the night at the train

239

station. If you could make sense out of it. If your mother ever mentioned me to you. It was so hard not to be able to talk to anyone about it. It happened so long ago. I didn't mean your mother any harm. I couldn't have." She took a deep breath. "I thought a lot about how I would tell my side if anyone asked. I knew I couldn't cry or get indignant. It's nobody's fault. Long ago I decided that if anyone asked me, I would tell everything as I felt and saw it from the beginning."

She got up and refilled both cups, then went and sat down in the armchair across the room, next to the table with the photographs. It was as if Aunt Carrie had been waiting for this moment; Virginia imagined her rehearsing her answer, year after year alone, in this room, from that chair. A wrenching fear passed through her, brief and raw.

"My daddy—your grandfather—ran off at the beginning of the Depression. I was thirteen, your father was nine. Mama began taking in washing, cleaning up white folks' houses, anything to bring in a few dollars. My older brothers and sisters were married off or sent out to find work as soon as they were old enough to walk without wetting their pants, it seemed. I had seven brothers and sisters older than me and I never saw them much, except on holidays. Mama let me stay home and tend to Ernie—your dad. He was the smart one in the family and we all loved him no end. Ernie was our shining star, and we did everything to protect him from things. So I stayed home and took care of him while Mama went to work. I cooked him breakfast and sent him out to school, and tried to help him with his homework. Ernie never heard a harsh word about his daddy—in those days men left their women for all sorts of reasons, and nobody blamed them much, because times were hard. But when Ernie finally learned that our daddy had left us holding the bills, he went furious and never spoke his name again.

"I was the runt of the family and the homeliest. I knew it—no one had to tell me. I could see it in the mirror and in the eyes of people when they came to visit. So when your father got to be grown enough to fix his own breakfast, there was the problem of Carrie. What can she do? Not smart enough for business, not pretty enough for marriage. But they found me someone to marry, finally. A widower, forty-odd years old, who ran a barber shop. Numbers racket on the side. I was seventeen.

"Folks said Sam Rogers was a good soul. He'd lost his wife of twenty years to an accident and was helpless without her. He needed a woman to clean and cook and to give him a little comfort. He couldn't have children, folks said, and that I was perfect for him. In a way, moving into his little house was so much like living at home that I barely had to adjust. He come home at night and I'd have a good dinner waiting—Dixie butter peas from the garden and baked yams, chitterlings on weekends. I washed his clothes and kept the house clean. He barely noticed me. It was like taking care of my baby brother.

"Everyone thought I was coping so well. The older ladies would wink and ask me how I liked having a man in the house, and I'd smile. I didn't let on that Sam hadn't touched me. Not that I minded. Sam Rogers was big and sweaty, and when he sat down at the dinner table he sometimes put me in mind of a big slimy frog. He had bugged-out eyes that were bloodshot, not from drink but because the air and dust could get to them so easy, and he grunted when he walked, almost like sounds would help him along. But he was kind, and I got used to him. Little by little he come out of his grieving. After a few months he began talking about his wife's cooking. 'Could you fry me some green tomatoes for tomorrow?' he'd ask. 'Edna used to make them.' I asked around to find out how to fry green tomatoes, and they'd be on his plate next morning. 'You cook nearly as good as Edna,' he'd say, and it pleased me to know I was doing a good job.

"Then one summer evening after dinner he was sitting in his chair and I was on the sofa, crocheting a doily for the armrest, when he turned to me and said, 'I want to tell you about Edna.' I put down my handwork; he was hunched down in that chair so that his head nearly touched his knees, almost as if he was in pain. He talked about Edna when he first saw her, at fifteen, and their wedding; how they tried to have children and the doctor finally told him he couldn't have any. He talked about how Edna lost all her shyness when the lights were out. I sat there and listened to him, a great big piece of a man humped over in that chair like a child with a stomachache, talking about what ailed him. He must have talked for hours. Did you ever notice how the air looks like it's full of feathers sometimes when it gets dark? Everything seems to come apart and float around, and heavy things like tables and chairs take on a grainy look, like old sugar. I listened and watched Sam melt too, just like the furniture. He seemed so delicate all of a sudden.

"When he finished, he looked at me without sitting up —just turned his head and looked at me from his knees. He smiled. Then he laughed. Then he reached out his hand and I went to him.

"I got to tell you all this because you've got to see what it was like. I mean, I'd been taught for so long to be thankful for whatever I got that I didn't think to ask for more out of life. I took whatever came to me and was satisfied. I didn't know what I was missing. Which was why, a couple years later, I about went crazy when he up and died. Lord knows I didn't have the world, but the little piece of it I had I didn't want to lose and have to start all over again. But there I was, a teenage widow with good as no money.

"So I went back home. I kept house and helped Mama with her washing sometimes, and I baby-sat the children in the neighborhood. Everyone started calling me Aunt Carrie. Aunt Carrie was there to do whatever needed to be done. Ernie was sixteen by then and was growing in his sleep, it seemed like. He was near to six feet already—and handsome, slim and tough, with straight black eyebrows and broad shoulders. But he was too serious for his own good. Every spare moment his head was in a book. He studied so much it got so he looked a little cramped, like some twisted-up fungus that grows in the dark. He looked pale under his color. Ashy. For all his book learning, though, he didn't know beans. Never went out with girls . . . never even looked at them. People'd say, 'That boy's going to make something out of himself,' but I'd worry."

She paused, and Virginia became aware of sounds from outside—children playing in the street, tennis shoes slapping the pavement, a shout.

"Anyway," Aunt Carrie continued, "spring came— not spring exactly, just the first blowsy days. I'd been washing sheets and had hung them out on the clothesline. But like I said, the weather was unpredictable that time of year—clothes will dry in a couple hours if a rain don't come up and drench them, or if a storm don't appear out of nowhere and dash them all into the mud. That afternoon about three o'clock, it suddenly looked like it might rain. I ran outside and began taking down the sheets, when I happened to look up and see the most beautiful man in the world walking down the street. He had on a white shirt, and his head rose out of that white shirt like a statue. I felt myself go weak, and I realized that I wasn't dead yet. I bent over the laundry basket, then peeked another look. He raised his free hand and waved.

"I was so confused that for a moment I couldn't lift my head. I stayed bent over the basket, playing with the clothespins. I was ashamed, but the feeling wouldn't go away. I could have stayed right there, kneeling in the mud, and cried. But there was this feeling, this strength inside the weakness, which made me stand up and reach for the next sheet. Soon I sensed him next to me. He was playing around, joking—like he'd take down two pins at once and hold the sheet above the dirt with his hands and teeth. But then he reached around me to get my end of a sheet, and I felt the heat from his chest rising up against my back, and something went inside of me and I held on to that clothesline like I was drowning. He thought I was playing and tugged at the sheet. I wouldn't let go—if I had I would've fallen down. I stood there listening to the wind slap that sheet against my face, and I could feel the bottom of the sheet flicking my shins. It was like being caught in a sail, and flying, flying over everything. He gave up and let go, and I finally got it all folded and ready. He carried the basket inside for me. I must have walked funny, because he asked me if I felt well. I said I was a little dizzy and might lay down for a spell. He said he'd help me make the bed.

"So he took the basket into the bedroom and I went to the bathroom to try to pull myself together. But I didn't know what I was doing. I went in to splash water on my face and found myself undressing down to my slip. I could still feel that sheet beating against me, like a bird gone wild. When I walked into the bedroom, he was kneeling on the bed, trying to tuck the bottom sheet into the headboard. He whistled and plopped over on his back. 'I don't see how you women do this sort of stuff,' he said. I didn't answer. I was in a trance. 'There's nothing smells better than freshly washed sheets,' he said then, turning his head to the side and sniffing. He didn't suspect a thing. And without expecting that I'd really go through with it, I bent over and touched his cheek. His face turned and looked into mine. That was the first moment he knew anything. I remember seeing the pulse start up under his Adam's apple. And you know what he felt like to touch? Like onion skins. Soft and dry."

For a while the two women sat without speaking. *What he felt like to touch,* Virginia thought. *Soft and dry.*

"But that's what was important for me." Aunt Carrie's tone became brisker. "What's important for you is what comes afterward. We were together most of that spring and summer. I think he never really thought much about it. It was pleasant, and when it was over, he forgot about it. I'm sure of that. I stopped it because I realized it was crazy. I don't know if anyone suspected us. Mama was away so much of the time, and the neighbors thought Ernie was inside studying." She paused. "After a long while I got it out of my head, too, and when he married your mother there couldn't have been anyone happier than the two of them. When your mother asked me to baby-sit you and your brother, I didn't think about it at all. I don't know if I'm explaining it right. It was like it had happened to somebody else—not to another me, but like he had been some-one else."

Virginia's thoughts exploded in a thousand different directions. She didn't know if she was shocked or not.

"How did my mother find out?" she heard herself ask.

"The time he went to Pittsburgh was the first time he'd been away from Belle since they were married. She was pregnant with your little sister, and she must have been lonely —I remember how clean the house was that week. When she got to shining up this picture of Mama, somehow she got it in her head to surprise him by getting a new gold-plated frame for it. That's when she found the note."

"Note?" *Get it straight, finally: all the facts, map-outs of procedure.*

"To Ernie. After that first time I was so confused, I ran out and didn't come back till right around dinner. When I got my senses back, I knew that whatever happened, I had to make sure he didn't feel bad or that he'd been a failure . . . whatever goes on in a boy's head. So I wrote him a note telling how nice it had been, that he was a man now and should always hold up his head. I slipped it under his pillow. He must have thought about hiding it from Mama, so he put it where he was sure she wouldn't look—behind the frame of her own picture. It stood on his dresser for years and went with him when he got married. I didn't know he had kept it. I don't know what he thought. But I know nobody would have known if it hadn't been for that note behind the picture frame." She took a deep breath. "That night at the station your mother gave it back to me."

Aunt Carrie sat very still, in an attitude of waitful repose, her eyes straight ahead. "I always wondered if you remembered that night." She spoke with her gaze focused on air; it was like watching a statue come to life. "Your mother couldn't be reasoned with. And your father loved her, he loved her more than anything in the world. He did everything to hold his family together—took the job in Arizona, cut himself off from his kinfolk. I haven't seen him since."

Virginia kept silent; she felt oddly at peace.

"What did your mother have to say about me when you children were growing up in Arizona? I know it's silly to care after all these years, but I'd like to know."

"She never said a word. We—" She'd nearly said, *We forgot all about you.*

Aunt Carrie was nodding slowly. "That would have been the best way." A deep and irrevocable sadness. "Well, I'm your crazy old aunt."

Virginia thought of Belle's grim determination when it came to matters of propriety: "Don't go anywhere with raggedy underwear on; you never know when an accident'll strike." How well she knew! One scrap of paper, and her scrupulously kept universe had shredded in her hands. So she had tried to flee to the farthest corner of the country but the pain came with her, and because she didn't know how to get rid of it, she clung to it as the one indelible memory from home.

"Mrs. Evans always said you didn't know nothing."

"Grandma knew?"

"Oh, yes. She's the one who told me later how her daughter found the note. She was there. When Belle called me up to ask if I wanted to go to the station, Mrs. Evans tried to stop her. 'Let lying dogs lie,' she told her, but Belle wouldn't listen."

Now you'll learn, Virginia, that you can't hide nothing from nobody in this world. People are too curious for their own good, and there's some things we don't never need to know but we're going to find them out one way or the other.

Suddenly, Aunt Carrie laughed. She laughed so hard tears rolled down her cheeks, and for a moment Virginia was afraid she was going to be hysterical. Then she stopped, as abruptly as she had begun.

"I've been thinking about telling it all these years, and when it gets round to it, I tell it all wrong." Her face turned back to marble. "After your mother handed me my own note back, she never spoke to me directly again. I didn't know how she had got hold of it, and I was too sick to ask. That night was the last time I saw Ernie, too, so I couldn't ask him. I don't know if I would've asked him if I could've. It didn't seem so important then. But later, after you all had moved and I had plenty of time to remember, I wondered. I didn't think I'd ever find out. Then your Granddaddy Evans died, and Mrs. Evans moved into Saferstein Towers. One day she called me on the phone. 'I'm lonely,' she said, 'why don't you come up for a visit?' I thought it was a little funny, but I went."

Your Aunt Carrie sitting all alone in that house on Furnace Street. Folks forget about you before you're even dead. It's a shame.

"She told me what she knew. She didn't want to hear my story. 'Old bones, dead and buried,' she said. So we became friends."

"Aunt Carrie—"

"Don't say nothing. I ain't expecting nothing."

Virginia started to go over to her, then thought better of it. "Would you like to come to the kids' puppet show on Wednesday, Aunt Carrie?"

She shook her head slowly. "No thanks, honey. I imagine you got to be going, though."

Virginia did go over then, and knelt beside her. *This*

hand, soft and cold and dry. She squeezed it, gently. "I want to see you again, Aunt Carrie," she said. "I'll call you, okay?" It was an inadequate thing to say, but she didn't know what else to do.

"Don't you worry about me, sweetie. I'm just glad I got a chance to tell you"—suddenly embarrassed, she changed tack —"and to see you. You've grown up to be a pretty little thing. Your mama must be so proud."

Fourteen

Virginia stumbled through the next day at school, taking advantage of the children's mounting excitement to conceal her inner tumult. It wasn't that she was shocked, exactly. Somehow she'd suspected all along that her father had slept with another woman. But that this woman had been his sister, and that it had happened before Belle . . .

Mrs. Woods intercepted her in the hall after recess. "I thought you might like to look at this," she said, holding out a lilac folder.

"My Life," it said, in white letters, and directly below the title in green, "by Renee Butler." There was a drawing of a bassinet with a curly-headed baby peeking out: bits of black yarn glued on for hair, a scrap of white cotton for the blanket. Virginia opened the folder.

On a hot summer day nine years ago, a new citizen of the United States was born: Me.

Before the age of one, I liked to roll around in my stroller. One day Mom left the basement door open and I rolled down, laughing all the way!

This wasn't as much fun as it seemed. From that day on, instead of sneaking out of doors I became a door closer. This soon became a problem too, because Mom found herself locked out one day when she went for the mail.

During my second and third years I was content to tag along behind my big brother, until my discovery of the back yard gate. Oh, how wonderful the outdoor world looked!

The next couple of years my grandparents took us on many fishing trips. I had my first horse-back ride and found out what poison ivy was.

When I was five, a great event happened: I started school. When I went to first grade, my grandfather died and I began spending Friday nights and Saturdays at grandmother's house. She always tells me wonderful stories. When I was in second grade, my uncle got married, and I was their flower girl. That Christmas our class bought a tree and decorated it.

I like school very much. My favorite subject is music. I got interested in music in third grade, when I won honorable mention in the Composer's Contest and went to a concert. This year I began Instrumental Music lessons, and next year I want to learn to play the violoncello like Miss King.

Nearly dark, and yet there was no light burning over Terry's front stoop. *He's probably peeved,* Virginia thought. Kevin answered the door. He stood there staring until Terry's voice bellowed from the back of the house: "Who is it?"

"Miss King," Kevin answered.

"Didn't your dad tell you I was coming?" Virginia asked as Kevin led her toward the kitchen.

"I wasn't sure you'd show." Terry stood at the top of the basement stairs, in jeans and an inside-out sweatshirt, holding a wet paintbrush. "There was no point in getting his hopes up."

"*His* hopes?"

"Kevin, take Miss King's coat and hang it in the hall closet. Hang it up, understand? Don't throw it at the hook." Kevin grimaced and took her jacket. "Come on down," Terry said. "You know the way."

Once downstairs, he started to embrace her, then hesitated. "You're lucky I'm covered with paint," he said ruefully, putting his hands behind him as he leaned forward to kiss her, "or you'd be in big trouble."

She heard tentative footsteps descending and tore herself away from Terry, who continued painting where he'd left off, applying gilt to the proscenium trim. A pair of high-tops appeared, followed by rolled-up corduroys. At the foot of the stairs, Kevin stopped. "Wow!" he gasped, and made a beeline for the stage.

"Hold on there, big boy," Terry said. "Wet paint." He caught Virginia's questioning look. "I wouldn't let him see it until it was finished. But I figured you're here, so he can have a preview. How do you like it, tiger?"

"It's great." Kevin's answer came out a whisper.

"Stand behind here. See, you put your football puppet up there. This part gets fastened at the posts. Watch the paint now."

The stage was a masterpiece, a full eight feet wide, with an arched opening in the middle and two hinged panels on either side that swung inward to shield the puppeteers from the audience.

"It's terrific, Terry," Virginia said. Kevin's eyes widened. She realized that Terry had avoided saying her name ever since she'd arrived, referring to her in Kevin's presence as Miss King. But adults called each other by their first names all the time, didn't they?

"Thank you, ma'am. Coming from you, that is high praise indeed. And my son approves, too. This is my lucky day." He grabbed Kevin's head in a playful hammer lock. "So you're gonna be a magic football, huh? The starring role." Kevin giggled and twisted free.

"Listen," Terry said, "I do have a few questions on this thing." He turned to Kevin, who was standing off to the side, watching. "Look, tiger, don't you have homework to do? Why don't you make like a cloud and float on upstairs. We've got some details to work out, and Miss King has a busy schedule, so we've got to get started."

He waited until Kevin had trudged upstairs and shut the door, then came out from behind the stage and crossed the cement floor to where she stood. "Look, I meant what I said yesterday; I do have high hopes. I want to be with you, understand?"

"I think we've both been thinking too much," Virginia said. *Whatever that means.* She smiled and reached up to wipe a fleck of paint from his eyebrow. But as he continued to stare, she realized that he wasn't playing; he was putting his chips on the table. He leaned down to kiss her and she closed her eyes, terrified. The airy corridors of the Oberlin Conservatory floated before her, music seeping from every closed door like perfume emanating from the pores of the skin.

. . .

253

For she's a jolly good fellow,
For she's a jolly good fellow,
For she's a jolly good fellow,
So bright in the afternoon!

Laughter, the rhythmic *thlop* of basketballs on the other side of the curtain. The class had lined up in the middle of the gymnasium and was beaming at her. Light from the high windows poured onto the floorboards and flickered over the children's expectant faces.

Mrs. Woods sidled up to explain. "They wanted to surprise you. It was all their idea." She turned to the children. "Look, class, Miss King is speechless! You surprised the words right out of her!"

"It was a wonderful surprise," Virginia replied. "I'm going to hate to leave you." These faces, growing old before her eyes! She forced a brisk gaiety into her voice. "So let's not think about it. After all, we've got a play to perform . . . and as we say in the business, the show must go on."

"Come on, don't stand there lollygagging!" Mrs. Woods clapped her hands. "There's a lot of work to be done before tomorrow evening! Can they help with setting up, Miss King?"

"Sure. Jimmy and Carl, you're in charge of the stage. And each puppeteer is responsible for his or her puppet. The rest of you help with the chairs." The kids scattered off in all directions. Virginia felt a tug on her sleeve; there stood Renee, with Kevin right behind her.

"Is it true you went over to Kevin's last night?" she demanded to know.

"Why yes, Renee," she began. "After all, Kevin's father built the stage!"

"See, I told you!" Kevin blurted, triumphant.

Just then Mrs. Woods came up. "Mr. Murray certainly did a fine job with the stage, didn't he, Miss King?"

"Yes. Yes, he did."

"You must be very proud of your dad," Mrs. Woods said, laying a hand on Kevin's head, who smirked. "Come along now, children—to your stations!"

Virginia popped the last dripping chunk of a double cheeseburger with lettuce and tomato into her mouth and finished it off with a clutch of golden French fries dipped in ketchup. The greasy food seemed to calm her. She'd been eating too much junk food lately—it was not the convenience but the company she craved, the urge to blend in. She basked in the impersonal warmth of the place, the bright orange booths and perky self-advertisements plastered over the window, the inconsequential chatter and fluorescent cheer.

What was Terry thinking of? Virginia shivered; the chocolate milkshake was so cold that her teeth hurt. *I'm in it for the distance*—Belle's image of her daughter as the Successful Career Woman, a nine-to-five job of the higher order, topped by a husband and 2.5 neatly dressed kids. No, she wasn't ready for that. Lucky thing Kevin had been there last evening, or she would never have gotten away.

Who could plan anything after one night? And yet she didn't want to end up like Aunt Carrie, squirreled away in a mental mausoleum erected to the memory of a few scant hours of pleasure. Now that the ghost of Belle's past had turned out to be an old woman with bad teeth couldn't the daughter, at least, learn to let go of the anguish? And how could anyone tell when letting go became running away once more?

An unexpected phone call had sent her reeling from her apartment into the impersonal hubbub of Burger King.

"Is that you, Virginia?"

"Nigel?" The British accent had been unmistakable.

"Really, my dear, you were the devil to locate! I called your mother in Phoenix, and she said she believed you didn't have a phone."

"What?" But the flash of anger Virginia felt toward Belle quickly faded into a vague, fleeting sorrow. She turned her attention back to Nigel.

"Then I called the Ohio Arts Council, and they referred me to Mrs. Peck, who was kind enough to provide me with your number."

Why was he calling? And he had gone to such lengths. Maybe . . .

"So how is the home turf? Have you managed to infect any young innocents out there in the heartland with dreams of stage and stardom?"

She laughed. "I hope so. After all, I've still got the bug, too."

"Ah."

"How are you?" she asked, suddenly feeling foolish.

"Excellent. I've landed a bit of a big fish—well, actually, a peculiar one. An odd play from an *enfant terrible* about the indiscretions of Watergate; it all takes place in Nixon's mind his last night in the Oval Office." A rueful laugh. "Right up my alley. Naturally, they figured I was just the director for it."

"Nigel, that's wonderful!"

"And there's a tasty little part for a person of your caliber, Virginia."

"But not my color, I assume," Virginia retorted, not quite taking it in.

"But of course, my dear," Nigel replied, chuckling. "Although I wouldn't hesitate to cast you as Joan of Arc if a producer would let me. Well, this role is positively *drenched* in blackness. You're to be a Black Militant, dashikied and spouting Marcuse. It'll be a challenge." He laughed.

It began to sink in. "You mean," she forced herself to sound cool, "you're offering me a part?"

"Yes, kind of. We'll start casting about Thanksgiving time, as soon as we get the patrons squared away, but I don't anticipate any difficulties. And Virginia—it's off-Broadway."

She made some rapid calculations: a month to finish up at Oberlin and study the script, then give notice to the Arts Council—*due to unforeseen circumstances . . .*

"I'll be there."

"Magnificent. But I must say—you don't seem very surprised at my call."

"Oh, I believe in destiny," Virginia replied smoothly, although she felt like doing cartwheels. "Especially when it works."

Back in her apartment, she set up the Sixth Suite and stood staring at the music. Kadinski's favorite suite had been the Fifth—its deliciously tragic melancholy suited his east European soul—and he'd spent an inordinate amount of time going over each phrase. She had graduated before he could start her on the Sixth. She had tried it out on her own, but the range lay extremely high, with more thumb position than she could handle without incurring blisters. On recordings this last suite was a *perpetuum mobile,* the open-string continuo like a sweeter version of the bagpipes. It was less indulgently sorrowful than the Fifth, more self-possessed and bittersweet and—adult, a chin lifted to the chill wind. It was the suite of departure, the conscious leave-taking of one who knows when it's time to move on.

Virginia shook her head. What nonsense! "Overinter-pretation," Kadinski had warned, "is the scourge of a soul that thinks too much for fear of feeling too little."

She gave up and went to bed.

"Mirrors are doors," Clayton said, and sleepwalked through the wardrobe mirror. Although she knew in her dream that it was just a dream, Virginia yearned to touch him, but they couldn't make love because of the large panes of glass he carried on his back.

"If you truly loved me," she said, "you'd remove that glazier's pack."

"I can't do that," he replied. "Glass is my business." Then he walked away.

She ran to the door to call after him, but her mouth wouldn't open; all she could do was stand there looking out as he made his way down the street. For a long while she could see her reflection in the windowpanes; sometimes the glass would shift on his back and throw a tree or the sky across her own image. Clayton grew gradually smaller, until there was nothing visible of him but a distant square of light that flickered and finally went out.

Virginia awoke in a darkness so complete, there was no boundary between her skin and the blackness around her. Even the weak light from the shaded lamp on the night table blinded her at first. She shivered and got up to shut the window.

The air was lightless and cold. Was Terry the man she'd been hoping for—if she was hoping for a man at all? Yes, her body rippled when she thought of Saturday night, but that was all. What did they have in common that might last? Neither books nor music, and certainly not how they perceived the world. Sex would never be enough. Clayton had been the perfect "soul-mate." And Virginia began to cry, marooned in the wreckage of tangled sheets.

Toward morning she tumbled into another dream: she was scheduled to give a lecture on "The Significance of the Sambo Figure in Prehistoric Primitive Music." The double doors opened into a school auditorium filled with the heads of adults screwed onto children's bodies. Belle sat front row center, next to a fat white man with a rolling eye; Nigel was there, as was Parker, his feet dangling from spindly ankles and his hands no more than a puppet's thumb and mitt.

Virginia distributed headsets, then stepped back up on stage, behind the lectern.

"The first thing to bear in mind about Sambo," she began, "is that Sambo is all of us. We all want to make merry, to wear bright colors and sing in the sun all day. The tiger does not care if we do—he only wants our beautiful red coat. The sun does not care if we do—it only wants our sweat. The palm tree does not care if we do—it only hopes we will not knock it down while merrymaking." She switched on the tape recorder and the room filled with the hollow sound of tom-toms. The audience tried to tap their feet to the beat, but they had no control over their atrophied muscles, and their feet twitched horribly.

"We prance around the palm tree in our bright new clothes. The sun is a gift from heaven, the umbrella a gift from earth. The breath of the wind materializes in the swish of the grasses, the rasp of the cicada. We dance! The tiger does not care, as long as we give him our fancy blue trousers. The sun does not care, as long as we continue to sweat. The tree does not care, as long as we look for shadow. The drum! The sun! The gong! The tiger!

"But there is Someone who cares, Someone who minds what we are doing. This Someone minds because he can't do it; he is jealous of our merrymaking in the sun! So he whispers into the tiger's ear, and the tiger demands the green umbrella. We give it to him. The Someone whispers to the tiger again, and he demands our purple shoes with crimson soles and crimson linings. We give them to him. Again Someone whispers to the tiger, but this time he tells him that he looks foolish. 'Mr. Tiger,' he says, 'can't you see that Little Black Sambo has made a fool of you? Those clothes were made to fit him. You have squeezed yourself into his blue trousers and red jacket, with purple shoes on your ears and an umbrella wrapped in your tail. Now Little Black Sambo's had his joke, and he dances to taunt you. Can't you see the smirk twisting his lips?'

"So the tiger strikes. He leaps after Sambo and Sambo runs, runs, runs, and the tiger runs, runs, runs, and the sun burns, burns, burns until the tiger melts to butter. Little Black Sambo has won again.

"Now Someone is very angry. So what does he do? 'The music must stop!' he screams, and it stops—for that is the power of the word."

The audience looked up, feet still twitching slightly. " 'This Sambo,' Someone writes in an essay, 'is a vain and silly

African. All day he loves to dance, which we recognize as the chief pastime of black people from time immemorial. Finally, we can see—as the best of his race would agree—that Little Black Sambo has no sense at all. He is ignorant. He doesn't even know that there are no tigers in Africa. And he lacks judgment. Look at how he dresses—red coat, blue trousers, green umbrella, purple shoes with crimson soles and linings! He loves bright colors, a surefire indication of frivolity and immaturity. And anyone who abuses the laws of composition so flagrantly deserves only a grass skirt. Or let him run naked, for that matter! It's hot enough in Africa, isn't it? He'll never know any better.' "

Leaning forward from his seat in the front row was an Apache with two long braids wrapped in turquoise ribbons. Virginia hadn't noticed him before. "Music!" he cried, his voice choking.

The others swung their feet faster and faster, sitting on their hands and shifting their weight from haunch to haunch in order to keep their legs going. Then, one by one, they scooted off the chairs and began crawling, flopping, wriggling toward her, sobbing, "Music! Music! Music!"

Virginia turned to run offstage but collapsed; her muscles were useless. Above the thicket of hands and heads she glimpsed Grandma Evans, perched on a windowsill in the far corner of the auditorium.

"Chile, ain't you figured it out yet?" Grandma Evans shrieked as she arranged her dark green skirt over her thighs, spread to make room for her cello: "They want your skin." She broke into the happy Gavotte of the Sixth Suite, scooping up the epic chords from the lower strings and flinging them into the air. Soothed by the grand, authoritative rhythms, Virginia closed her eyes and dreamed that she dreamed she was flat on her back under a snow-white blanket, looking up at a row of bright plastic balls in all colors of the rainbow, strung on a wire. Now Grandma Evans was plucking the cello like a ukulele and singing, forcing Johann Sebastian Bach into a mischievous tune:

> *There is a gal in our town*
> *She wears a yallow striped gown*
> *And when she walks the streets aroun'*
> *The hollow of her foot makes a hole in the groun',*
>
> *Makes a hole in the groun'.*

Fifteen

The children were wild with excitement; only their stage fright kept them manageable. Virginia hustled them into position and waited breathlessly for the conclusion of Mrs. Peck's welcoming remarks.

Then the lights dimmed, and Virginia listened to the muted rustle of programs and the scraping of chairs as the parents settled into their seats for another Washington Elementary Fall Extravaganza.

ROGER: She won't give me the time of day!

FAIRY GODFATHER: Then wow her. You've got the magic football—listen to the football, and you'll be the hero!

ROGER: Will she like me then?

Giggles, quenched by Marianne's sharp "Shhhh!" Crouched in the darkened shelter behind the stage, Virginia felt the swift thrill that flooded her every time an audience grew quiet, the curtains parted, and the first actor—person or puppet—made his or her wobbly entrance.

This backstage was the smallest she'd ever been in; she had to stoop, Gulliver among the Lilliputians, to avoid being seen by the public. Late that afternoon Terry had stopped by the school to add to the stage's line of defense, razoring open two large cardboard boxes—the kind used to pack refrigerators —and setting them upright, like Spanish screens, on either end of the plywood partitions. Now Virginia and the children were almost completely surrounded by accordion walls. *Rabbits in a top hat,* Virginia thought, helping the fairy godmother onto its eager hand.

When the children were making the puppets, Virginia had agonized over the racial constellation of the play. The fairy godparents transcended social pressures, with their silvery-blue complexions and rainbowed tinsel hair. The majorette, cheerleader and football teams had a healthy mix of brown, white and tan faces. Tommy, a freckle-faced blond, had been chosen to play Roger, the main character, and a black girl named Cassandra was to operate the puppet representing Karen, Roger's lady love—but Virginia had hesitated over what color these puppets were to be. Was Washington Elementary ready for an interracial love story?

The children, however, both black and white, knew exactly what color the main puppets should be: white. Virginia was crestfallen, but she didn't want to push it. After all, she had thrown her first black doll out of the window. So much for consciousness raising!

She looked over at the line of kids on stools, their faces alight with excitement, holding their puppets up to the scaffold for their moment in the limelight. *Imagine—me as a black militant, an Angela Davis character plotting revolution on an off-Broadway stage.* And reviewed in the *New York Times* maybe, finally, finally clicking into place—but first she had to help these kids act out their fantasy, this world where people got what they wanted simply by wishing it into being.

FOOTBALL: Hey, pick me up, kid! Now toss me back. That's the stuff.

Virginia smiled. The real star was the talking football, and Kevin plunged into his lines with reckless joy. What a transformation a mask and a curtain could effect! She knew it might look like she'd chosen Kevin for the part because she had secret designs on his father—that's what Ida Lee and Sarah believed, anyway, and there was nothing she could do to convince them otherwise. What did Renee think? Virginia cut a furtive glance over to where Renee waited with another girl to wiggle the majorette squad across the stage. Could she be imagining that Kevin was going to get Virginia as his new mother? Nonsense, Virginia told herself, unable to extinguish the memory of Terry's lips on her skin, his warm breath tunneling deep. . . .

ROGER: I . . . I caught it!

FOOTBALL: Of course you caught me, kiddo! Now run . . . run . . . *TOUCHDOWN!*

CROWD: *HURRAH!!!*

Halftime entertainment. The marching band started up, a chorus of kazoos, and Virginia crept over to cue the majorette squad, giving Renee's shoulder a friendly squeeze the girl barely tolerated before slipping away with a diffident shrug and moving to her station. Virginia picked up a kazoo to lend melodic support to their rather too spirited rendition of "Hold That Tiger." True, she had been a little standoffish with Renee the last few days. *Renee tends to fixate on people,* Sarah Butler had said. Was she mad because Virginia hadn't played the cello for her yet? Maybe she could arrange something for tomorrow —thank Sarah for her help and invite mother and daughter for cookies and music.

The audience roared when the majorettes and the cheerleaders bumped into each other and fell down. Virginia took off the whistle around her neck and handed it to John, who, at her nod, blew it three times. Halftime over!

ROGER: Hi, Karen. Are you enjoying the game?

KAREN: Hello, Roger. Your playing's dynamite.

Now it was time for the hero to approach the girl. Unlike the members of Puppets & People, whose backstage expressions usually belied the emotions portrayed on stage, often becoming more ferocious the more tender the gesture was that needed to be articulated, these children identified with their characters so intensely that their actions mirrored those of the puppets. Virginia studied the anxious look on Tommy's face. How coyly Cassandra manipulated the Karen puppet! How sweetly serious their voices as the two children knelt side by side, shyly trying not to touch. *Two plays in one,* Virginia thought. But which one was the shadow of the other?

She had worried a bit about the children's precocious interest in love, how relationships worked and, more unsettling, how they faltered. She'd mentioned it to Terry last night, but he just rolled his eyes and laughed.

"They know more than you can imagine in your worst nightmares, girl," he said, and when she protested, added, "It's no big deal. How old were you when you thought you knew what happened after the violins started playing and the camera swerved out the window to show the waves crashing onto the beach—ten years old, eleven? And what did you actually know about the . . . logistics? Now, what these kids are *really* aware of are all the preliminaries—how to strike up a conversation, how to flirt, how to play hard-to-get. After all, they watch TV: they get the general idea. They might not know what to do when they finally get tangled up, but they sure know the ropes."

Now the entire cast gathered for the grand finale. For a moment Virginia forgot her own troubles as she watched the children jostling for positions, all the puppets—boy and girl, magic football and fairy godparents, majorettes and cheerleaders and football team—crammed together under the small proscenium.

Boy meets girl and finds that love
Isn't what he thought it was!
A bit of magic and good advice—

She would have to tell Terry—tonight, maybe, if the timing was right. He'd already scheduled himself for every weekend in November, though she had drawn the line at Thanksgiving dinner. "I've got family here," she'd protested, thinking she'd have to go to New York that weekend, and by then . . . by then this whole business with Terry had to be resolved one way or the other. There was hard work to look forward to, creative work—an entire future. Not that she didn't enjoy Terry's attentions in some dazed way; but wasn't part of the thrill the fact that she hadn't expected someone like him to be interested in her? Hadn't she met his insistent ardor more with gratitude than with passion?

That's how boy gets girl and saves the day;
We hope you have enjoyed our play!

Laughter, applause: the overhead lights gushed in, bathing the circle of blinking puppeteers in yellow glare. Virginia went over to guide them through the curtain calls, but the children had thrown down the puppets and bolted, pushing aside the cardboard screens in their rush to find their applauding parents. It was a pandemonium of screaming kids and shrieking kazoos. Yes, it was undoubtedly a success, and success feels like success no matter the circumstances. Virginia was so elated, she wanted to hug the whole class and their parents, even Mrs. Woods; but first she set to rescuing as much as she could from the trample, scooping up puppets and depositing cloth and tinsel and papier mâché into cardboard boxes.

A hand on her shoulder gave Virginia pause; she straightened up into a smiling circle of familiar faces.

"It was marvelous! You had everything under control," Mrs. Woods enthused.

Sarah Butler embraced her. "You've done a fantastic job."

"Thanks to your costumes," Virginia replied; she felt her face blushing.

"Pooh! Those scraps of cloth." But Sarah was proud. "Renee will never forget this month. I hope you'll come back and visit us some day. Did she tell you we're going to let her take up cello after Christmas? I understand you play. Renee says she wants to grow up to be just like you."

Virginia found Renee folding chairs in the back of the

gymnasium. The child looked up gravely when she heard her name.

"Renee? You did a great job with the majorettes. Your mom is so proud." Renee waited. "Your mom also tells me you've decided to play the cello."

Renee nodded; she looked anxious.

"Well, I think it's terrific you've made that decision, and I'm flattered that it's my instrument you've chosen, but have you thought really hard about it?"

Renee's gaze clouded. *No, that's not right. Try again.* Virginia looked straight into those wide-set eyes.

"I mean, I told you how I happened to choose the cello, but I didn't tell you everything—like lugging that hulk home every weekend or always having to cut your fingernails short, and wearing pants or wide skirts in order to play it. It can get to be a drag."

"You think I won't be good at it?"

"No, honey, that's not what I think at all. I'd just hate for you to take it up and blame me later." *Stupid!* "I mean, of course I think it's great that you're interested in good music, and the cello can certainly hold its own against the violin—or even the flute, for that matter."

Renee stared at her. Then she turned and contemplated the row of chairs she'd been folding up. "You think I'll be no good. You went to Kevin's house and didn't come to mine anymore," she said to the chairs.

All of a sudden Virginia was smothered in a massive embrace. "Wait till I tell that husband of mine what he missed, the lazy dog!" The heavy scent of Moon Drops, mingled with ironed-in perspiration. Virginia felt the ropy imprint of pearls against her cheek.

"I don't think I've enjoyed myself so much in a long

time," Mrs. Parnell went on. "You're a genius, Miss King—Sammy was right!"

Renee was gone.

"Would you excuse—"

Mrs. Woods rushed over. "I just saw Renee run out the door. Is anything wrong?"

"I'll get her," Virginia said, breaking free from Mrs. Parnell and heading for the hall. But everyone seemed to be after her; parent after parent shook her hand, pulled at her sleeve, barred her path while asking questions.

Terry caught up with her at the foot of the stairs.

"What's the rush?" he said.

"Terry, I'll be right back. I've got to—"

"Lighten up! The show was great; now you can relax." Renee must be standing at the top of the stairs, peering down from the gloom—could she hear them?

"How about a nightcap? Kevin won't mind . . . " He moved closer, the whole of his body giving off a spiced heat.

From the corner of her eye Virginia saw Mrs. Woods step out into the hall and look their way. She tore loose and ran up the stairs. As she rounded the landing, she made out the small form crouched at the top.

"I can do it," Renee hissed. "Watch me!"

She jumped. Virginia lunged across the banister, too late—startled, Renee balked in midair, catching her foot on the last step. She sprawled face-first across the landing, the foot twisting under her.

"Miss King?" a voice cried.

Virginia couldn't answer. It seemed as if she were far away, gazing through the wrong end of a telescope, looking down not at a child but a tossed-out doll, a splintered configuration.

Sixteen

Is she all right? Call the ambulance . . . there, her eyes are opening—say something, sweetie. . . . Now why would she go do a foolish thing like that. . . . Don't worry, Miss King, you've done all you can do. It's just her leg. Why don't you go home? We'll take it from here.

The ringing telephone yanked Virginia awake.

"You sure disappeared in a hurry." It was Terry, sounding gruff and a bit wounded.

"Oh, Terry, I'm sorry. The excitement with Renee and all just wore me out. I crashed as soon as I made it back to my place." She fumbled for her watch. Seven-thirty.

"So how about dinner tonight?"

"I can't. I'm heading out today—"

"Today!"

"I've got to, Terry. I'll start at Oberlin High first thing Monday, so I need to meet with the teachers and principal tomorrow. I'll be back, though . . ." she trailed off.

"This is not acceptable behavior, young lady," he growled, so comically that even in her groggy state Virginia had to laugh. "I can't get away from here till four. Can you hold your horses till then?"

She did some quick calculations—the school, the Butlers, Grandma Evans—and agreed. "I'll be here packed and waiting," she said, and hung up.

At the school she ducked into the principal's office to say goodbye and went to collect her things. Mrs. Woods's class had baked her a cake frosted like a jack-o'-lantern; all the children were in their Halloween costumes. "For she's a jolly good goblin!" they sang.

Renee's ankle had been fractured. "It's a complicated break," Mrs. Woods explained. "The doctor said the whole area could fuse together without proper care and cause that leg to grow shorter than the other. As long as it's X-rayed every six months, though, things should work out just fine. If worse comes to worse, they'd have to put in a steel pin."

Virginia drove to the Butlers. The house, with its gray porch and gables, seemed to stand out against the stripped branches more starkly than before.

Sarah opened the door. She looked surprised and cautious.

"I wanted to come by before I left town," Virginia explained. "How's Renee feeling?"

Sarah stepped back to let her in, but remained standing in the vestibule. "Fine, considering."

"I'm so sorry this happened."

Sarah shook her head. "Kids are always trying to impress people. Especially someone they look up to."

Virginia shrugged. "I don't know what got into her."

"Boy, are you young," Sarah replied. Virginia was about to contradict her—*We can't be more than five years apart!*—but the other woman's gaze silenced her. "You think you can start something up in one corner, then put it on hold while you go dabble somewhere else." Virginia felt devastated. What had gone wrong?

"Renee would've licked the ground you walked on. Now, I know how children can fixate on someone, I'm not blaming you for that. But you encouraged her—first asking her questions about her family, then telling her about yourself and walking her home. And then, when you saw how much she was investing in you, you thought you could stop, just like that. I'm no child psychologist, but one thing I know about kids: what you start, you better finish."

Stunned, Virginia dropped her eyes. "May I see her?" she asked.

Sarah hesitated, studying Virginia's anxious face, and finally nodded. "I think she'd be delighted."

Renee was in good spirits, proud of the stir she had caused and even prouder that Virginia had come to visit her. She presented her cast for autographing, and Virginia signed Gina's name as well. "I'm her secretary, so it's okay," she joked.

Renee promised to give her a piece of the cast when it came off in December.

"Where will *you* be in December, Miss King?" she asked.

"In New York, I think."

"New York City?" Renee tried to sit up, wincing. "Kevin said you might come live with him and his dad."

"When did he say that?" Virginia asked, astounded.

"Yesterday, right before the play."

"Well, that just goes to show you that talking footballs don't know everything."

Renee smiled and dropped back onto the pillow. "Are there really as many people as they say there are in New York?" she asked.

"Probably just as many, if not more," Virginia replied gently. "I'll send you a postcard with my address, okay?"

Renee beamed. "Make it a picture of the Empire State Building. Will you come visit for Christmas?"

Back in the car Virginia glanced at her watch: two-thirty. She wanted to be packed and ready to roll when Terry came by, so she decided to return to the apartment. That way she could stop by Grandma Evans's on her way out of town, and Terry couldn't talk her into staying for dinner. She felt a twinge of guilt. Was this what her majorette friends meant by romantic maneuvering? All she had wanted was a little space for thinking, a little time to figure out who this man was and what her feelings could be—then Nigel phones and throws the whole affair into the past tense.

You think you can start something, then put it on hold while you go dabble somewhere else. Sarah's words swirled up and Virginia stopped just inside the door, key still in hand. She hadn't asked for Terry's advances; in fact, she'd tried to dodge him—hadn't she? Why did it seem like she was always running away? *But when everything you've dreamed of suddenly comes together, how can you not drop everything else?* She had to give it a try; she had to go to New York.

The apartment was chilly. On her way out that morning she had turned off the heat, afraid she'd forget it later. Shivering, she decided to trade skirt and blouse for jeans and a turtleneck; as she sat down to pull on a pair of boots, she felt like a cowboy about to strike camp and saddle up.

There was something exhilarating about stripping the closet hangers and folding away clothes. Virginia considered the possibilities of the upcoming month, this "interlude" before the real challenge: She'd talk theater with high school kids, and there'd be recitals and concerts, movies and student plays to see at the college. She didn't quite know how to make Terry understand that their relationship couldn't last, but she'd find a way without simply running from him.

She hummed while she swept out corners and crouched to wipe down the pale green tiles in the shower stall. As the efficiency resumed its pearly anonymity, she felt herself become more buoyant, her mind clearing; even her heart—which she'd been protecting like a porcupine, quills whetted to camouflage the tender core—seemed to grow a little braver.

Terry was a nice guy. Was she using him? No, it wasn't that vulgar; it was far more complicated and also much simpler. What she felt for Terry was not love, and even love didn't always warrant life-changing sacrifices. She knew: she had loved Clayton.

Virginia started to lift the suitcase from the bed but undid the clasps instead, rummaging until she found the baggy purple sweater she'd worn while shopping for wood with Terry. She stared at it for a moment, then pulled it over her head.

The red MG roared up just as she had finished wedging the cello into the passenger seat.

"Getaway car's all packed, I see," he said, unwinding his legs from the low-slung chassis in a sinuous sweep that made Virginia swallow. "And I suppose I can't talk you into dinner before you go."

Virginia shook her head gently. "I don't want to roll in there too late," she said. "I've got meetings all tomorrow." She couldn't tell him about New York now—not in an apartment carport with her hand on the door handle. He'd take it as a brush-off, and it wasn't that she didn't want to see him again; she just didn't want it to be forever.

"Tell you what"—Terry rested his elbow on the open

car door and leaned toward her—"I'll drive up tomorrow night and help you settle in."

"I've got a better idea," she countered. "Why don't I come down on Saturday and we explore Akron a bit more? Oberlin's a sleepy little burg"—she moved into his arms—"in fact, I believe it's dry."

"Oh, man! All right, I give in."

Saturday. Maybe she'd tell him about New York then, maybe not. It wouldn't be easy. But they had time.

The smell of fresh coffee wafted through Grandma Evans's little apartment. This time the old woman sat in the flowered armchair herself, allowing her granddaughter to serve her.

"Carrie came by last night. I haven't seen her that happy as long as I can remember. How she must have hurt, all these years." And with a sharp glance at Virginia: "But don't forget your mother in all this, chile. Some people get damaged by the darndest things. Stuff that might seem silly to you and me.

"Love is such a little thing," she went on. "That's why we're all the time running around looking for it. And it's delicate. But pain . . . pain is strong; pain goes on a long time. And it's selfish, it needs itself to feed on. So the pained folks can get to nursing their wounds too long."

Grandma Evans paused, as if considering whether she should say what was on her mind. "I thought Arizona was a mistake. I told Ernest so; I told him to smack that daughter of mine if it came to it, but don't go to Arizona. Don't look at me that way, child! I told him, but he was not the kind to do it. A shame. You see, if you're one of the damaged, you have to confront the damage to find out what you can use before you put the rest away. There's always something you can use."

She shook her head. "I couldn't seem to help Belle much. I didn't know how to tell her to give up the pain, which was a false affliction anyway, being born of hurt pride and not a little bit of vanity as it was. You see, I was younger then. I didn't have the experience to back up what I felt. But I reckon it wouldn't have mattered." She looked up. "I'm glad you came, Virginia," she said, and reached for her granddaughter's hand. It was the first time she had addressed her by their shared name, and she lingered over the syllables, stretching them out until the word seemed both a benediction and a farewell.

It was twilight when Virginia pulled out of the parking lot of Saferstein Towers—not yet dark, but those drawn-out minutes of deepening gray. "Everything seems to come apart and float around like feathers," Aunt Carrie had said.

At the corner something dashed into the street. Virginia slammed on the brakes; a humpbacked dwarf huddled, gawking into the glare of the headlights, his eyes terrified slits. Then a tiny crone ran up to shake her broom at the car, hooked nose wobbling.

"Trick or treat, trick or treat,
Give me something good to eat!"

And the dwarf joined in:

"If you don't, I don't care,
I'll pull down your underwear!"

They shrieked with laughter, holding up their paper bags, and ran into the intersecting street. Virginia watched them scurry down the sidewalk; the entire neighborhood seemed to writhe like a giant octopus, dozens of orangish pods flickering as it adjusted its coils.

There were devils and fairies, butterflies and cheetahs, Caspar the Friendly Ghost and the Tin Man and princesses and bionic Six Million Dollar men. They came from all directions and proceeded from porch to porch. Every now and then an astronaut or a Frankenstein would stop to execute his own rapturous little jig, while from the sidelines the grown-ups watched and waited.

About the Author

Rita Dove was born in Akron, Ohio, in 1952. She has published four poetry books and a collection of stories and won the 1987 Pulitzer Prize in poetry for *Thomas and Beulah*. Other honors include Fulbright and Guggenheim fellowships, as well as grants from the National Endowment for the Arts.

A professor of English at the University of Virginia, she lives in Charlottesville with her husband, the German writer Fred Viebahn, and their daughter, Aviva.